COASTAL CATS

COASTAL ADVENTURE SERIES VOLUME 5

DON RICH

Library of Congress PCN Data

Rich, Don

Coastal Cats/Don Rich

(A Mallard Cove Novel)

Florida Refugee Press LLC

Edit/Proofreading by: Tim Slauter

Cover By Aurora Publicity

This is a work of fiction. Names, characters, and incidents are either the product of the authors' imaginations or are used fictitiously. Any resemblance to actual persons, living or dead, businesses, companies, events, or locales is purely coincidental. However, the overall familiarity with boats and water found in this book comes from the author having spent years on, under, and beside them.

Published by FLORIDA REFUGEE PRESS, LLC, 2020

Crozet, VA

Copyright © 2020 by Florida Refugee Press

❀ Created with Vellum

To all of you who read and enjoy what I write, and especially to those who take the time to leave reviews or go the extra step of emailing to let me know that these stories mean something to you. Without y'all, the Mallard Cove crew would only continue to exist in my mind, not on your screens or on paper. The characters and I thank you for your continued support!

Also to my eagle-eyed team of secret Beta Readers, who make my books better reads. Like great babysitters, I never reveal their identities because then they'll get snapped up by my writer friends, and when I need them they'll already be busy. Y'all know who you are, and hopefully you know how grateful I am to have each and every one of you on my team.

For me, writing is a solitary endeavor until that last word is written, and then it becomes "all hands on deck." I'm so fortunate to have such an extremely talented group of professionals and volunteers to make my writing look better than it actually is, and to not make me feel too inept in the process!

July 31, 2020
Crozet, Virginia

PROLOGUE

He never realized it would be so difficult dragging a body up from below, and it didn't even weigh all that much. He silently damned whatever naval architect had designed this European monstrosity. The hardest part still lay ahead, having to drag the body up the narrow and curving steps in the corner of the aft deck and over the transom peak; there was no way for him to carry it safely. Again, that designer was an idiot! These steps were a damn nightmare to navigate, especially after having had a few drinks, like he had this evening. Once you reach the top of these three irregularly shaped steps, there is only a tiny postage-stamp-sized flat deck to balance on. Alongside it is a knee-high railing which can just as easily trip as save you, sending you plunging into the water six feet below.

Yes, large sailing catamarans are popular in part because they are extremely stable, so normally dealing with the dangers and challenges of these steps shouldn't be an issue. And of course, no one designs boats for the convenience of body disposal. He thought however that a pair of walk-through open transoms would have been a major improvement right now. Instead, descending ahead of him were five steep, teak-covered transom steps of varying heights and depths that ended at the water and were lit only by the dim moonlight. Having to deal with all of these obstacles reminded him of the "stupid human tricks" police use at DUI checkpoints.

Somehow though he managed to get both his burden and himself safely down to the bottom stair, a foot above the water. Then he went back up the steps to help his accomplice deal with the larger and heavier second body. Fortunately, this one had fallen down from the raised helm above the aft deck, and was now less than a twenty-foot drag away from those nightmarish stairs. With a lot of grunting and swearing, the two of them managed to get the second body down alongside the first.

His accomplice retrieved the anchor, chain, and rope from the yacht's rigid-hulled inflatable tender. It was another tough task, but they managed to bind the two bodies together on those narrow and steep steps. The hundred-fifty feet of one-half-inch nylon line and the eight feet of galvanized chain attached to the anchor worked perfectly. The crowning touch was tying the chain around the necks of both bodies using a clove hitch knot on the links, leaving the anchor and a few spare feet of chain extending beyond their heads.

The two climbed up into the twin helm seats and started the inboard diesel engines. Using the electric winch they retrieved the plow anchor, then motored slowly out of the secluded cove toward the deep shipping channel in the middle of the calm Chesapeake. They needed a deep spot to dump the bodies where they wouldn't be discovered by fishermen, oyster, crab, or clam boats.

This early in the boating season, the water wasn't yet above fifty degrees. This was the reason it was so important to tightly bind the bodies together. Soon the bay's famous blue crabs would be rising up out of the muddy bottom, their winter hibernation finally over. Crabs awaken with a big appetite, and they were counting on these shellfish to pick the bones clean before the deeper water got warm enough to let decomposition gasses start forming. They couldn't risk those bodies coming loose and floating to the surface before the crabs could finish their work. With any luck, if there was any current down that deep, the anchor might bite into the mud and secure the crustacean's feast, making their job even easier.

Fifteen minutes later, after checking the radar to make certain there were no boats nearby, they pushed the two bodies the rest of the way down the steps, and off the transom. They disappeared head-first into the calm, dark water; the weight of the anchor and chain enough to drag them down quickly. He now had the vision of the woman's lifeless, bulging eyes illuminated by the moonlight burned into his mind. They had stared straight ahead as she had slipped beneath the surface. The feet of her half-nude body were the last of her he saw before she was gone. The man's body had been facing away, though the sight of him disappearing probably wouldn't have bothered him as much. Then again, bothered wasn't exactly the right word; that would imply that he had a conscience. He didn't. He was a modern-day pirate, and this boat was a means to an end, not the end itself. And he wasn't about to let anyone get in the way of that. The couple had merely been an inconvenience. But still, it seemed more of a waste that the woman had to go so quickly, especially since she had been so obviously eager. He could've cared less about the man.

Back in their helm seats they started idling slowly south, back to the resort and marina where they had left their small center console outboard. They had used it to follow this boat up the bay after first spotting both it and the bored couple at Cape Charles. Their "coincidental" meeting up at the Bayside Resort the next evening had been well planned. The faint flicker of recognition coupled with obvious excitement from the woman provided the perfect opportunity for introductions, drinks, conversation, and dinner. The way she kept looking at his partner throughout the evening left little doubt in either of their minds as to what dessert would be. He could see on the man's face, this wasn't a first-time thing, and not something he objected to. Her suggestion of an after-dinner "booze cruise" aboard their sixty-five-foot catamaran yacht was the clincher, and the opportunity both pirates had both been hoping for.

After anchoring in the cove, the woman said she first wanted what she called "some one-on-one time" with his partner before the rest joined them. The pirate and the man had another drink while sitting up at the helm, biding their time to join in the fun and games, or so the man thought. After going below with the second pirate, the woman had first removed her jewelry, she wanted nothing to get in the way and impede their fun. She insisted on putting it all in the safe that was hidden behind a panel in the cabinetry. Apparently, she had deemed the pirate safe enough for sex, but not trustworthy enough for her to leave her jewelry lying out on the table. Sadly for her, she had been only half right. She also hadn't blocked the view while she punched in the combination, and it would end up being the last mistake she ever made.

The scream that soon came from below could never have been mistaken for passion. The man jumped up in alarm, turning toward the step intending to go to her but that was as far as he got. Instead, the pirate pulled an icepick from his pocket, driving it deep into the man's back down into his heart, stopping it. He plunged forward, missing the step, and ending up in a heap, face down on the deck behind the helm.

The pirate went below to the master stateroom, finding the topless woman on her back in the bed, the life having been strangled out of her. His partner had the safe open and was now pulling out jewelry, passports, banded stacks of cash, as well as the boat registration and title. The paperwork was a bonus, and exactly what they had hoped to find. He lifted the woman's warm body off the bed, leaving the second pirate to look for even more hidden valuables while he prepared to dispose of the bodies. The stairwell was too tight for him to be able to carry her up, so he had to drag her by the wrists the rest of the way.

An hour later after leaving Bayside with two fresh drinks in hand, the two modern-day pirates toasted their good fortune, sitting in the helm chairs, slowly cruising south with the outboard safely in tow. They would anchor out tonight, then arrive at their destination near Norfolk at dusk tomorrow. They would drop the boat off at a small boatyard that had been picked by their black market broker for its lack of after-hours visitors and security video surveillance. And this wasn't the first job they had done for that broker, a shadowy figure who they had never actually met in person, which suited the pirates just fine. They knew there would be a duffle bag filled with cash waiting for them in a shed, and that's all that mattered. Better not to put a face with whoever was behind the messages on the secure internet messaging app. Within two weeks this boat would be somewhere on the Mediterranean with new owners. The new name and new papers would be supplied by this boatyard, which specialized in these things. But that wasn't their concern.

It was just as well, the first pirate thought. The interior of this "cat" had been done in Danish modern; all satin finish varnished teak and grey metal. It was like sailing around in a damn floating Ikea store. He was no fan of the austere Euro-style. When it came to yacht interiors he liked his more American, more "over the top" with glossy wood finishes, granite countertops, and vivid colors. The only things he liked that were made in Europe were watches, cars, and women. Especially the women.

1

THE TRIP FROM HELL

I f I thought I was happy to see Murph and Lindsay arrive back at Mallard Cove last spring, that was about to go double for this year. Things had gone completely berserk soon after they left, and it's been "off the chart crazy" ever since. But wait, I'm getting ahead of myself, and besides, that's all a story for another time, and you need to know what's happening here now. Let me first start by introducing myself. My name is Marlin Denton, and I'm the Executive Director of a private foundation dedicated to protecting Atlantic coast fisheries. I know, it sounds boring, but it's not. Last year we bought the hottest reality fishing show on cable to use as an education vehicle, which is how I also ended up becoming an Executive Producer of the show. In addition to my "day job", I also own the *Pelican Fleet,* a group of boats and crews located here at *Mallard Cove Marina* on the southern tip of the Eastern Shore of Virginia. A place more commonly known as ESVA. We cater to the tourist trade and offer everything from para-sailing, to paddle boarding, eco-tours, sailing trips, and light tackle fishing.

As if this wasn't enough to keep me occupied, I'm getting married in a little over two months, oh and I'm also in the middle of creating another television show. Yeah, it's nuts around here, and I've been without my two best friends and confidants who have been gone for over three months. Okay, two of my *three* best friends that is, I'm marrying the other one. My fiancée's name is Kari Albury, and she's as busy as I am. Kari's the head of M&S Partners, a private company that acquires, designs, develops, and manages marina properties around the Chesapeake and mid-Atlantic coasts. Her office is one floor above mine, in the same building here at the Mallard Cove complex, which M & S also manages. We live here in the marina aboard a large tri-decked house barge called *Tied Knot*.

So, back to Murph and Lindsay, who are due to arrive at any minute in their sixty-foot Merritt sportfisherman named *Irish Luck*. They've spent the majority of this winter fishing billfish tournaments down in South Florida. I envy the warm weather they enjoyed while they were there, but they paid for every single degree of it, working their tails off. They do private charters with *Irish Luck*, meaning that there's no sign on the dock behind the boat advertising this. They don't need one since they've either won or placed in many of the tournaments they've fished the past few years. They have a full list of charter clients. They're one of the hottest teams on the water; Murph as captain and Lindsay working the fishing cockpit as mate.

Neither of the pair really need to charter anymore since they are now the majority owners in the Mallard Cove complex, which has become a tremendous financial success. They bought the property two years ago for a steal, back when it was just a crumbling marina with a dying boatyard. The majority of the property was overgrown back then, hiding its true size and value. Murph realized that he needed help with it so he brought in his old boss, Casey Shaw, who had just reopened an upscale resort north of here called *Chesapeake Bayside Resort and Marina*. Casey put together a great group of investor partners, then put a young and unbelievably talented young woman in charge of figuring out how to get the most out of Mallard Cove. Kari. Her solution included a hotel, two restaurants with bars, a seasonal beach bar and café, plus an in and out boat storage barn. The place has blown away even the most optimistic expectations, earning Kari a small percentage of the project. Surprising, since she was only twenty-four years old when she started, but not surprising that two years later she's heading up M&S after building it from scratch. Now she's developing a huge marina, retail, and residential project many times larger than Mallard Cove, just across the Chesapeake Bay Bridge Tunnel from here in Lynnhaven. She's even busier than me these days.

While Kari and I are usually the last ones to leave our offices, today I cut out early. I'm sitting on a huge boulder that's part of the riprap breakwater which runs behind the marina's private dock. From this spot I have a great view of the channel between both Fisherman and Smith Islands, which is where I'm expecting to see *Irish Luck* appear at any time. It's March, and still well before the start of the season, so I was startled to hear someone come up behind me.

"Slide, Clyde, there's plenty of room for two there."

I turned and saw a smiling Kari, her long black hair getting blown in the cool, heavy breeze. I quickly made room for her, and she leaned in against me, putting her arm around me as she sat down. The warmth of her body next to mine felt good; it was a chilly afternoon and spring wouldn't officially be here for a few more days. The stubbornly cold temperatures of the Atlantic and the Chesapeake waters will still keep our corner of the world chilled down for at least another month or two.

"You're out of the office early, too," I said.

"It's Friday, it's not that early, and I'm meeting with clients that are arriving. What's your excuse?" She grinned in a teasing way.

Not to be outdone I said, "Oh, I'm waiting for a couple of my best friends who I'm going to tell that you called them 'clients' instead of pals."

"Okay, I'm waiting on pals, partners, and wedding party members, is that better?"

I nodded. "I think they'd be good with all that. I'm just trying to get you out of your 'office mode' and into a celebratory mood instead."

"Oh, I'm there already. I've really missed these two. Video chats now and then just aren't the same thing as being together. And they both seemed really tired when we talked to them last week. I'm worried that they're getting burned out."

I nodded. "I am, too. Losing that transmission didn't help things. Murph was frazzled about it. Running down there and back every season is hard on the boat as well as them. I wish they'd just stay here year 'round."

Off in the distance I spotted an approaching boat, probably five minutes or more away at its present speed.

Kari noticed it too and said, "Looks like them."

Since we were only watching for boats coming from the south, neither of us had noticed the movement from the east until a catamaran shot out of the Virginia Inside Passage, or VIP. This section of the VIP is essentially a wide canal cut through a marsh that leads over to Magothy Bay. But what caught our attention was how fast the cat was accelerating in the open water with its higher wind speed. That, and the fact that both hulls were rising out of the water by a couple of feet, the lee hull having a hydrofoil extended beneath the surface.

By the time the boat passed us, it must've been moving at well over thirty miles per hour, more than twice the speed of the wind. It looked to be around twenty-four or twenty-five feet long, and maybe twelve feet wide. There were two men in wetsuits suspended horizontally by cables that were attached high on the mast. They were counterbalancing the boat, their bodies hanging out over the water while their feet were braced against the side of the windward hull. That had to be such a tremendous rush for the two of them moving that fast while suspended just a few feet above the water. Only their cables and harnesses were between them and a very cold swim. Kari and I could only sit quietly, both of us transfixed by the sight of the speeding and almost silent vessel as it flew past us. It was quickly out of sight, going around the point heading toward Fisherman Inlet Bridge.

Kari spoke first. "That was incredible. Carlton told me that one of his new renters was working on some kind of a super-fast catamaran, and this must be what he was talking about."

Carlton Albury is Kari's cousin. He owns the best boatyard on ESVA up on Magothy Bay, about seven miles up the Virginia Inside Passage. It's where we and most of our friends have our boats repaired, and where Kari and I had *Tied Knot* built. Carlton is a great guy; he knows everyone around here and he's head of the Northumberland County Board of Supervisors. He had recently added a huge metal building adjacent to his boatyard where he is subdividing and leasing individual units. His goal was to attract specialty marine businesses that would complement his own, making it even more of a boat mecca than it already is.

Again our attention was drawn back south and the approaching sportfish, which we could now easily see was indeed *Irish Luck*. Just as she started to slow down to enter the basin, the sailboat reappeared, going even faster than before but in the opposite direction. It passed close behind Murph and Lindsay, the hulls both raised well above their wake, not touching nor affected by it at all. Finally, its hulls settled back down onto the water when it slowed down upon entering the narrow inland section of the Passage. Most of its wind was now blocked by the trees on the shore. Even down off the foil it was still moving fast. It disappeared from sight in under a minute.

As Murph and Lindsay entered the basin Kari and I got up and went over to the slip next to their house barge, *On Coastal Time*. It had been the original inspiration for our own *Tied Knot*. As Murph backed in, a smiling Lindsay waited in the cockpit with their mooring lines after having already positioned fenders to sit between the painted fiberglass over wood hull and the floating dock. We made the lines fast around the dock's cleats, then plugged in their shore power cable before Murph killed the generator and the big diesel engines. Kari hopped aboard and wrapped Lindsay up in a hug as Murph called down to me from the bridge.

"Marlin, did you see that crazy catamaran? It had to be doing forty when it cut through our wake! I wonder where it's from?"

"Yeah. Murph, I missed you too!"

He looked sheepish, "Sorry, Marlin, that thing just caught me off guard, I've never seen a hydrofoil catamaran before."

I laughed, "No worries, it's the first time we've seen it, too. Kari thinks it's from up at Carlton's. Some guy just put in a new shop there."

Lindsay stepped onto the dock and now wrapped her arms around me. "Well, my annoying brother, since you won't come to me, I'll come to you! I really missed you, Mar."

We weren't actually related, but we were very close and at times we bickered like siblings. "You too, Linds. Been boring around here without you guys."

She stepped back, still smiling. "You have no idea how great it is to be home again."

"Well, let's get you guys unloaded so you can start to relax and tell us about your trip. Dinner's on me and Kari over at the *Cove*."

Murph called down again from the bridge, "We aren't unloading anything tonight. We're just gonna wash her down, then I'm getting the hell off this pig! I've been dreaming about my waterfall shower head on *OCT* for weeks now." Nicknames and abbreviations have a way of sticking around here, like "Mar" and "Linds" and "*OCT*" for *On Coastal Time*. I came up with that one. But I knew right then that this must've been the trip from hell. Murph loves the big Merritt sportfish and had never spoken this way about their boat before.

Kari said, "In that case, we'll help with the wash down so you two can get off here faster. Cocktail hour starts as soon as we're through and can get to the *Cove*."

AN HOUR later Kari and I were seated at a table next to the big glass paned rollup doors in the *Mallard Cove Restaurant*. Another two months and these doors would be open on most days, taking advantage of the access to the adjacent deck and the view of charter boat row just beyond. We kept an eye out for our pals, but we also didn't wait for them before ordering our drinks.

"Did you get the feeling too that something has changed," Kari asked.

"Oh yeah. I know he was really upset when they blew that gear, it must've been a whopper of a repair bill. He loves that boat, and it would have taken a lot for him to start calling it a 'pig'. Probably tired from that long trip though. We'll know soon enough, here they come."

We watched them walk in, then waved them over. At thirty-seven, sandy-haired Murph was three years older than me but usually looked much younger. Not tonight. While he and Lindsay were both tanned from their time down south, he now had dark bags under his eyes. Lindsay, on the other hand, still looked younger than her twenty-seven years with her sun-streaked blond hair and eye-catching figure. Our server quickly came over and took their drink order when they sat down.

Lindsay remarked, "Wow, still really busy in here, even this early and before the start of the season."

Kari nodded. "Wait until you see the numbers from this winter, we were busy every weekend. In fact, we all need to sit down next week and talk about expanding. I don't want to lose our momentum and leave an opening for anyone else to start taking business away from us. But we can talk about this in a day or two. How was your trip?"

Murph answered before Lindsay could. "Great up until we lost that transmission and had to sit out a week's charter because of it. Then our biggest client showed up to fish with his obnoxious business partner. The guy had been hitting the rum before he ever got on the boat. Then he switched to hitting on Lindsay instead, and decided to up the ante by playing grab-ass. I knocked him on his ass and ran them back into the dock. The jerk left, taking my charter with him, but not before canceling a month's worth of charters he had booked for this summer.

"You guys know how much I love to fish, but only with good people. Running almost a thousand miles then having to deal with an idiot like that isn't worth it. And between the downtime during the repairs and then getting stiffed by my biggest charter client because of his friend, we barely broke even for the trip. On top of that, we didn't even end up in the running in any of the tournaments we were able to fish."

This wasn't the Murph I knew, the one that left here over three months ago. He is almost always upbeat, rolling with the punches and willing to adapt to changes. He sounded negative and down, something I hadn't experienced from him before. I noticed Lindsey looked concerned too. But I had an idea of how to lighten the mood.

"Hey, what do you guys say to taking a field trip over to Carlton's place in the morning? I don't know about y'all, but I'd like to have a close up look at that catamaran. Even better, I'd love to try getting invited out on it. That would be the ride of a lifetime."

Murph and Lindsay's drinks arrived at that point, both vodka on the rocks with lemon. Linds took a sip of hers, but Murph drew his down an inch and a half before coming up for air. Yeah, he wasn't a happy camper right now.

I pressed the issue. "What do you think, are you guys up for it tomorrow?"

"I am! That thing was wild-looking, and I wouldn't mind seeing it up close. How about you, babe?" Linds looked hopefully at Murph, who gave her an unenthusiastic nod.

This was so uncharacteristic for Murph, who was normally really fun to be around. Not tonight. He polished off two drinks for every one that I had at the *Cove* and continued to pound more of them after we all went back to *OCT,* becoming more and more incoherent as the night wore on. It's not that I've never seen Murph plastered before. Hell, I've been right there with him on more occasions than I'd like to remember, or that I even *can* remember. But most of the time we were celebrating something or just having fun. In this case, however, it felt like he was drinking strictly for the sake of getting annihilated, and the root cause wasn't evident. Not good. I helped Linds and Kari get Murph into bed after he passed out, then left the two women to chat in *OCT's* salon when I headed back home.

. . .

"LINDSAY SAID the first month of the trip was normal, except they were having a tough time getting on the fish." Kari had just returned, an hour after I had left the two of them alone. "She said that losing the transmission compounded that, then the bozo messing with her topped it off. His buddy had them booked for two weeks down there. Between him and the gear going out, they lost a third of their charter time. That was bad enough, but she said she felt that Murph was starting to resent her for something. They had been having small arguments when they left here, and it got worse after those problems happened. She's halfway expecting Murph to break up with her."

That was a stunner. Other than me and Kari, those two are meant to be together more than anyone else I know. I make it a point not to get involved with anyone's relationship issues, but if those two split, it would have a big impact on me and Kari. I wasn't exactly sure how that would pan out. We'd still end up hanging with each of them, only it would have to be one at a time. They're both fun people separately, but together they are a ball. At least they've always been that way before tonight.

"I'll talk to Murph, one on one, and see what happened. There has to be more to this. But it's going to be important that we take a step back. With them being not only friends but also your partners, this could get ugly for us, too."

She agreed. "I know, though I'm more concerned about the personal side right now. I hope you can get some answers out of him tomorrow."

2

BACK TO BASICS

I normally wake up around five a.m., and most of the time Kari is already awake, watching me for signs of life. Today was one of those rare Saturdays when her mental alarm clock had failed to go off. I carefully slipped out of bed and dressed without waking her. Rather than make breakfast in the galley and have the aroma of bacon cooking wake her, I decided to let her sleep. I headed for the *Cove* without even making my first cup of coffee. The restaurant opens early to feed the crews and anglers who head out long before sunrise.

Walking out onto the small entrance deck, I was glad that I had picked a heavy chamois shirt to wear, since it was in the thirties. I stepped over onto the finger pier that *Tied Knot* shares with my vintage forty-two-foot Chris Craft, *Why Knot*. In the light from the dock, I saw frost crystals glittering on her canvas aft deck cover. I put a little more spring in my step as I hurried past my Chris, Lindsay and Murph's Merritt, their houseboat, and the few other boats between theirs and the security gate. A hundred yards beyond the gate I was greeted by the warmth of the *Cove*. I took the same table that we had last night, intending on watching the sun come up through the rollup door's glass windows. From here I had a perfect view of where it would rise above the water between Fisherman and Smith islands.

I hadn't gotten halfway through my first cup of coffee before Murph walked in, looking like something that had been dragged in. He made a beeline for my table, signaling the server for coffee along the way. He plopped down in the chair opposite me with a chagrinned look.

"Hey. Sorry about last night."

"What," I asked.

"Uh, getting schafozzed and being grumpy."

"I didn't notice you being any grumpier than usual, though you have been gone a while."

"Funny guy."

I chuckled. "One thing I've learned about you, Murph, is that you always have a reason for whatever you do, so there's no reason to apologize about anything."

He grunted in reply and studied the menu as our server came up to take his order. "What're you having?"

"Short stack of Caribbean pancakes with the fruit and the toasted coconut. Super large fresh-squeezed orange juice. Breakfast of champions. Had a few vodkas myself last night, and right now those carbohydrates are my new best friends."

"In that case, I'll take the same thing, but a tall stack and two orders of bacon."

As our server headed off with his order I asked, "Does bacon help?"

"Dunno, but it can't hurt. Besides, it's *bacon*."

"Good point." I let that last sentence hang in the air, leaving the door open to further conversation if he wanted, or a nice stopping point if he didn't. He knows I'm a friend, and that's all that matters right now.

After a minute or two, he asked, "Did Lindsay talk with Kari last night?"

"Yeah. First opportunity they've had in three months."

Murph nodded. "Missed being able to bounce stuff off you, too.

That whole video chat thing feels like I'm talking from a jail cell, so I don't like to do it." When I just nodded he continued, "Everything has just been shot to hell lately, you know what I mean? We shortened the season down south by a month because everything has gotten so expensive there. Then the already short season got shortened even further after we had that breakdown and then when my charter took off. Still cost me the same amount to run the boat down and back, but I only got half the charter income and no prize money from any tournaments. And Lindsay and I got into it a lot."

He let that hang just like I did, but again, I wasn't going to pry. I'm here if he needs an ear. Apparently, he did.

"Things changed after we left. I think a lot of it was because you and Kari are getting married and we aren't even engaged. I think she resents that."

"Sorry if that's part of it." Not that there's much that I could do about it if it were.

"Not your fault. Not my fault, either. But her attitude definitely changed. Truth is, I don't think that whole dustup with my charter's partner was all his fault. I think she might have led him on."

"*Lindsay*? Lead some guy on? Are you nuts? She'd never flirt with another guy."

"Oh, like she's never flirted with you."

"No Murph, not seriously. Kidding around, yes. But that's because we're such close friends and we both know it isn't serious. But with some guy she doesn't know? I didn't even have to be there; I can tell you she'd never have done that."

"Maybe not consciously, but subconsciously she might, Marlin. It would be a way of getting back at me for not asking her to marry me. Every time she got off the phone with Kari, that's all she wanted to talk about was your wedding. I hate it! Not the fact that you're getting married, but that she's so obsessed with the whole thing."

"She's the Maid of Honor, Murph, of course they're going to talk about every detail of it. And she's only had you to talk to about it face to face for three months. Weddings are all about the women; it's the bride's day, and the smartest thing guys can do is let the girls talk about anything and everything to do with the wedding if that's what they want. It's like us doing our part without having to do anything. Besides, I even offered to elope, so it isn't like I didn't try to avoid all this."

He started to say something then stopped, surprised. He said, "You what? Really? I bet that went over well." It was the first time I'd seen even a hint of a smile from him since he got back.

"Yeah, uh, that's a big noooo."

He laughed out loud then suddenly looked serious. "You know I just realized, that's the first time I've laughed in months, Marlin. That's telling me a lot. I'm not happy, and I need to make changes in my life. I want to, no, I *need* to laugh more than once every few months."

Now I was worried. "What kind of changes?"

"I don't know, whatever it takes to make me happy. I want to get back to where I was before I left last fall."

At least he and Linds had been together then, so hopefully that didn't include a breakup. Fortunately, our food came at that point. I know that when I'm hungover I always think more clearly after I consume a pile of carbohydrates. We ate in silence. It wasn't that further conversation would be uncomfortable, it was because the food at the *Cove* is just that good.

Murph leaned back and smiled after the last bite was gone. "You see, this is part of what I was talking about, Marlin. This is the best breakfast that I've had in months. It's stuff like *this* I need to get back to so I can be happy again."

I said, "Sounds to me like your annual trip south makes you unhappy."

He looked thoughtful. "I think you're right. It was fun a couple of years ago when it was all new to Lindsay and we were learning to be a team, discovering how well we worked together. Of course we had no problem getting on fish then, either. This year it was all different. We were out of step with each other, and everything seemed to go wrong. I dread thinking about going back next year."

"Then don't. You said you barely broke even anyway. We may not have a lot of billfish here in the winter but we do have big tuna." It seemed logical to me.

"You may have a point, Marlin."

He looked like he was brightening up the more he thought about the idea. I figured that exploring this further couldn't hurt. I remembered something Kari told me about Murph.

"I seem to recall that Casey Shaw was able to talk you into the concept of taking on partners in Mallard Cove so that you would have a nice income stream without the headaches of running this place yourself. Something about having more time and money to fish?"

"What's your point?"

"From what Kari told you last night, it sounds like the place is doing much better than expected. Meaning, more money. Less need to charter."

"Yeah but I *like* fishing."

"I do too, it's why I still fish a small group of clients that have been with me from back when I started guiding and chartering. Now that I don't depend on the income from charters to live, it's more like fishing with my friends except they pay for all the gas. I enjoy it so much more. What's your favorite part about fishing, Murph?"

He laughed again. "Catching."

"Mine, too. That, and putting my friends on fish, especially Kari."

"Yeah, I never will forget Lindsay's first white marlin on the old boat. That was one of my best days of fishing, ever. She was so excited, and I was so damn proud of her, and proud of myself too for putting her on that fish. The look on her face as it swam away after she released it was unreal." He paused for a moment, then continued, "I see where you are going with this. I've let it get to be a job instead of something I love doing."

"So, how do we get you back to that point?" I smiled as I saw it dawn on him.

"For one thing, I need to only fish the people I like fishing with."

"Who is at the top of that list?"

"Lindsay. I'd rather fish with her on a bad day than anybody else on a good day."

"I'm glad you still feel that way, I was beginning to think it wasn't like that anymore." Lindsay had put her hands on his shoulders, making him jump. She had silently walked up behind him a minute before and heard this last part of our conversation.

Murph stood up and hugged her, no conversation needed. I got up and walked past the two of them and said, "You're buying my breakfast, Murph. While you're at it, buy hers too."

I looked back from the doorway on my out and saw they were sitting down, holding hands across the table. As I walked across the deck I saw the first part of the sun peek above the horizon. This day had started with a lot of promise.

∿

An hour *later on the other side of the Chesapeake...*

"Not a bad payday. I'm a lot closer to my F50."

"I'm very glad for you. I will also be very glad for me when you hand me my cut."

"Is it only about the money for you?"

"You know that it is not."

He sighed and handed over a zippered canvas duffle bag. "Here. By the way, you'll be happy to know I've chosen the next one myself, and I think we can line up buyers for it ourselves without our usual broker. A bit riskier, but a lot larger payday. Are you in?"

"Am I not always?"

3

A NEW INVESTMENT

The four of us climbed out of my old Ford Sport Trac. We were parked in front of Carlton's new building in the part of his boatyard that's known as "*The Slab*". It's several acres of concrete and gravel, mostly covered with boats this time of year since some have been stored "up on the hard" for the winter, and others are in the process of being prepped for the season.

The new structure is a huge light blue metal building resembling a tall airplane hangar. There were a series of regular-sized doors and several giant sliding doors facing out onto the slab. Each of the bigger doors was large enough to allow access for the Travelift into the units. One of the large doors was open halfway, a large sign proclaiming it to be the home of *ESVA CATAMARANS*. We headed for that door.

Most of the time boatbuilders welcome visitors to their facilities because they never can be sure who might be a potential customer. I've seen people that looked like vagabonds in boatyards and marinas who were actually extremely wealthy. A smart boatbuilder won't let first impressions fool him or her. I was reasonably certain that whoever owned this business would probably fit in that category. Carlton had been looking for sharp operators as tenants, and he was picky.

As we walked in and our eyes adjusted from bright sunlight to electric light, we found in front of us what we had come to see. The catamaran was sitting on a motorized wheeled dolly, its dark blue hulls even more thin and sleek looking up close than they had been out on the water. It was longer too, about twenty-six feet. A man I judged to be in his latter thirties came walking toward us, a big smile on his face.

"Hi, I'm Richard Rollins, the owner. What can I do for you folks today?"

I took the lead. "Hi, Richard, we saw this rig down by Mallard Cove last night and had to see if we could find it and get a closer look."

"Oh yeah, you two were on that sportfisherman, and you two look like the folks that were on the breakwater. Beautiful boat by the way, for a 'stinkpot'. Glad you all came up, and please call me Dickie, all my friends do."

Many sailboaters and powerboaters have a bit of animosity toward each other. The terms "blowboater" and "stinkpot" are frequently used to describe the other camp, though in this case, I took the way Dickie said it in more of a friendly rather than derogatory sense. I introduced our group.

"You know, Dickie, for a blowboat, this one sure is sleek. But where are those foil things?" Murph had given it a good once over, noting the foils weren't anywhere in sight.

Dickie smiled, "Those daggerboards and the rudders are part of a new proprietary technology we've developed which makes this model the fastest cat in the new eight-meter class. We take them off as soon as she's out of the water. The competition is pretty fierce among us builders, designers, and racers. While we're waiting for the patents, we're keeping the new foil devices under wraps. Sorry about that."

I said, "No problem, we aren't going to go into business against you anytime soon unless we can figure a way to mount rod holders and outriggers on them."

Dickie laughed. "Marlin, for the right price we can equip one with a waterproof widescreen TV and a beer 'fridge if you want."

I liked Dickie right off the bat. "You said 'this model'. Do you make other sizes?"

"This is the only one equipped with foils, at least for now. And like I said it's not ready to sell quite yet. We're focusing on making this a whole new racing class, designed from the very start as a foil boat. We've been making a more family-friendly eighteen-footer for a few years that's been paying the bills."

Suddenly a light went on in my head. "You have one of those around? I'd love to see it." I caught the questioning look that Kari was giving me, and I winked at her.

"Um, yeah, we have a couple in the rigging room next door. Come on in, I'll show you and give you the full tour."

These eighteen-footers were sleek and, this is tough for me to say as a devout powerboater, even *sexy*. The more I looked over the three his crew were rigging, the more excited I got. I pulled Kari over to the side and told her what I had in mind.

"If you want to, it's your business," Kari said.

"No, it's *our* business, and I'm asking your professional opinion."

"My opinion is that Chris will kill you."

Chris Wagner was our head of operations and oversees all of our boats and crews. This would definitely mean more responsibility, but also a jump in pay and probably another person added to his growing crew.

"Nah, he loves a challenge. So, what do you think?"

She said, "They are kind of synonymous with waterfront fun. But please tell me that jet skis aren't next on your list."

"Oh, hell no! That would be the fastest way to chase off all the fishermen. But these things wouldn't be bad."

I went over to where Dickie was in some kind of serious discussion with Murph. But I was the only buyer in the room, or so I thought. "Hey, Dickie, you want to sell me six of these?"

"Marlin, I would love to sell you six of them!"

"Hit me with a number for six in bright red, with the Mallard Cove logo on each mainsail. But I'll need to ride on one first, and you have to throw in a ride on that rocket ship next door for Murph."

He smiled. "I was already talking with Murph about that very thing. Give me a minute."

He walked into an office over at the side. We could see him through a large window writing in a notepad and using a calculator. He came back out a few minutes later with the notepad, showing me the figure. I liked it.

"We just need to do that sea trial, and if it goes well, you'll need to train my operations manager on how to teach guests to sail them."

Dickie said, "Already figured into the price. This isn't my first fleet sale, and I figured all of you would want a ride on both models." He had a wide grin going. I figured I had made his week. But I was wrong, he had bigger fish already frying.

Kari was looking over a pair of hulls that were lying against the wall with various parts piled on top of them. "Hey, Dickie, what are these?"

"Those were an earlier pre-foil version of our twenty-six footer we called our Eight X Six. That was back when we thought we just needed to go wider in order to go faster, and that one had a twenty-foot beam. The foils changed our way of thinking and made those hulls obsolete. With the foils, less boat in the water means reduced friction and increased speed. We needed to cut the weight down and were able to go much narrower on the hulls themselves since we didn't need as much buoyancy. The trick is in getting the lift angle of the foils dialed in compared to the weight of the boat and the amount of wind.

"On smaller boats like this, you used to have to pre-set the daggerboard foil and rudder elevator angles. The problem with that is when the wind speed fluctuates, the foil angle doesn't change and the boat can begin to porpoise then finally stall just like an airplane, then she 'falls off' and the bows dig into the water. Doing that at high speed can be really violent when the boat stops almost within its own length. On the big boats like the F50 class, they have one crewmember whose only job is to continually trim the daggerboards and the rudders to keep her flying. But as I was just telling Murph, we've developed a technology that makes them self-trimming, utilizing the hydraulic force of the water itself. It's a completely autonomous mechanical system. This will revolutionize sailboat racing almost as much as the invention of the foils themselves."

Murph was hanging on Dickie's every word. To be honest, so was I. "What's the F50 class? Do you have one of those here?"

Dickie laughed. "Don't I wish! Actually, that's a dream and a goal of mine. F50's are the catamaran equivalent of an Indy car, and each one costs well into the millions. Made of carbon fiber and titanium, forty-nine-feet long by twenty-nine-feet wide, and they can go over sixty miles per hour in far less than half that much wind. But it takes five crewmembers to race one, which is partly why our new invention is so exciting. One less crewmember means less weight and even more speed. And more speed is what it's all about."

Kari asked, "What are your plans for those old round bottom hulls over by the wall?"

What the heck was her preoccupation with those things, I wondered.

"I need to get them out of here, but I don't have the heart to cut them up. We learned an awful lot during test runs on that old boat. Those hulls were the first ones we retrofitted with foils, but we've now stripped everything off of them. See how wide they are on the bottom? That's designed to add floatation that's needed when it's up on one hull. But it's now just unnecessary weight and drag, and completely outdated with the foil design.

"We came up with this new design when we realized the hulls would spend minimal time in the water. If you look at our new eight-meter you'll see those hulls are a third as wide because the boat's supposed to be flying as opposed to floating. Weight and drag are the enemies. Plus, with it up on the foils in high wind there's just too much stress for aluminum crossmembers to bear. If you look next door you'll see that boat has integral carbon fiber arched crossmembers that replaced the aluminum ones." Dickie paused a minute then asked, "Do you have some kind of use for the old hulls, Kari?"

"I might. I should know by Monday night."

"In that case, if you decide you want them, I'll throw 'em in with Marlin's deal for free. They're just taking up space here."

I was curious, and more than a little worried about where they might end up. "What the heck are you going to do with them?"

Kari smiled. "You'll just have to wait and see. I have an idea."

The way that she said it I knew there would be no more details forthcoming until she was darn good and ready to share them. I hoped that it didn't somehow have something to do with our wedding, though I couldn't imagine that it might. Then again, between the two of us, she's the one who has the most "vision" and imagination, so I can't wait to see what's up her sleeve.

"Do you all have wetsuits, or do you need to borrow some? We can dunk an eighteen footer and the eight-meter and take a spin around Magothy Bay this morning if you'd like," Dickie offered.

Murph said, "We all own them, but they're back at Mallard Cove. Marlin, if you and Kari wouldn't mind picking ours up along with yours, Linds and I can stay and help Dickie get these in the water."

IN THE TRUCK on the way to the marina I asked Kari if she got the same feeling I did, that Murph was trying to get rid of us for some reason.

"Yes. And the three of them sure huddled up quickly as we were leaving. I wonder what's going on there."

I said, "Just like I'm still wondering what the heck you are going to do with those pontoons."

"They're hulls, and I need to meet with all the Mallard Cove partners first before I say anything."

"Aha! This has to do with Mallard Cove." I was relieved that it wasn't wedding related after all.

"Potentially. Or, maybe the new Lynnhaven project. I like the fact that they're from ESVA and have a story behind them. It's the story that sold me."

This kept getting more and more interesting. What did she have in mind? I glanced over and noted her cryptic smile, knowing it all too well. There would be no getting anything further out of her until she was ready to talk about it.

OUT IN MAGOTHY Bay with Dickie and Kari, I was impressed with how easy the *ESVACat 18* was to sail. There was no doubt in my mind now that these will be a moneymaker for the *Pelican Fleet*.

"I can see why this model pays the bills, Dickie. I love it!"

He laughed, "Wait until you sail on the eight-meter, that one is intense. While this model can sail about as fast as the wind, that one can go almost twice as fast. We've got around fifteen knots this morning, meaning that it's going to be a fun ride."

I waved Murph and Lindsay over; they were in a rigid hull inflatable chase boat. Kari and I swapped places with them, letting them take a turn on the smaller cat. We then took the outboard back in to help Dickie bring out the eight-meter rig. It was easier to tow that one out through the channel using the chase boat than to have to tack back and forth in a zigzag pattern against the wind through the narrow cut leading out through the marsh. The smaller cat would have a straight downwind run coming back in to the dock.

We had the tow rope already attached to the eight-meter by the time they got back, and Dickie quickly mounted the daggerboards and rudders. This was the first time I got a closeup look at the system. Each daggerboard was over six feet long, made completely of black carbon fiber. But instead of being a straight fin, each one curved in underneath the boat and looked almost like an inverted question mark. The rudders had what looked like thin wings on the bottom. There were channels within the material which carried the water that powered the actuators, automatically adjusting their angles of attack.

We all strapped on harnesses before boarding the chase boat and the cat. Murph was the first passenger to ride with Dickie. The eight-meter was equipped with a double trapeze; those were the cables attached to a point high up on the mast that hook onto a ring in the center of our harnesses. It was what we had seen Dickie hanging from yesterday. After releasing the tow line the two of them connected their harnesses to their trapezes, and Dickie started his run. Both of them "hiked out" and were now suspended horizontally, mere feet above the surface of the water.

Over the noise of our idling outboard we could easily hear Murph hollering with excitement as the cat picked up speed. The hulls were staying up above the water and were level the entire time even through some very tight turns where I expected them to want to squat or dive as they slowed slightly. This stability must be due in part to that proprietary system, so it was no wonder that Dickie wanted to keep it under wraps for now.

After all of us had a chance to ride on the eight-meter, we helped Dickie get her back on the dolly and into the building. The daggers and rudders went into a locked room.

"I can start delivering your boats in about two weeks, Marlin, if that works for you," Dickie said.

I nodded. "Perfect. That way I get them all before Memorial Day, which is the real start of our season. We'll line them up on the beach in front of the bar, they'll be great eye-catchers."

"Yeah, that will be a good advertisement for our company as well. Maybe we can take some promo pictures there."

Murph spoke up, "We'd love that. How about bringing the eight-meter up and shooting it at the same time?"

"Great idea, we'll do it."

MURPH SAT up front with me on the ride back to Mallard Cove, and he had a funny grin on his face. I'd seen it before. Suddenly I was worried.

I asked, "What did you do now?"

His grin got wider. "Keep it under your hats, but Lindsay and I are buying into ESVA Catamarans. Dickie needs more cash to finish the auto-adjuster patents and to make the eight-meter project successful, and we like the concept as well as the idea of owning a chunk of those new patents."

Okay, I was right to be worried. "What the hell do you know about sailboats?"

"Enough to see that catamarans are a growing trend. You should have seen how many there were down in Florida this year. And I know that when the catamaran world gets a look at that auto-leveling thing, every builder is going to want to license it. You can see why they'll be putting foils on a lot of boats now. That's where I see the value and where I think we'll get a great return on our investment. If the eight-meter class takes off, that'll just be the icing on the cake."

"I hope you two know what you are doing." I wasn't sure they did.

Murph answered, "I know more about this than you knew about television shows when you bought into that, and that's worked out well for you."

He had a point; I had gotten lucky buying *Tuna Hunter Productions* for the foundation. But my dad always used to say that he'd much rather be lucky than smart. I'd never heard of anyone being out-luckied.

"I knew exactly what I was getting into. You guys don't even know anything about Dickie. I mean, he seems like a nice guy that knows that he's doing, but it sounds like you are going to be putting a lot of your savings into his business. At the very least you should get Rikki to check him out." Rikki Jenkins was a friend of ours that owns ESVA Security, a private security firm. They were actually a lot more than that, but this is what they told the public. Within an hour her firm could give Murph and Lindsay a complete rundown on the guy, all the way down to his shoe size.

Murph thought about it a minute then agreed. "I'll call Rikki when we get back to the marina."

I was relieved. "Good. He's probably an okay guy, but it pays to be cautious."

Lindsay spoke up, "You're right, Marlin. Thanks for reminding us of that."

She sounded excited about the idea of the investment, but not nearly as much as Murph. It was good that he had her to help temper his enthusiasm a little. Going a bit slower wasn't a bad idea until they knew exactly who Dickie Rollins was.

4

CATS & CRABS

Monday night Kari came home with a big grin on her face and carrying a huge sketch pad. I knew that she had held a partner's meeting for the Mallard Cove group up at Bayside and that Lindsay and Murph had gone up with her to meet with the other four members of the group. Apparently things had gone very well. Just in case they didn't though, I poured her a vodka when I saw her coming down the dock.

I asked, "I trust all went well?"

"They couldn't have been happier. We will be breaking ground on the Lynnhaven project a little ahead of schedule, right after we get back from our honeymoon. And, the profit numbers at Mallard Cove are far ahead of my most optimistic projections, so everybody is pleased. Our biggest problem now is that we're too crowded at the *Cove Restaurant* in season. We need to add more dining room space before Memorial Day."

"How are you going to do an addition that fast?" I had a hunch, and I hoped I was wrong.

"We're going to cover the deck with a canvas awning so we can use it either rain or shine. Oh, and we're going to knock out the wall between the dining room and the Captain's Lounge and take over that space. Instant addition."

My worst fears were now realized by the second part of her statement.

"Baloney is going to kill you."

In addition to being a true lounging area, the Mallard Cove Captain's Lounge was the meeting place for an unofficial group called the Beer Thirty Bunch. It had originally been made up of the local charter boat crews, and was headed up by Captain Bill Cooper, who was more commonly known around the docks as "Baloney". Bill reveled in his leadership capacity and was very protective of the lounge. But as soon as we started shooting the *Tuna Hunters* show and some of the old cast members joined our group, more and more people started crashing, hoping for a chance to get to meet their favorite stars. Kari and I had stopped going because things had gotten so crowded.

"I kind of hoped that you might volunteer to tell him."

"*Me?* You're the one taking his playroom away, you go tell him."

"He likes you better."

I hate it when she gives me that sweet puppy dog look. "We both know he adores you, so you can look as sweet and innocent as you want, I'm still not telling him."

She said, "I'll make you a deal; you tell Bill, and I'll show you what I'm using those catamaran hulls for."

She knew that had been driving me nuts. "Okay, but you have to tell me before I go over there. I don't want to die without knowing."

Kari chuckled, and reached for the sketch pad. "Okay, you know how the *Cove Beach Bar* turned into such a money-making machine last summer? We still lost some business because the bar wasn't big enough, and it sometimes took way too long to get a drink. Another thing that happened was we've started getting more and more sailboats in the marina and it's now split about fifty-fifty between sailboats and powerboats. I noticed that some of the sportfish crowd and a few of the sailboat crowd didn't always get along and weren't always comfortable around each other. Originally I thought about just expanding the *Beach Bar* but then I thought, why not create another beach bar with a sailing theme? It's going to be next to the existing one with a covered breezeway between the two. Here's the new *Catamaran Bar and Grill*."

Kari held up a sketch of a very tropical looking bar with seating on three sides and a service bar at one end. Benches ran down both sides of the bar, only they weren't benches, they were Dickie's obsolete eight-meter hulls with cushions on top.

"That is too cool! So, you had this idea in mind all along."

She said, "It hit me as soon as I saw them. We'll have the canvas shop over at Carlton's make custom removable cushions. And we'll hang an old jib sail up on the ceiling. It'll have a galvanized metal roof, ceiling fans, and the whole place will have a real open-air 'down island' feel to it. Best of all, it'll be simple, quick and easy to build."

"I like it! Everybody gets a place where they're comfortable. Except the captains and crews. What about them?"

"We'll add on next to the dockmaster's office, that way it'll be in the middle of the marina between the powerboats and the sailboats."

With few exceptions, the eastern part of the marina had mostly become the sailboat side with the west side now filled with powerboaters and charter fishing boats. It seemed to make everyone happier this way.

"Sounds like you have thought it all out, as always."

"You know I try to cover my bases, dear. But there's a bit more to this now. Remember Chef Carlos Ramirez, the head of the restaurant group? He invented a new seafood steamer that will be able to cook dozens and dozens of crabs, clams, oysters, and shrimp at a time. So we're adding a screened 'Steamer Shack' with a brick charcoal pit for fresh seafood, too. It and an attached walk-in cooler for the shellfish will go between the *Catamaran* and the marina."

This was news to me. "You think you guys will sell that many steamed shellfish at a time to make it worth having its own building?"

She nodded her head, "Heck yes. We're the first restaurant as you get off the bridge or as you're running into the Chesapeake by boat. It'll make us even more of a destination. It won't hurt to have a view of the commercial boats unloading in the marina and the bags and baskets of shellfish going straight into the cooler. Nobody will have fresher crabs. You know the old saying, 'if your crabs ain't kickin' then you shouldn't be cookin'. Most restaurants have crabs that first get unloaded off boats and into a chiller at a fish house. The next day or so they get trucked around for who knows how long, then they go into another cooler. They can be days old before ever hitting the steamer. Our crabs aren't just going to be kicking, they'll still be fighting when they get steamed. That's how you want your crabs."

She showed me the sketch of the shack, which was a simple screened building with a metal roof, designed to match the *Catamaran*. I think she may be onto something.

Kari said, "I'll make you a 'to go' cocktail for your walk over to tell Bill. And if you pick out some beer to take him, it should help blunt the news." Kari grabbed my glass and headed to our bar.

I KNOCKED on the side of *My Mahi's* wheelhouse. "Hey, Bill, you home?"

My Mahi is Baloney's "flagship" and home; a decade old fifty-four foot Viking sportfisherman that he salvaged after it had sunk in front of Carlton's boatyard. He had done a great job of rebuilding her, with a lot of us around here pitching in to help. We got her finished just in time for him to join the cast of the *Tuna Hunters* show, and he quickly became its most popular cast member. With his recently increased annual contract, next season he will become its most highly paid cast member as well. His head appeared from under the angled canvas cockpit cover.

"Oh, hey Shaker, it's you. C'mon aboard." He spotted both my cocktail and the six-pack of beer I was carrying. "Uh oh. You're bringin' me beer and it's not to a meetin'. Expensive beer, too. This can't be good."

Bill knows me too well. Enough to call me "Shaker", which is short for "Shake and Bake", a nickname he gave me back when I used to carry a few extra pounds some years ago. One afternoon I jumped on his old boat, the *Golden Dolphin*, and when my feet came to a stop, some of the rest of my body kept moving. Kinetic energy and gravity when combined can be such a bitch. He had scowled and said, "Take it easy on the teak there, Shake and Bake!" His nicknames for people tend to stick. By the way, I didn't hurt the *Dolphin*. Right now she's floating in the slip next door, run for Bill by his old mate, Bobby "B2" Smith.

I followed Bill into the salon of *My Mahi*, the living room area of the wheelhouse. "Where's Betty?" She's Bill's wife of over two decades, a sweet lady who adores him as much as he does her.

"Grocery run. You gonna tell me the bad news now or what? The show get canceled or somethin'?"

Bill sat in his favorite spot on the built-in couch then grabbed one of his favorite cheap cigars from the box next to him, nervously popping it in his mouth, unlit. He never lights up unless he's out fishing. This is the one rule Betty has strictly enforced, so my sense of smell was safe for the time being. Trust me, you don't want to be anywhere downwind whenever he breaks out his lighter; his "sticks" are noxious.

I laughed nervously. "No, nothing like that. Uh, they're going to make some changes around here."

Bill eyed me suspiciously. "Well, spit it out. I ain't movin' the boats you know, it's in my dockage contract. I got guaranteed these two prime spots."

"No, your slips are safe, it's uh, well, about the Captain's Lounge. We're going to be getting a new one, but until it's built, we'll be without one for a while. They're expanding the restaurant." I waited for the eruption.

"Good. That gives us an excuse not to have the afternoon meetings anymore, at least not officially. It's gotten so I don't recognize half the people there. Besides, all the old gang have keycards for the security gate on your dock, so we can meet up on your top deck."

"Oh, good, I thought you'd be mad...wait, what? Where?"

Baloney grinned. "You know, the top deck on *Tied Knot*. Youse two got a lot of room up there."

Did I mention that Bill has a bit of an accent? He spent twenty-some years in his native New Jersey before moving to Virginia a little over twenty years ago. But to hear him talk, you'd think he left the Garden State just yesterday. You can take the boy out of Jersey, but you can't take the accent out of the Baloney. And he had just volunteered my entertainment deck as the new Beer Thirty Bunch hangout. I'm not crazy about the idea, and I don't think Kari will be either, but I'll deal with one problem at a time, especially since he took the whole lounge thing in stride. I went on to explain in detail about the expansion plans, the ones for the dining room, the steam shack and the *Catamaran Bar and Grill.*

"Love the idea of that steam shack; I can eat my weight in steamed shellfish. And it's great them blowboaters are gonna have their own place that's all dolled up just for them so they won't wanna be in our *Beach Bar.* Lots of 'em moving in here now, too many that is. I never heard so many people cry an' moan over the price of a beer as that bunch. The wind's free, so they think everything else should be, too."

I struggled not to grin or laugh. I had no doubt that Bill believed what he had just said was true, but there was more than a ton of irony attached to it. First, Bill hardly ever buys beer himself. Even before he became a cable star and had people fighting over the chance to buy him a beer, he always mooched off everybody else in the Beer Thirty Bunch. He never brings his own beer to our gatherings, instead he drinks everybody else's no matter the brand nor quality. We all know this and have come to expect it. He's the central figure who provides a lot of comic relief, so we look at it like paying the court jester's fee.

As to his blanket statement about the sailing community being cheap, that's been a long-held prejudice of many in the sportfishing community. The truth is that many of the boats on the sailboat side are worth far more than a lot of those on the motorboat side. And there were plenty of frugal folks in both camps, as well as some outright cheapskates. Bill not only mooches beer and labor from his pals, but he also assembled *My Mahi* from two wrecks and a ton of used materials, only paying for new parts when he was totally out of options. Not that you could tell, since he did a great job of putting her back together, but he certainly knows how to stretch a penny until Abe Lincoln begs for mercy.

"Kari just showed me the plans, I think it's going to be a cool place for everybody, Bill. She got some catamaran hulls from ESVA Cats over at Carlton's that'll be the benches for the bar, and there'll be a lot of tables too, just like at the *Cove Beach Bar*."

"Yeah, Carlton's lost his mind, puttin' a blowboat builder in the new place. It'll run off more business than it'll bring in."

"Uh, I don't know. I just bought a half a dozen of them for the *Pelican Fleet*."

"Don't even joke like that, Shaker. That'd be all we need, Sunday sailors playing 'pinball wizard' in the marina, bouncin' off everything and everybody in those things."

I swallowed. "Uh, I'm not joking, but they won't be anywhere near the marina, we'll keep them up on the beach which is where they'll operate out of."

"You really *are* serious! What, now that you bought that Irwin sailing head boat thing you've become one of *them*?" He asked incredulously.

Coastal Dreamer was the *Pelican Fleet's* fifty-four foot Irwin sailboat.

"Hey, don't knock it until you try it! I took a ride on their new eight-meter boat with the hydrofoils last weekend and it was a blast! I'll take you for a spin on one of our new cats when they get here," I offered.

"Not unless I'm dead or unconscious! You've lost your mind. The only boats I'm ever riding in or want anything to do with all have engines. What's next, jet skis?"

I was starting to get irritated with how closed-minded he was acting, but he was already past the point of irritation himself. "Well, I figured you'd probably like jet skis since they have engines. But me and the fish schools around here wouldn't, so no, we aren't going to add any of them." Okay, I admit it was a cheap shot, but he'd taken a few, too. I decided it was time for me to go before things escalated further. "Enjoy your beer, Baloney."

Bill just glared at me as I left, remaining in his chair. I knew he wouldn't stay mad long, and he hadn't used my full "Shake and Bake" nickname or called me Marlin, which he only does when he's *really* mad. Besides, if he is serious about meeting over on my top deck, he knows he's going to need to play nice or get banned. And as Executive Producer of *Tuna Hunters*, technically I was his boss. But that was something I'd never hold over his head; that's not my style. So far we haven't ever allowed business to affect our personal relationship, and I hope we never will.

"So, how did he take the news?" Kari was sitting on our couch when I walked in, a worried look on her face.

I went to the bar to rebuild my vodka. "The part about the Captain's Lounge went over very well. Like us, he hasn't been happy about how large the Beer Thirty Bunch has grown. Almost as unhappy as he is about us adding catamarans to our fleet. I guess I missed the part about him being a 'never sail' kind of guy. He's glad that you're adding a 'sailor's bar' and he hopes that it will help cut down on the sailboat crowd over in the *Beach Bar*. I never realized he had such an issue with sailboats and sailors before."

She looked surprised. "Neither did I. But Bill certainly can be full of surprises at times."

"You can say that again. Like wanting to go back to the core group of the Beer Thirty Bunch and having the meetings here on our entertainment deck." I waited for the reaction; it didn't take long.

"Wait, the what is going where?"

"He wants to drop it back to the core group that we used to have. He volunteered our entertainment deck, I didn't, and part of his rationale is that it'll be easy to limit it to just the people who have keycards for the security gate on this dock."

She thought about it for a minute. "We'll see how that goes. If it starts being a pain, they'll be going back to the new lounge after it's finished. I don't want our home turning into a clubhouse twenty-four-seven. I don't get why he should care about the catamarans, either. They aren't going to be anywhere near him."

"Because he's Baloney. Then again, I didn't do the best job explaining it at first. I think he got a mental image of the marina filled with newbie sailors instead of them being over at the beach by the bar. He'll get over it, especially when he sees they aren't in his hair."

She looked skeptical. "I hope you're right."

I hoped so, too. But it's funny what challenges the Fates can throw your way when you least expect it. There was a curveball coming, and I was going to have no control over it.

5

NEW BEGINNINGS

Murph and Lindsay heard back from Rikki early in the week. Dickie checked out, and everything he told them about himself was true. They were now moving ahead with their plans to partner up. And by the end of the week the old wall and the Captain's Lounge were just a fading memory, as was the little dust up between Baloney and me. Having the Beer Thirty Bunch on *Tied Knot* didn't turn out as bad as Kari and I had feared. The group was now down to Kari and me, Murph and Lindsay, Baloney and Bobby "B2" Smith from the *Golden Dolphin*, Captain Kim "Hard Rock" Collier and his mate Fred "Mad Gaffer" Everett from the *Kembe II*, and Timmy "Spud" O'Shea, the owner of Spud's Trolling Baits here at Mallard Cove. A much smaller group, more relaxed, and a heck of a lot more fun. But I knew better than to think the "relaxed" part could last.

"I need a beer, Shaker." Baloney was coming up the stairs, and he didn't sound happy.

"You always need a beer, Baloney." That's when I noticed the trail of smoke that was following him. His cigar was still lit. "What's with the cigar? Betty throw you out?"

"Huh? Aw, damn, I'm so mad, I forgot to put it out."

Now I was worried. He's never gotten off the boat with a lit cigar that I can recall. "Sit down and relax, here's your beer. What's got you so upset?"

"Not what, Shaker, *who*. That sumbitch on that pile of junk that cut me off comin' into the marina. I had to jam it in reverse and back down to avoid hittin' him, and one of the gals in my charter fell down when I did. She coulda sued me if she'd gotten hurt but luckily she didn't."

Bill was pointing over to the far side of the basin where a big, ungainly looking Chinese Junk was now tied up at the outside end of one of the sailboat docks. It had to be over seventy feet long and just shy of thirty feet wide. I hadn't seen this boat before. I looked at Kari who shook her head. She didn't know it either.

"He wasn't under sail, was he," I asked.

"Well, yeah, he was. But I think he mighta been using his motor, too. It was real obvious I was headin' into the marina, straight down the channel. And he shouldn't have had his sails up goin' through the breakwater, especially into someplace he doesn't know. The guy was just showboating. Cut in front of me from off my beam, he wasn't even in the channel. Then as soon as he clears the breakwater, he drops all three sails, jams his engine in reverse, and slides that thing sideways against the dock like that was what he planned all along, the crazy SOB. Then he's got th' nerve to yell back at me, like I was in the wrong after I gave him what for. Nobody cuts me off when I'm comin' in, especially not some damned blowboater!"

Hard Rock spoke up, "Good thing you didn't hit him or *he* coulda sued you. You know the law Baloney, any boat under sail has the right of way over one under power."

"Yeah, Kim, I know the damn law. I also know that he shouldn't have been under sail comin' in here, especially since he has an engine, and like I said, I'm not sure he wasn't usin' it. It's why I thought he'd bear off for sure, but he kept coming. He's a reckless jerk. You can hardly understand that SOB, too. Got an accent you can't cut through with a chainsaw."

When Bill starts using your real first name, you had better watch out, it means that he is seriously ticked off. Then again, so does the lit cigar when he's not on his boat.

Murph asked, "What was he speaking, Chinese?"

"No! That's the crazy thing, he was speakin' some kinda Spanglish. I could only catch every other word, and I didn't like any of 'em."

I didn't think it was that weird for anyone of any ethnicity to own a Junk style boat; everybody has their own boat design tastes. But I didn't want to have that debate with Bill right now. I looked over at Kari whose face was buried in her smartphone. After a minute or two she looked up.

"I just texted Barry. The fellow's name is Marco Vasquez, and he's rented that slip for the season." Barry Rolle was the marina's Bahamian born dockmaster.

"Oh, that's just great. Well, I hope 'Marco Polo' and his piece of junk stay at the dock most of the time, at least when I'm comin' in or goin' out. He tries that crap on me again and he's gonna lose a side rail." Baloney exhaled a cloud of cigar smoke to punctuate his threat.

Kari wanted to steer the conversation away from Bill's confrontation quickly. "On a happier note, we're starting construction on the new bar and cook shack tomorrow. They're using a big crew, so start to finish should only take three weeks. There's not much to the *Catamaran* building but a metal roof and the bar since it's all open air. And there's even less to building the cook shack. They should be done just in time to open for the season along with the *Beach Bar*."

Baloney replied, "Good. Then those blowboaters can stay out of our bar."

So much for steering away from confrontation.

B2 said, "If it draws those sailboat girls away from the *Beach Bar*, I may end up spending some time over there. Lots of pretty girls came in on sailboats last year, and that bar might help draw more of 'em."

Bobby is a handsome guy in his mid-twenties, recently "singled-up" by his now ex-girlfriend. Having two beach bars in his backyard was happy news for him, and he apparently didn't care what kind of boats their female patrons preferred. Baloney glared at him.

My ringing phone saved me from wading into the middle of this. It was my old friend, Johnny Knowles. We went back together all the way through elementary school in Richmond and growing up we used to be thicker than thieves. Then I moved to Virginia Beach and started guiding while he went to college, dropped out and built a software company. He called me several months back, asking if Mallard Cove could accommodate a big catamaran, which of course I said they could. I got up and moved to the front of the deck so I wouldn't interrupt the others' conversation.

"Good to hear from you again, Johnny. In fact, it's good timing, too. I'm getting married May twenty-seventh, and I'd really like you to make it if you can."

Johnny laughed. "Of course I'll be there. And I wasn't laughing at you, by the way. Karen and I got divorced last year, so I had to sell the company and split the proceeds with her as part of the settlement. I'm having this big cat built because now I have the time and money to use it, after being kind of forced into early retirement." He paused a minute, "A year ago I was working seven days a week, but now I'll have the time to watch you get married, all because I got divorced. The irony of that is really thick."

"Johnny, I'm sorry, I hadn't heard."

"Don't be, Marlin. Back then I thought life was all about algorithms and spreadsheets. It turned out that I didn't know the difference between merely existing and truly having a life. Somehow I thought they were the same thing. So, Karen lives down in the Keys now with her new beau, and I'm footloose these days. I even had *Wanderer* built for single-handing. That's what I named my boat, *Wanderer*, because that's exactly what I plan on doing. Equipped her with power winches, roller-reefing fore and mainsails, with all the lines tailing back into the cockpit. Sixty-five feet long, and I don't even need to bring anyone along if I don't want to; I can handle her all by myself. I'm my own floating private island. She gets launched in two weeks over on the Rappahannock River. I'll do some short shakedown day trips, then head over your way. I'm going to take her around the Chesapeake starting at Mallard Cove, then hit Cape

Charles, Bayside Resort, Smith Island, St. Michaels, Baltimore, Annapolis, and be back in time for your incarceration. Oops, I mean marriage."

"Hey! You haven't even met my future wife!"

"No offense meant to her, Marlin, I was commenting on the institution of marriage in general and so many that are trapped in it."

"Rough divorce, Johnny?"

"I can't imagine any other kind, Marlin. But I'm putting that behind me now. I've got a new start to a new life, and I intend to enjoy it. That boat is going to be freedom for me, and water past her twin transoms is just that. I'm looking ahead to where I'm going, not back at where I've been. And then this fall I'm heading over to Bermuda for the winter. Palm trees, warm breezes, no snow, beautiful women, and gallons of Gosling's rum. Hell, maybe I should send Karen a 'thank you' note."

"That's where we're going on our honeymoon, Bermuda. But it sounds like we'll be over and back before you get there. Oh, and speaking of Bayside, the wedding is going to be up at the Bayside Club next to the resort, so you may want to book your slip up there now. I know the place pretty well, and they only have one dock that can handle big cats, they'll be starting to get busy by the twenty-seventh."

Johnny whistled, "I've heard about that place. When you get hitched, you don't spare any expense! Never figured you for a club type of guy."

"Some friends own it. Kari works for them and is a partner in a few of their properties, so we kind of had to have it there, but we got a great deal."

"Well, that's one party I am not going to miss! I'll book that slip first thing in the morning, and I'll book one at Mallard Cove for three weeks from now. I'm really looking forward to kicking back and catching up with you. Kind of like the old days."

He couldn't see it of course, but I was smiling, looking forward to spending time with my old friend. "I can't wait, Johnny. I'll see you then."

I rejoined the group after I hung up, and by that time Baloney had calmed down and was more his old self. Kari gave me a look as if to ask about my call, so I gave her a wink and a nod to silently let her know that it was all good. I'll tell her about Johnny later after everyone leaves.

~

"THE BOAT IS in the final rigging. I was able to get some good pictures and video of her, pretending to be a lost tourist from a boat. I sent the photos to our buyers along with our final offer, and we now have a deal."

The second pirate said, "That's great news. Did you tell them about the pickup point?"

"Yes, and they agreed. It is so nice to not have to ship it and to pay a middleman. They said they know others who are also interested in a deal like this one."

"Well then, I guess we'll just have to find them one, won't we."

6

THE NEW NORMAL

Three weeks later...

SEVERAL THINGS HAVE BECOME Kari's trademarks since she started working for Casey and Dawn. The biggest are the accuracy and speed at which she gets things done, and her high degree of organization which allows her to work that fast. She schedules her contractors so that they aren't working on top of each other, then makes them stick to their allotted timeframes. Since they aren't held up by other crews on a job, it allows them to work faster and make a larger profit, which is part of why her crews love working for her.

The *Catamaran* and the steam shack were right on schedule to be completed tomorrow, the day before the season opening of both beach bars on Friday. I have to admit, I'm excited. I love steamed shellfish, and I'm looking forward to seeing this new steamer in action. Carlos swears it will keep up with all the demand for shellfish they can throw at it. And I can eat a lot of it.

And as Kari had hoped, the hull benches have become a real conversation starter. Everyone who has tried sitting on them is surprised by just how comfortable they are. Kari also had the sign painter paint the name *Mallard Cove Express* on the side of each one. That's another one of her strong points: attention to detail.

The last two of our *Pelican Fleet's* catamarans are also due to arrive tomorrow. The first four are already sitting on the beach and will be available for rent starting this weekend. But they won't be the only ones on display. The eight-meter and another eighteen-foot demo model are now going to be based out of here too. The eight-meter will be sitting on its motorized cradle that will allow it to be easily launched from the beach. The cradle is needed since this model is so much heavier than the eighteen footers. Those can easily be dragged up on the sand by two people.

When they did their deal, Dickie and Murph realized this would be the perfect spot for doing demonstration sails for their catamarans. They have a straight shot off the beach, without having to deal with navigating the cut at Carlton's. And a quick right turn puts them into the Chesapeake, while a left puts them into the Atlantic. On most days we can find some wind on one or both of these bodies of water.

It also made sense because the design of the boats is complete. With the exception of maybe a quick tour, most of the customers are going to be more interested in sailing the finished product instead of hanging around the itchy fiberglass dust over at the boatyard. And any tweaks made to the eight-meter at this point will only be changes to the foils and the rudders, which are easily transported back and forth.

Part of the reason Dickie wanted the capital infusion from Murph and Lindsay was to finance the building of a pair of eight-meters. They needed the new ones to be able to better promote the class, as well as have at least one "on the floor" to sell as soon as their patents come through. Having the demo boats on the beach alongside our *Pelican Fleet's* cats was just the icing on the cake of their deal. It looks like everything is coming together nicely for all of us.

This evening Lindsay and Murph stayed on after the rest of the Beer Thirty Bunch made their way home. The four of us planned on grilling and hanging out together for the first time in over two weeks. It hadn't happened sooner because everyone had such full schedules, working long days.

Murph said, "I got into this catamaran thing thinking that it was going to be a passive investment, but I've found out that I enjoy spending time over at the boatyard, watching and learning from Dickie. It's taking up the slack nicely as Linds and I back away from working so many charters. I've been able to give Dickie some good input, like my idea of using our beach for demos. Linds and I are definitely not doing the Florida gig anymore, at least we won't be fishing anyone else besides us if we do go back down there."

Kari said, "It'll be great to have you guys here next winter, and by then we'll be in full construction mode over on the Lynnhaven project. I'm glad that you'll be here to be able to be involved with it."

While other project managers might not want the oversight and input of their project's investors, Kari welcomed it, especially from Murph and Lindsay. Over the past several years they had lived aboard on a few different boats, staying in various marinas up and down the Atlantic Seaboard, so they brought a lot of experience and knowledge about the most popular amenities along with them.

Lindsay added, "I'm glad that we'll be here too, but mostly so we can spend time with you guys in person, not just over a video call. This next Christmas will be the first one we'll have seen here at Mallard Cove. These last couple of years we've left just as Bill was putting up Santa."

Baloney had a few interesting, if not outright peculiar traditions on the *Golden Dolphin*. And some of them have also found a home on *My Mahi*. If he catches a wahoo, instead of a pennant or flag he hoists a black brassiere on the outrigger line. Then every Thanksgiving he puts an inflatable Santa with a beer can glued in his hand up in the tuna tower of the *'Dolphin*, with two floodlights trained on it. At night you can even see Santa as you are coming back over the bridge from Virginia Beach. And Santa doesn't come down from the tower until New Year's Day.

"So, this is going to be the 'new normal' then," I stated.

Lindsay replied, "Since when has any of us had anything 'normal' going on? Speaking of which, what's your old pal like, Marlin? I mean, we'll know soon enough on Friday, but what's his story?" She had a point about things being normal. We really didn't seem to have a routine, even though that suited me just fine.

"I grew up with Johnny, we lived in the same Richmond neighborhood, went to the same schools and were close pals throughout those years. But I got into fishing while he was more into computers and electronics. He became a major geek. Really shy with other people and especially with girls. Though while our paths went in different directions after high school, we still remained friends, just at a distance. He married a girl he met at college right before he dropped out, then he went on to build a big software company. He and his wife ended up getting divorced last year, and he told me had to sell the company to free up cash for the settlement. Now he's built a big catamaran sailboat, and I guess he's retired. Said he's going to sail around the Chesapeake this summer, then head over to Bermuda for the winter. I get the feeling he's trying to make up for the time he spent building the business.

"Other than me, he never had a lot of friends in school. Then I think he jumped into marriage way too early, and now a little over a decade later that's over. I guess he's in some kind of a 'finding himself' mode. He didn't date a lot in high school, not for lack of trying, but more because he was so geeky. I was a little surprised that he got married so young, I figured it would have taken him a lot longer to find a girl who was into him. I never met her; they eloped and then he dove into building that business every waking moment of his life. He doesn't fish, at least he didn't back then, though some of his family did. I guess that's a big part of why we drifted apart; we were getting deeper into two completely different fields. I just want to warn you about him being so shy and such a big geek. But once you get past all that I think y'all will like him, he's really a good guy."

Murph frowned. "Sounds more like a sad sack."

I disagreed. "I haven't seen him in a few years, but he sounded very upbeat on the phone. And he's the one who reached out to me, so he's trying to do some reconnecting. That doesn't sound like anyone who's a downer, more like someone who's trying to be more outgoing. Give him a chance, Murph. Everybody gave you one, though it helped that you were giving away free beer and barbecue about the time I met you." I couldn't help but grin as the girls chuckled. Murph and Lindsay threw a big barbecue soon after they bought Mallard Cove, to attract potential customers like me and show us how they planned on fixing the place up.

The word "nightmare" comes to mind when describing the property's condition when they bought it. Now, two years later, the transformation has been nothing short of amazing. Even before we started filming *Tuna Hunters* here last fall, the *Beach Bar* had already become the "it" place on the Lower Shore. The extreme popularity of the show is sure to add to this as more people become aware of what they've been doing here. Adding the extra dining room space and the new beach bar were brilliant moves on Kari's part, I think they'll need every bit of it this summer. I have a feeling that we'll get a good indication of what's in store for this season on Friday, especially if it's already busy this early. I'm really proud of my friends, and what they've accomplished.

THE NEXT MORNING as I was headed to my office I saw a crab boat unloading a pair of wooden bushel baskets of crabs at the dock slip nearest to the new walk-in cooler. A busboy loaded the baskets onto a hand truck and wheeled them up to the cooler as Mimi Carter paid the crabber in cash. Dealing directly with the boatman means it is always strictly a cash deal. There were no credit cards or credit of any kind at this level of the industry. As he left I greeted Mimi, the head of Mallard Cove restaurant operations.

"Hi, 'Meems'. Loading up for tomorrow's opening?"

"Hey, Marlin. This is hardly 'loading up'. I've already ordered ten more bushels for tomorrow, then we'll see what we're going to need for the weekend. I got these just to make certain we'd have some crabs ready to go at lunch tomorrow in case my big order didn't arrive by then. And I've got clams and shrimp coming in the morning."

I whistled. "You guys are really optimistic about the start of the season, aren't you."

"Well, there's a really good buzz going around about the *Catamaran*, not just on ESVA but over in VA Beach and beyond. Thanks in part to your show, the restaurants are no longer the best-kept secret on the Shore anymore. That opening introduction shot totally shows the place off."

The opening scene of *Tuna Hunters* is taken from a camera drone that slowly rises from behind the charter dock as the cast members' boats cast off and file out in a line. The drone keeps rising, showing a great overhead view of the marina, the *Cove Restaurant* and *Cove Beach Bar*, with Fisherman and Smith islands, the Chesapeake Bay Bridge Tunnel, and the Atlantic Ocean beyond. It was purely a staged shot, taken a few days before the season when the lighting conditions were perfect and the water was calm. Welcome to the world of "reality TV." In "the real world" the boats go out anywhere from a few hours before sunrise to just after dawn, which is not the greatest time to try to get them on video as they race out, heading into the sun.

"I'm glad that worked out for you. It was the perfect show intro, the boats leaving the marina, headed out into the ocean. But wait until we air the last show of the season, that cast chat we filmed inside the *Cove*. That one should boost things even more."

"I love it. Hey, speaking of boosting things, are you going to be around for the opening tomorrow?"

I nodded. "Looking forward to it. With our cats lined up on the beach, I'm hoping we get some rental business from your customer pool this weekend."

"You mean before they start drinking."

"Uh, yeah, that would be a requirement, Meems. You can have them to feed and get them 'lubricated' after they come back in from the water. But I need them stone-cold sober to sail our cats."

"I'll tell the bartenders to try to keep an eye out for your sailboaters, Marlin. Though you know how crazy it got last summer in the *Cove*, and I bet it'll be the same at the *Catamaran*. I sure hope so."

I said, "We both do, for everyone's sake. We've all got a lot riding on this."

Mimi headed back to the restaurant as I continued toward the office. Up ahead I saw a commotion happening around *My Mahi*, and I could hear loud voices. Bill was standing in the middle of the cockpit, having been in the process of taking down the canvas cover. He was wagging a finger at someone on the dock.

"I'm warning you that if you pull that same crap again, I'm not coming off my throttles, you got that?"

I could see Baloney was not a happy camper right now. The guy on the dock was giving it back to Bill, in heavily accented English. Obviously, this must be Marco Vasquez.

"An' I'm tellin' you if you don' and you hit my *Zopilote*, I will own this piece of garbage you call a boat! A sailboat gots the rights of way, you should know dat!"

"Yeah, well, this time I saw you were under power with the sails up, and that makes you the same thing as a motorboat. And I wasn't just in the channel, I was ahead of you, so that gives *me* the right of way. *You* should know *that* if you even have a Virginia license to operate that thing, which I doubt, you're too dumb to have passed the test. So, I'm tellin' you, if you pull that stunt again you crazy sumbitch, I'll put you and your hunka junk on the rocks but good, you got me?"

Vazquez answered by jumping over *Mahi's* stern into the fishing cockpit just as I reached the boat. I leaped aboard at the same time that Baloney came across the cockpit at him. Vazquez looked to be about an inch taller than Bill's five-foot five-inches, and was maybe ten years younger, somewhere around his mid-thirties. In retrospect, maybe I should have let the two of them go at it and get it out of their systems, but I didn't want to take a chance on my friend getting hurt. I got between them and put my hands out toward each of them to keep them separated. I turned toward Vazquez.

"Bad move, jumping uninvited onto someone's boat, Vazquez."

He stopped his advance and looked at me. "Who th' hell are jou? An' you jus' made a bad move yourself, stickin' jour nose in where it don' belong. Tha's a good way to get it punched, jou know?"

Baloney went ballistic. "Get the hell off my boat, you channel hog!" He lunged toward Vazquez, but I was still blocking him.

Vazquez stuck his chest out. "You real brave now that you gots jour frien' here wit' you!"

Bill tried to sidestep me, but I blocked him again.

"Oh yeah, well, I don't need any help to mop my deck with you! Lemme at him, Shaker!"

"Yeah, Chaker, let me an' him settle dis right now, mano a mano, without jou helpin' him," Vazquez taunted.

"Both of you just cool your jets! Vazquez, get the hell off his boat, and Bill, why don't you go back in the salon."

Neither budged, which is just what I was afraid of. Fortunately, I saw Murph coming down the dock and I yelled to him. "Hey, Murph, how about a little help here?"

Murph started double-timing it our way. Vazquez, seeing more reinforcements en route suddenly saw the wisdom in retreating. He stepped over onto the floating dock just as Murph arrived.

"This ain't over. Jou come near my *Zopilote* wit' dis barge again, an' I'll put *jou* on de rocks, jou got dat?"

"Try it, you crazy ass, and see what happens! You're damn right this ain't over," Baloney yelled at Vazquez, who was now making a beeline for the *Cove,* and breakfast.

This was about as mad as I'd ever seen Bill. Good thing he hadn't grabbed a cigar yet today or he probably would have bitten it in two. He backed up a couple of steps and glared at both Murph and me.

"And what the hell right have you two got to jump into my fight and keep me from defending my own territory? Don't ever do that again. If I ever need your help, I'll ask for it. But I don't need it!" He went into the salon and slammed the door.

I looked at Murph and shrugged. "No good deed goes unpunished, I guess." I stepped over onto the dock next to Murph.

48

"I guess." Murph asked, "Was this about what happened a few weeks ago?"

I shook my head. "I'm guessing it happened again yesterday. And Vazquez had better watch out. If he was under power, even if he did have his sails up, he was wrong and Bill was right. And I don't for a second doubt that he would ram Vazquez."

Murph agreed, "I don't either. It sounds like Vazquez is a show-boating hothead. I'd throw him and his junk out of the marina, but this isn't about anything that happened inside the breakwater, other than them yelling at each other. Not a Mallard Cove problem unless this starts becoming a regular event. Then we'll have to step in."

I nodded. This wasn't a position I wanted to be in, but I intend on protecting Bill as my friend first, and as my highest rated cast member, second. Both were good reasons to take the stance I did, and no matter what Baloney says, I'll do it again if I have to. He'll just have to get over it.

THE MESSAGING APP chirped on the pirate's burner phone. *"I have another one for two days from now. In Annapolis."*

The pirate grimaced. They had never turned a job down before, but the timing on their own job meant this wouldn't be possible. Besides, they had done too much preparation to drop it now, especially since the money was so much better. *"Can't get to it for two weeks."*

"Must be done in two days."

"Not possible. But will be available again in about two weeks."

The pirate knew the broker must be furious, but it was unavoidable. He had put just as much planning into this, their first solo job, so he knew the broker was not going to be happy. They'd always been available on twenty-four hours' notice before, and this time the broker had given them twice as long.

In the ensuing silence he started analyzing his position. Maybe it was a good thing, and the time may have come to keep working on their own, and break away from the broker entirely, especially as they built up their reputation. Better boats, dependable delivery, and fair pricing. Maybe they didn't need the broker as much as he, or maybe she, needed them. He saw the three dancing dots, meaning a reply was coming.

"Two weeks then. Delay will cost you."

He didn't like what that might imply, especially since the broker had sought him out, then suggested he hook up with a partner, which had worked out very well. The broker had researched both of them as closely as the target boats and their owners. He knew who both pirates were, and that wasn't a very comforting thought. He messaged back, *"I'll be back in touch as soon as we're available."*

"Time is cash. Remember that."

The pirate looked at the curious message on his app, shook his head slightly and closed it.

7

THE SPY

The next day Kari was anxious over the opening of the two beach bars, especially the *Catamaran*, but I wasn't concerned. I knew that everything they had done was top notch, and it should be a huge hit. Besides, for late April, the weather felt more like June, and today's sky was crystal clear. She couldn't have asked for a more perfect day. At this rate, the water would be warming up fast, which meant many species of fish would be showing up earlier along with more gulls, pelicans, and summer fowl. The arrival of the gamefish migration will be welcome news for Mallard Cove's growing charter fleet. With school not even out yet, the *Pelican Fleet's* weekend parasail, eco-tour, and sailing trips were already booking up. All the signs were pointing to an early and busy summer season.

KARI RODE the elevator down to my office at *Tuna Hunter Productions* a little after four. "Feel like knocking off early? I need to go over and show my face at the *Catamaran's* grand opening. I figured since it's Friday we can have a prolonged cocktail hour, then split the new steamed shellfish platter for two."

I replied, "Sounds like a plan. Johnny just texted, he's about ten minutes out. We can help him tie up then bring him along with us."

"Barry set him up at the end of D Dock. He'll be backed up to your buddy's boat."

I frowned. By "your buddy" I knew she meant Vasquez. I hoped he wouldn't be around when Johnny pulled in. We hurried over there just as Johnny was passing through the breakwater's inlet. Unlike Vazquez, his sails were already furled and out of sight, and he was moving strictly under power. He pulled up almost to the floating dock, then pivoted and slid her sideways slowly using a combination of *Wanderer's* diesel engines and her twin bow thrusters, gently laying her pre-positioned fenders up against the dock. There was no sign of Vazquez, but now I almost wished that he were here, to see how docking is done, properly and cautiously.

Now that we were up close to her we could see that *Wanderer* was definitely a custom boat. The window lines were more like those from a sportfisherman, and unlike any I'd ever seen on a sailboat, though they flowed nicely. Kari and I quickly cleated the bow, stern, and spring lines before plugging in the large shore power cable that Johnny handed down from the deck. At least I think it's Johnny. The guy who appeared at the side rail only bore a slight resemblance to the friend I grew up with.

Gone was the geeky, pasty-white look of someone who had spent the better part of his adult life indoors, at least until now. He was quite tan, maybe not as deep as Lindsay and Murph, but bear in mind that it was snowing here only a short two months ago. By Virginia standards, Johnny was already very dark-skinned for this early in the season.

Gone also were the long wrinkled pants and tee shirts advertising space adventure movies or emblazoned with computer jokes that only seem to amuse those people who write code. In their place were name brand fishing shorts and a short sleeve vented fishing shirt. Canvas deck shoes and a huge gold wristwatch rounded out his ensemble. He looked like he just stepped out of a preppy catalog.

"Who are you, and what have you done with Johnny Knowles?"

He grinned at me. "He died in a courtroom a year ago. I'm his evil twin."

I shook my head. "A distant cousin, maybe. There's only a slight resemblance."

He smiled as he looked over at Kari. "You didn't tell me your fiancée had a daughter."

I saw Kari's eyes narrow, if only slightly. Johnny had hit on the one thing that had originally kept me from asking her out, the more than seven-year difference in our ages. But Kari also isn't a fan of either fast or smooth talkers. Probably part of what first attracted her to me since I'm neither. Apparently, Johnny had lost more in his divorce than just half of his company. He'd also lost his shy, introverted personality, and I suddenly missed that about him.

I said, "Johnny Knowles, meet Kari Albury, my fiancée and business partner."

"Nice to meet you, Kari. Hey, do you have a sister or a friend? I'm new in town."

I saw Kari stiffen, really not liking what she saw of Johnny so far. He was starting to rub me the wrong way, too, not at all like he used to be, though I was still willing to give him the benefit of a doubt. I'd known other friends who had gone through a weird and wild phase following a divorce, acting completely different than they had been before becoming single again. Most of them eventually chilled out, became more grounded, and reverted back closer to who they had been before. But so far everything he said to Kari had been about the worst things he could have picked to say.

Before Kari could answer I said, "It sounds like you won't have a problem meeting someone without any help. Speaking of which, we're heading over to a new bar that just opened here, come on and go with us. We can kick back and catch up there."

I think I had Johnny at the point where I said, "new bar". He hopped down on the dock and said, "Let's go, I can give you two a tour of *Wanderer* tomorrow."

Kari quickly moved to my left side, leaving me to walk in the middle between her and Johnny. A sure sign that she was definitely not a fan of his.

"I've watched *Tuna Hunters* a few times. You know that fishing has never really been my thing, but after I heard you were involved with it I gave it a try. It was the opening shot that convinced me I wanted to see this place for myself. It's even better than the video."

"This was all Kari, she did the whole project, concept to completion. You should have seen it when she took over, it was a complete disaster, and that was just two years ago."

"That's amazing. Yeah, everything looks great, you did quite a job with it then, Kari."

"Thanks." She said it in the way you might say it to an annoying relative that you wanted to stop talking, but Johnny didn't pick up on that, which would have made my life so much simpler if he had.

WHILE THE TRIO kept walking to the *Catamaran*, they were too preoccupied to notice that a small center console with a single occupant had idled into the marina, tying up at an empty slip toward the end of B Dock. A pair of eyes followed them as they entered the covered breezeway between the two bars.

"HEY KARI, I figured you would be here so I reserved a table back in the corner for y'all."

Mimi led us through the already packed bar to the far corner and a six-seat table next to where the edge of the bar's concrete patio meets the sand. From here we can watch the whole bar crowd and also the beach. It was exactly the vantage point I would have chosen myself.

If there were any doubts about how this new bar would do, they were now gone. It wasn't even "rush hour" yet, and already all the tables were occupied, as well as most of the spots on the hull seats. The *Beach Bar* was nearly as packed, too.

Our fleet of catamarans sitting on the beach in front of the bars gave both places a real "down island" vibe, though I was looking forward to tomorrow when they would hopefully be out, starting to earn their keep. I noticed that the launch cradle for the eight-meter was empty, and there was a slight breeze blowing.

"This is a great sailor's bar! I love the way you used those hulls as benches," Johnny said.

I saw that Kari wasn't planning on answering him so I said, "All of it was Kari's idea and design, and yeah, it's a great place, I love the feel of it. And speaking of designs, that window line on your boat is really cool and unusual." I wanted to switch to a more neutral subject.

"Thanks, that was my own design, or rather, I copied it from the old Andy Mortensen sportfisherman that my grandfather had when I was a kid. You might remember it from his house up on the James River. I wanted to incorporate something that reminded me of him every time I saw it. As you know, I was never much of a fisherman, but that boat meant everything to him and he meant everything to me. I wanted to take a part of him with me on my trips in my new life. I miss that old man so much." Johnny launched into a very long story about his grandfather that meant a lot to him, but not so much to Kari or me, though we listened politely.

It was funny, when he got off his boat he had sounded like a braggart and walked with a swagger. But as soon as he mentioned his grandfather, I could hear his voice soften. It gave me a glimpse of that shy kid I grew up with, the one I missed. I saw that Kari had picked up on it too, as she now tilted her head slightly while listening to the story. That he didn't pick up the fact we weren't as into what he was saying was so much more like the Johnny of old. When we were kids he would tell me about the latest discovery in computers or electronics, rambling on until my eyes glazed over. But he was my pal and those things were important to him, so I never interrupted him. I was one of the few that he felt the need to communicate with back then, and I wasn't going to be an ass by stopping him, neither then, nor now.

As it was, I didn't need to, Johnny interrupted himself. As he was coming to the end of one of his grandfather stories he stopped mid-sentence as he looked out over the water.

"Whoa! That is the coolest cat ever!"

We followed his gaze, spotting Murph and Lindsay approaching in the eight-meter with Linds on the tiller. Despite it not being a really strong breeze, the cat was up on her foils, going almost twice the wind speed. The boat had caught the attention of many in the bar, and I saw one woman was now filming it.

Murph had seen the packed bar from offshore and told Lindsay to show the crowd what the cat could do. She made for the shore and executed a fast ninety-degree turn, now paralleling the shore and accelerating on more of a reach. Another quick turn and she was heading back out the channel between the islands as the two of them hiked out on the trapezes, trying to squeeze every ounce of speed out of the boat. Several of the sailors at the bar had been watching, including Baloney's new "pal", Vazquez.

"Wow! La chica can navegar," Vazquez exclaimed from his seat at the bar. Seeing the funny looks he was getting from some of those around him he said, "I said dat girl can really sail. Dat boat is not bad too, eh?" This time he got several nods in agreement.

A MINUTE later Lindsay brought the cat back in toward the beach, this time much more slowly, but the cat was still stubbornly staying up on the foils. She finally had to point the bows up into the wind to be able to slow enough for the hulls to settle into the water. The foils had been adjusting their angles automatically according to the speed, just as they had been designed. And instead of nosediving, the hulls settled into the water completely level. Murph then raised the extended daggerboard and foil. Linds turned the boat and brought it to a stop on the mobile cradle while simultaneously popping the rudders up.

Murph quickly hooded the proprietary mechanism on each of the rudders and daggerboards with heavy black canvas bags, after releasing all the foil components from the hull. This fact wasn't lost on the woman who had been filming the boat from up by the bar.

She had been surprised to see an eight-meter here and stunned by its performance. Not once did it nosedive or stall in the relatively low wind. Obviously, whatever the man had covered was something that allowed this boat to outperform all the others she had seen so far. Now she wanted to find out more about whatever it is that he was hiding. She approached the couple who had already secured the boat on the cradle and were now motoring the wheeled contraption up above the high-tide line before locking it.

"Bon jou... er, good afternoon. This is such a beautiful boat, an eight-meter, no?" Her English had a thick French accent.

Lindsay looked surprised, "Yes, yes it is! You certainly know your boats."

The woman angled toward Lindsay, for the moment ignoring Murph, who was on the other side of the boat. He looked her over from there as he gathered up the rudders and daggerboards, and he liked what he saw. Somewhat short, barely above five feet tall, with blue-green eyes. She had short-cropped, naturally tightly-curled blond hair that looked like it had seen its share of sun and salt, but not in a bad way. Canvas deck shoes, suntanned legs leading up to nicely filled white shorts, a button-down oversized coral fishing shirt knotted at the bottom and buttoned only halfway up, revealing a light yellow bikini top barely covering her smallish but perky breasts. The whole look screamed of someone who had spent a lot of her probably thirty or so years around boats. And that accent, he could sit and listen to her read from the dictionary all afternoon long...

"Weren't we, MURPH!" Lindsay was glaring at him.

"What?" Uh, oh.

"I was saying to Danielle that we are in a hurry to meet up with some friends, otherwise we would love to sit and chat with her about the boat. She is *quite familiar* with eight-meters." Lindsay's voice carried an implied warning, and it wasn't even about the way he had been leering at Danielle. That conversation would no doubt happen later.

Murph caught the inference and unconsciously tightened his grip on the four hooded carbon fiber units now in his arms. "Yes, yes we would love to talk at some point. Are you going to be around this weekend?"

Lindsay shot him a look that said, *wrong answer*, before smiling her best fake smile and saying, "Yes, will you be around?"

"Perhaps." Out of the corner of Danielle's eye she saw the man from the big catamaran stand up and head this way along with another man. This wouldn't do. "But you have reminded me, I too am supposed to meet a friend. I must run now, but I will find the two of you again. Au revoir, Lindsay and Murph. I look forward to chatting with you in the future."

Danielle turned and walked in the direction of the original beach bar. She made sure not to get too close to Johnny. Meeting him now in front of his friends would not be good, she didn't want them to be able to recall seeing the two of them together.

After she was out of earshot Murph asked, "How did you know her name was Danielle?"

"She introduced herself. If you hadn't been so busy checking her out, you might have paid more attention to what she was saying instead of how she looked. She was asking why our eight-meter stays up on the foils longer and in lighter wind than any she's seen before. So she's *very* familiar with eight meters, too familiar for comfort if she could detect that much of a difference in its performance. We need to lock up the foils and rudders in *OCT*'s big dock box. I don't trust anyone that knowledgeable with 'eights' getting such a close look at those until the patents are issued."

"Hi, guys! Lindsay and Murph, meet my old friend Johnny Knowles." We had arrived at their boat just after the pretty blond left. Johnny had been following her with his eyes as she walked away, and now reluctantly turned to face them. Or rather, he turned and faced Lindsay.

"Very nice to meet you... both." At the moment it looked like

"New Johnny" was back, judging by the way he was now eyeing Lindsay.

Murph said, "You, too. Marlin has been telling us a lot about you."

Johnny turned to Murph and smiled, "Anything good is pure fiction, Murph. I was just a geeky kid he went to school with. He pulled me out of a lot of the lockers I got stuffed into."

Murph had seen Johnny visually check out Lindsay when he walked up, so he was prepared to dislike him. Instead, he was caught off-guard by his remark and the disarming grin that came with it, and he found himself chuckling.

"He always sees the best in people and said that you were a great guy. He also said that you just built a catamaran?"

Johnny nodded. "Yeah, it's not quite as sleek and fast as this, but it's comfortable, and now it's my home as well. Glad you had room for it here this weekend, you're really busy for this early in the season."

Lindsay answered, "You should have seen it last summer. We had to add this new *Catamaran* bar just to keep up with the demand for beach bar space. Though you wouldn't know that it only opened a few hours ago by looking at it now, it's already packed." She too had seen how full both it and the *Cove Beach Bar* were on their first pass offshore in the cat.

I said, "We're lucky they saved a table for us. Speaking of which, why don't we head that way and get a cocktail? We hadn't even ordered yet before we saw you guys pulling in." I was ready to kick back and relax.

"Johnny, why don't you and Lindsay head over to the table, and how about giving me a hand with the rudders and foils, Marlin? We'll be back in a few minutes, guys. Linds, order me the usual, would you please?"

Murph and I carried the units up toward the breezeway between the bars while Johnny and Lindsay went to join Kari. I knew something was up since Murph asked me to go with him rather than stay with Johnny and Linds. He kept looking around nervously, apparently watching for someone.

"Murph, what's up?"

"Wait until we get past the bars and to where no one can overhear us." After we finally made the turn toward the security gate at the base of our dock he said, "Did you see that hot little French blond that was at the boat right before you guys walked up? She knows eight-meter cats. As in, knows *everything* about eight-meter cats. She knew that ours outperforms other eight-meters, and I think she was snooping around to find out why."

"I saw some woman with you guys, but I was too busy talking with Johnny to notice much about her."

"That's because you're all but married off already, Marlin. This chick was hot, and I didn't pay that much attention to what she was saying to Linds. But the more I think about it, something just wasn't right about her. She might be a spy for the competition."

That caught me off guard. "What competition? I thought Dickie was trying to stir up interest in this class, and he was the only builder?"

"He is, and he's not. It's popular in Europe already, and only a matter of time before it fully catches on here in America. That's another big part of why we wanted to invest in the company. But we've heard rumors of someone over on the west side of the bay that's supposedly going to start building them. That's why getting the patents locked down on the auto-angle device is so important. Then we can license them to the European builders, and for that matter to most all of the hydrofoil equipped sailboat builders, even ones that make monohulls."

We had arrived at the gate, and Murph paused to fish his keycard out of a pocket. We went past it before he continued, "So, we have to be really careful to protect this technology, it's the real future of the company. It's why Linds wanted me to run these straight back and lock them up at home."

Murph locked the foils in the huge dock box where they barely fit. I waited on the dock while he took a minute to "hit the head" on *OCT*. I waited for Murph on his aft entrance deck. When Murph rejoined me I asked him, "Wasn't that girl wearing a pinkish or coral colored top?"

"Yeah, I think so, why?"

"Because I'm pretty sure I just saw her trying to get through the security gate while I was waiting here for you. Whoever it was turned around and took off though when they spotted me."

Murph looked worried. "Good thing I locked those up when I did. I thought Linds was being paranoid, but there's no good reason for that chick to be trying to get past the gate, especially with that 'Private Dock' sign on it. Did you see which way she went after she left?"

I replied, "No. It was hard to see through the screening on the gate and the fence. I only saw the color of her top through it."

"Let's get back to the bar, fast."

8

ITINERARY

Vazquez swayed a bit as he stood up, having had a few drinks on his boat before coming to the bar and having two more. He then weaved his way through the crowd a bit unsteadily as he headed to the far corner table. He addressed Lindsay when he arrived.

"Bonita chica, jou handle that boat good! Where'd jou learn to sail like that?" Marco Vazquez's accent had gotten thicker in direct proportion to the amount of alcohol he had consumed. He grabbed the empty chair next to Lindsay and started to pull it out from the table. Johnny hooked one of its legs with his foot under the table, preventing it from moving any farther.

"This is a private party, why don't you go back to the bar," Johnny said.

"Because haim a party animal, an' I wanna party wit chica here." He smiled drunkenly at Lindsay, and yanked the chair again, this time freeing it from Johnny's foot and pulling it to him. But before he could sit down Johnny jumped up from his chair and was around the table, pushing the chair back in.

"Time for you to go, pal." While Johnny was only of average height, he towered over the Spaniard by several inches.

Lindsay said, "And we mean like leave the bar. You're cut off for the rest of the day. Go settle your tab and hit the bricks."

"Who you tink jou are, orderin' me 'roun chica?"

"Somebody who owns the place. Now do as she says, go pay your tab, and you'll only be banned for the night. Cause any more trouble and you and your boat will be outta here for good," Murph said. He and I had gotten back just in time to see Johnny facing off against Vazquez.

"Jou two again? Dis ain't over." Vazquez wagged a finger at us but he didn't look that sure of himself anymore, and his machismo wouldn't let him back down without first protesting to Murph.

"If it's not, then you can untie your boat and shove off right now. But behave yourself, and you'll be welcome back in here tomorrow," Lindsay said.

Mimi was right behind us. "C'mon pal, let's go."

As Mimi led Vazquez over to the bar to settle up, the rest of us all sat down. I said to Murph and Linds, "You guys are a lot more lenient than I would have been."

"At least he started out as a friendly drunk and kept his hands to himself. He just had a bit too much liquid 'ego booster'. Mimi will make sure the bartenders keep an eye on him. But if we threw everybody out of here that tried chatting up women who weren't up for it, or all those who picked a fight with Baloney, the place would be empty all the time," Lindsay said.

Johnny looked puzzled. "What's a Baloney?"

"I'm a Baloney! I got tired of waitin' for youse guys to come over to *our* bar and buy me a beer, so I had to 'slum it' and come over here. Wow, it's a real blowboaty lookin' place, too. I guess the food's all vegan, huh Shaker?" Baloney plopped down in the remaining empty chair.

I said with a straight face, "No, it's not all vegan. There's also sushi and sashimi." The shocked look on Baloney's face was priceless.

"Bait? All they serve here is *bait* and plants?"

I couldn't hold it together anymore and started laughing. "Relax! It's similar to the menu next door, Baloney." I introduced Baloney to

Johnny and gave him the abbreviated explanation for my nickname. I figured a few minutes with Bill and there'd be no need for an explanation of his. Then our waitress appeared and took everybody's order but Baloney's.

"Hey, aren't you gonna take my order," he asked.

The young server said, "You may not remember me from last season over at the *Beach Bar*, Captain Baloney, but I sure remember you. Your usual order is to bring you the most expensive beer we have and put it on Murph's tab. Unless you are going to switch on me now."

We all roared when Baloney said, "I'll just have the usual, and Murph, make sure you leave her a big tip, she's good!"

When the laughter died down I said, "You just missed your pal."

Baloney replied, "Which one?"

"Marco Vazquez. He stopped by to drool over Lindsay." I grinned at her.

"At least someone was willing to drool over me, Marlin. Murph was too busy drooling over Danielle." She frowned at Murph.

"Glad I missed that damn Marco Polo jerk. But what's a Danielle," Baloney asked.

Lindsay told the nearly full story of the run-in, and I added the part about seeing her or someone dressed like her at the security gate. Then she briefly mentioned the foil devices without explaining them in-depth.

Baloney grunted, "Something top secret? That won't last long in the blow-boater world. They'll want it all for free and they blab about everything."

"Uh, Bill, did I mention that Johnny here owns the big catamaran *sailboat* that came in this afternoon? You know, the one that cost more to build than both your boats combined?" I watched Johnny, not knowing what to expect. I didn't have long to wait.

"Ah, don't worry about it, Bill. It's true that a lot of sailors and motorboaters are like that. But so many people do get into sailboats thinking that once they buy the boat, that's about it as far as the costs go. They've never heard about the ten-percent rule. You know, the rule of thumb that says it will take ten percent of the purchase price every year to maintain a boat properly, whether it's a sailboat or a motorboat. And that's even before you start to use it.

"But sailors aren't the only ones who can't keep a secret. Look how many boatbuilders steal ideas from each other, and that includes sportfish builders, too. My background is in computers, and I know guys that have been offered big bucks to hack into different marine architect's and boat builder's computer networks to steal new designs before they're even built."

Baloney nodded, but I could see Lindsay was suddenly concerned.

"Johnny, do you know anybody who could look over the network at ESVACats and make sure it's secure," she asked.

"Absolutely, I'll give you a friend's number before I go. He's as good as they get at protecting networks because he used to make a living breaking into them."

Baloney remarked, "You know, you don't act or dress like some blow-boating cheapskate. And I like that watch you've got there, guy. Nice one."

Johnny had an oversized extremely unique and square gold watch on his wrist. He glanced at it as a cocky grin spread across his face. "Thanks. It's a handmade Racon Jadaux from Switzerland, one of only two like it in the US. They only make one per year in this square model, carved out of solid gold. It's as rare as they come. They made this one last year, the very first one. It's kind of a trophy of mine.

"When my wife and I got divorced, it was in the divorce decree that we had to sell the company and split the proceeds. I didn't want to sell, but I didn't want to take on the huge amount of debt needed to keep the company for myself, either. We got an offer from a big privately-owned company, and I knew we would have to take it, even though I didn't want to.

"I kept dragging my feet as hard as I could, so eventually the guy from that other company took me out for drinks, just me and him. He told me that he understood why I didn't want to sell and he had been divorced once too. I said that my wife had been cheating on me, and now because of it we had to sell something that had taken a decade of my life to build. To me, my company was like my child. He understood that completely.

"So the guy asked me, 'You only have to split the proceeds of the sale, right?' When I said that was the agreement, he took this watch off his wrist and placed it in my hand saying that it was a 'gift' and had nothing to do with the deal. Then he winked and laughed. So, I wore this watch to the closing as a tweak to my ex who didn't even notice it. That's when I saw our buyer was wearing an identical one. He saw me looking at it and winked again. He had wanted to keep anyone else in the country from owning this same watch, but he wanted my company even more than he wanted that other watch. Darn thing cost almost half of what my boat did."

Baloney stared at the watch. "How? It'd have to weigh a hundred pounds."

Johnny laughed, "Probably more like fifty. But it's not about its weight in gold, it's about the perception of value to others. Being so rare is the real clincher for the people who would want to buy it. Even if I'd had the cash without having to sell the company, there's no way I'd buy a watch that costs this much. But my ex got to keep half the cash and ride off into the tropical sunset with her 'boy toy', so I never told her about the watch. She wrecked the life we built together, and keeping this doesn't even the score, but I like looking at it. In twenty years when her boyfriend has gone off with somebody else's wife or when both of them are looking pretty rough from all that Florida sun, I'll still have my Racon Jadaux, and it'll look every bit as good as it does today."

"I'll say this for you Shaker, you have some real interesting friends," Baloney remarked.

"That's what they tell me. Usually after they find out I'm friends with you!"

A WOMAN in long khakis and a tee shirt walked up to the bar and ordered a beer. Big sunglasses covered a good portion of her face, her ballcap covering much of her head but not the long blond hair that spilled out the back and sides of it. She paid for her beer and wandered out onto the beach, slowly making her way down to within earshot of the corner table. She stopped, taking a long draw off of her beer.

"So, how long ya gonna be around, JC," asked Baloney.

Johnny sounded surprised. "What's with the JC bit?"

"Short for 'Johnny Cat'."

"Be glad. Getting a nickname means that Baloney likes you and that you're always welcome around here," I said.

"And it also means you're welcome to buy me a beer. Like right now. Tide's low!" Baloney raised an empty glass.

Johnny signaled our server and pointed at Bill. Then he pointed at Murph, and she laughed, understanding the part about it meaning that it goes on his tab. Again.

Baloney continued, "So ya didn't say how long you're here for, JC."

"Just until Sunday, then I'll be in Cape Charles on Sunday night, and go to Bayside Resort after that. I want to make my way around the bay, ending up in Annapolis, scouting out a good spot to come back and watch the F50 catamaran races there in June. Then I'll head from there back over to Bayside for these two's incarceration, and back to Annapolis and hang out until the race. After that, I'll finish up the rest of the west side of the bay, head over here for a few days before I take off for Bermuda."

I glanced nervously at Kari when he made the crack about 'incarceration' but she looked amused instead of insulted. She had been very quiet, listening to everything and everyone. She's good at listening before she makes decisions, and I hoped she was deciding to like Johnny now.

. . .

THE BLOND WOMAN made her way to the covered breezeway, pausing to drop an almost full beer bottle in the trash on her way out. Five minutes later, no one at the table noticed a center console outboard as it got up to speed after leaving the marina. Its sole occupant was a blond woman in a ball cap, her long hair streaming behind her in the wind, and she was now wearing a red windbreaker. Once out of sight of Mallard Cove, she removed the ball cap and the wig underneath. Making a turn to the north once she was past the point of the peninsula, she set a course for Cape Charles. It was important for her to get the lay of the land up there before Sunday.

IT WAS ALMOST midnight before Kari and I got to bed. Lying there I was rerunning in my head what I thought had been a really successful day. Both beach bars, as well as the *Cove Restaurant,* had been slammed, and the new steamer had proven that it could easily keep up with the rush. Chris had texted earlier to let me know the boats were well booked for the weekend, including several of the new cats. It looked like it was indeed an early start to the busy season. I reached across Kari and drew her closer.

"He didn't mean anything by it you know."

She sounded confused, "Who? What?"

"Johnny. That incarceration remark. And the one about a daughter and asking if you had a friend."

She propped herself up on an elbow, looking amused in the faint light coming in between the window curtains. "I had him figured out five minutes after we sat down at the bar. You too, by the way."

"*Me?* What was there to figure out about me?"

"Why you were answering for me and giving those long explanations. You protected him back in school when he was picked on as geek, and you're still doing it now. Even with me, which you don't need to, by the way. He may not dress like a geek anymore, but it's still in there, a big part of him. Every time a new woman gets around him he gets mentally flustered and says dumb things. I suspect that his ex-wife was probably the only woman he's had a long term relationship with, and she broke his heart then forced him to sell his company. So, it's a natural reaction for him to be flustered around women now, at least until he gets his confidence back. He puts on the swagger act as a cover.

"What we saw at the table was the real him, a nice guy trying to transition into both the cruising and dating worlds, but not yet really knowing how. So, you can relax, Marlin, I like him. And I think he's relaxed now as well around me. But it's sweet that you are still acting as his protector after all these years. It's just part of what makes me love you so much."

Now it was Kari that was pulling me closer to her in the faint light, the look on her face telegraphing exactly what she had in mind. Sleep is far too overrated anyway.

9

JC'S NEW HOME

The next morning we met "JC", Lindsay, and Murph for breakfast up at the *Cove*'s deck. Our table was near the edge and had an unobstructed view of the charter docks and the marina basin beyond. The spring morning was warm enough so that the dining room's rollup doors were open for the first time this year. Just a week earlier the huge canvas awning over the deck had been finished. With its ceiling fans, this ensured the space could now be used rain or shine, even in the heat of the summer.

Johnny remarked, "This is such a neat place, I love it here. This is the most relaxed I've been around new people in a long time. You really know how to pick good friends, Marlin."

I replied, "Been doing that since grade school, JC."

He laughed. I didn't know if it was about our long-term friendship or the use of his new nickname. He's going to have to get used to the latter; I don't think Baloney will ever call him anything else.

"Hey, if you guys don't have anything planned, you want to take *Wanderer* for a sail down the coast? Nice breeze, warm day, and this place looks like it's going to be crowded." Johnny looked hopeful, wanting the chance to show off his new home.

Kari replied, "Only if you'll let us throw together a cookout for you tonight on *Tied Knot* as a sendoff party when we get back. Linds, Murph, you guys up for it?"

"All of it! I'll get the kitchen to make some box lunches for the sailing part too," Lindsay said.

AFTER BREAKFAST WE BOARDED *WANDERER*, but not before spotting a bleary eyed Vazquez standing on the aft deck of *Zopilote*. He stared at us for a few seconds then disappeared down below without any comment nor acknowledgment that he'd even seen us.

Murph nudged me, "I bet he's a hurting puppy this morning."

I said, "Ah, we've all been there. Except for the part about being such a jerk. The guy's got a hell of an ego."

JC gave us a tour of *Wanderer*, which turned out to be as plush and roomy as most motor yachts that were much longer than she was. Both the salon and galley were huge, due in part to her massive width. She sleeps ten in five staterooms in the twin hulls plus two crew in their separate bow quarters. The master stateroom is incredibly comfortable and includes a large private lounge area. Johnny wasn't "roughing it" a bit.

I was happy for my old friend's footloose future, but sorry that his life had taken such a sad turn for him to get to this point. After seeing how flustered he had been around the gang at first, then how relaxed he had become since, I knew he'd end up eventually finding the right woman to spend the rest of his life with. Being a little gun shy at first isn't such a bad thing for him right now. It was because he had been too quick to jump into marriage when he was younger that he now found himself where he did. I don't think he'll be one to make the same mistake twice.

After our tour, JC showed off just how maneuverable *Wanderer* is using her bow thrusters and engines to slide her sideways off the dock. Once past the breakwater, he then showed us how well she is set up for single-handing. From his off-centered bridge set slightly to starboard, he was able to unfurl and set the mainsail as well as the two foresails with the flick of a couple of switches. The sheet lines all tailed back to powered winches mounted next to the helm as well.

JC offered me the wheel, which I readily accepted. *Wanderer* turned out to be an absolute dream to sail. We had a nice offshore breeze, and we headed south along the coast at about nine knots, just a few knots shy of what she could do at cruise using the diesels. At sixty-five feet long and thirty-one feet wide, she had almost no noticeable roll in the three-foot beam sea.

Opposite the bridge above the salon was a padded sundeck, and there was a lower covered teak deck surrounded by cushioned bench seating aft. Both were easily seen from the bench seat at the helm, meaning the captain was never left out of the conversation. It was easy to see why he loved this boat.

"Johnny, it's cool how you can see everyone on the upper and aft decks from here," I said.

"This offset helm station was part of my design changes, along with the different window lines. I knew I'd be mostly sailing by myself, but I wanted the ability to communicate easily with anyone else that might happen to be with me, like today."

I looked over his state of the art electronics and noticed one omission.

"You aren't equipped with AIS?" Automatic Identification System is a transponder that is required on most commercial vessels, and certain larger sized private vessels.

Johnny said, "Isn't required since *Wanderer* isn't big enough nor commercial. But I do have an automatic EPIRB." An EPIRB is an Automatic Position Indicating Radio Beacon. It can be activated manually or automatically if it ends up in the water.

"An EPIRB is good if you get in trouble, but I was thinking that since you'll be single-handing all the way to Bermuda, you're going to have to sleep during some of the trip, and AIS would broadcast your position, speed, and course to other vessels while you catch some shut-eye."

He replied, "I've got radar with a collision alarm. I'd rather use that than broadcast who, where, and what I am since I go slow enough to be easily boarded by somebody. We still have pirates around in our oceans these days you know."

He had a good point. Sometimes stealth can be an important part of a good defense. AIS can give away a lot of information that sometimes is best kept to yourself.

"True. Are you thinking of crossing the Atlantic? I know parts of the African coast are pretty rough."

Johnny got a faraway look and said, "Right now, I'm playing life by ear, taking it day by day. I've always wanted to see Bermuda, and I'm looking forward to a winter with no snow. If that works out, I might make it an annual thing. I don't think I'll ever be going back to Richmond, at least not for any length of time. There are just too many painful memories for me there now. Most of my friends were connected to my business, and the others my ex got in the divorce. Hearing my old friends talking about what's going on now at my company isn't something that I want to go through.

"I wasn't kidding this morning when I said I loved Mallard Cove. I really like your friends, too. I might make it home base from now on. Especially since you're there, it's always nice to be around friends."

"Those folks aren't just my friends, Johnny, they like you as well. You'll get a chance to meet more of the gang tonight at the cookout. And you fit in well with everyone. Baloney has even forgiven you for being a blowboater."

He laughed, "He's quite a piece of work; funny as hell."

"You're right on both counts, but he's also an extremely loyal person, as you'll learn over time. He took to you very quickly, which sometimes happens, just not often. You usually have to have bought him at least a case of beer by that point."

We both laughed. JC because he thought it was a joke, and me because he believed that it was. Then I motioned for him to take back the helm.

"What, are you tired of sailing her already? I'm insulted! No, you just keep sailing until we find a good place to turn around and have lunch on the way back. Meanwhile, I'm going to spend some more time getting to know these guys while you do all the work."

He grinned then went to sit with Kari, Linds, and Murph. He was an entirely different man than the one who had stepped off this boat eighteen hours ago. I hope he does decide to make Mallard Cove his home base; I think we all would be good for him, and I know he would be good for us as well. Several memories had come back to me about us growing up together, and I realized how much I'd missed him over the last decade or so. I'm glad that he's around now, and I hope he'll keep coming back around.

Looking up to check the fill of the mainsail I saw I didn't need to make any adjustment. Don't tell Baloney, but I love sailing. Especially how quiet it is, with the only sound being the water against the hull. *Wanderer* is equipped with a diesel generator, but JC chose not to run it and instead draw what little power was needed from the big bank of DC storage batteries. The electronics all ran off of DC power, and the AC power came from a silent inverter for these times that Wanderer wasn't plugged into shore power and the generator was offline. Having even the muffled rumble of the generator running and the smell of its exhaust would have spoiled the moment. I hadn't been out on a big sailboat since I bought *Coastal Dreamer*, and I had almost forgotten...

"Having a Jack Sparrow moment?"

Kari had silently come up beside me as I was looking up at the sails, startling me. "That's *Captain* Jack Sparrow to you, swab."

She sat beside me, looking around at the view from the helm. Ignoring the swab jab she said, "We need to take *Dreamer* out sometime when she's not booked, just you and me. I had almost forgotten how much I love sailing on a big boat, and how quiet it is. So peaceful."

"Done deal." I paused then asked, "It's a good life, isn't it?"

"Can't imagine a better one."

I motioned for her to take the helm, and she jumped at the chance, as I relinquished the large stainless steel wheel.

"Okay, it just got better."

"Spoken like a true badass Shore woman," I said, then watched as she looked first beyond the bows then up at the sails as I had been doing a minute before. Only she looked like it came so naturally to her when she did. From the moment we first started dating, she always jumped at the chance to take the helm of one of my two outboard charter boats. She had to braid her black hair into a pony-tail to keep it from tangling at high speeds, and that just contributed to the badass look. Today however it was loose and free to spill down to the middle of her back. The sun shining on her hair gave it an almost blue-black hue, just naturally beautiful.

She glanced back down and caught me staring at her. "What?"

"Nothing. I'm just lucky, that's all."

"Just now figuring that out, are you," she teased.

"Nah, just now reaffirming it." I moved closer and lowered my voice so only she could hear me. "Sometimes you have to see what others have lost to understand just how good you have things. I promise I'll never take that for granted."

Just before she kissed me she said, "Me, too."

WE CONTINUED south across the mouth of the Chesapeake Bay, picking up land again at Cape Henry and the Fort Story Military Reservation. Quickly the hundreds of beachfront houses of North Virginia Beach came into view, eventually giving way to the tall condos, hotels, and the iconic Virginia Beach Boardwalk.

The density of VA Beach was such a sharp contrast to the sparsely populated Eastern Shore. It brought into focus one of the largest reasons Mallard Cove had become so popular, so fast. Because even on our busiest day, you could still feel the open space of ESVA. You only had to go as far as the Cove's northern and eastern property lines to find woods or marsh, and a five-minute outboard ride up the Virginia Inside Passage would leave you in fishable places without another boat in sight. We know that ESVA isn't for everyone, and so do our customers; we all prefer it that way.

Down off Croatan Beach, we came about, slowly making our way back to Mallard Cove. Even though the boat was new to him also, JC was content to just chat with all of us, letting everyone else take their turns at the wheel. We had a very leisurely and informal lunch, perched around the bridge and the seats on the aft deck. By the time we pulled back into the marina, it seemed almost as if JC had known the rest of our group as long as I had. There was little doubt in my mind about where he would be calling home after his Bermuda trip, and I couldn't be happier about it.

We returned *Wanderer* to the end of the dock tee, then Kari and Lindsay made a grocery run for the cookout supplies while JC, Murph, and I gave the catamaran a quick but thorough washdown. This boat is so stable that she would spoil most monohull sailors, but by being more rigid, she accumulates a bit more bow spray. Though I thought about how easy it had been to get accustomed to making good speed without having the boat heel over by fifteen degrees or more. There are tradeoffs to everything. But I could now see why these big cats were becoming so popular; I really liked this one.

COCKTAIL HOUR STARTED a bit early today since several of the Beer Thirty Bunch have already begun to trickle in. We are gathering on the upper deck of *Tied Knot*, which had been designed with this kind of entertaining in mind.

An open stairwell at the dock end leads up to this deck. A third of the open space nearest the stairs is set up like a living room, furnished with cushioned outdoor furniture. It's nice and airy, and there's plenty of room. The middle third of the deck is covered and contains a bar, outdoor kitchen with grill, widescreen TV, and more outdoor furniture. The final third is uncovered and has a three-foot high solid wood privacy rail around a sundeck with chaise lounges and a hot tub. An enclosed stairwell between this area and the covered middle also contains a compact elevator, and both lead to the lower two decks.

Kari and I had wanted to make it as welcoming and friendly a place as possible. A place old friends could easily gather close together, but also where new people can find as much space as they need to be comfortable.

While JC had been a bit nervous and awkward yesterday when he first met my closest friends, today he didn't show any of that as he met Baloney's wife, Betty, and our pal, Timmy "Spud" O'Shea. Then Bobby, "B2", showed up with a girl named Sandra that he had met last night at *"The Cat"*, as the new beach bar has quickly become known. She was a little star-struck over Bobby's newfound *Tuna Hunters* cable fame. But his quiet demeanor helped JC relate to him quickly.

Only the Williams brothers' arrival threw JC off slightly. Not because of either of them, they're both pretty laid back and fun members of the *Tuna Hunters* cast. But they arrived with their new girlfriends, a pair of "blond bombshells." The women were identical twin sisters named Mandy and Brandy who were also dressed exactly alike. If you thought Sandra was star-struck over B2, these two made her look totally uninterested. Either one of these them by herself would be considered "high octane", but together they pack more energy and enthusiasm than an entire NFL cheerleading squad. I don't mean that in a bad way, they're fun and funny, but also a bit overwhelming, especially to JC. Every time he tried to speak with either of the brothers by themselves, Mandy or Brandy would appear and dominate the conversation. After just such an interruption one was called across the deck by her sister to settle an argument.

A shellshocked JC asked KT, "Which one was that?"

KT shrugged, "I have no idea."

"But you're dating one of them! How do you tell them apart?"

"It's not that important. They know who they are." KT took a long sip of his cocktail. "They found us two weeks ago in a waterfront bar over by Rudee Inlet. This is part of being on *Tuna Hunters* that neither Junior nor I had figured on, the whole 'getting recognized in bars and restaurants' thing. But I can tell you this, I'd really miss it now if it went away."

IT WAS WELL after midnight before everyone had left. By then JC had even gotten used to the twins dominating the Williams brother's conversations. Well, as much as anyone ever gets used to that. I think that eventually KT and Junior will have had enough of the twins, but I also think they'll have their hands full trying to break up with them. And you thought that *Tuna Hunters* was the real reality show...

Right before he left, Johnny thanked us both profusely for the party and for introducing him to everyone. He said that Mallard Cove was definitely the place he planned on calling home. Then he slowly and somewhat unsteadily made his way down the stairs. I watched him as he weaved his way to the security gate, then I joined Kari in cleaning up.

I made Kari and me a pair of nightcap vodkas, and we leaned on the far railing up by the hot tub, looking out over the darkened marina. There were a few scattered parties still going on in some of the boats, with intermittent laughter and loud voices carrying across the water. From our angle we couldn't see JC make his way back to his boat, but we did see lights turn on and off on his back deck, the salon, then finally a light shone through the porthole of his master state-room. It went back off before we finished our drinks.

Kari said, "He really hit it off with Murph and Lindsay today."

I replied, "What's not to like about any of them?"

"Not much, especially now that he's relaxed around everyone. I even saw him holding his own in conversations with the twins."

"Then he's a better man than I am. Those two wear me out."

She gave me a sly grin. "And you're not even one of the Williams boys."

"There are things in this world that I am very grateful for. That one is high on the list."

Kari set her glass on the railing and put her arms around me, looking up at my face in the low light from the deck. "What's another?"

I tilted my head, gave her an adoring look, and said softly, "Rock-fish season."

She jerked back and swatted my shoulder. "You better have another answer, pal!"

"Hmmm, how about I'm thankful that I get to share rockfish season with the most badass Shore woman on ESVA?"

The hug was back. "That's a little better. Make it white marlin season and you'll be completely forgiven."

"Done. What about you? What are you thankful for?"

"That we built the shower in our stateroom big enough for two. The twins aren't the only ones who can wear you out."

10

TANK

We managed to get a few hours of sleep last night after some "shower aerobics" and still got up in time to meet Lindsay, Murph, and Johnny at the *Cove*'s deck for his "bon voyage" breakfast. Even though he'd only been here a day and a half, it seemed like it had been much longer. Not in a bad way, but because he had really "clicked" with the gang. I was looking forward to seeing him at the wedding.

"I know that Baloney and B2 are going to be bummed that they missed seeing you off. They both had full day charters today," I said.

"I understand. I'll see them again at your wedding, right?"

Kari answered, "Absolutely. All the Beer Thirty Bunch will all be there, and a few more of our friends you haven't gotten to meet on this trip. Though I promise, none of them are as stressful as the twins!"

Murph said, "Nobody is as stressful as those two. Hey, since you're going to be up at Bayside, I'll tell Casey Shaw that you're coming. He's an old pal of mine and he owns the place. I know he'd love to show you around. Just watch out for Dawn, his fiancée. Redhead. Tough one."

Lindsay hit him on his shoulder. "Hey! That's no way to talk about my good friend who also just happens to be your ex-fiancée!"

JC raised his eyebrows and looked curiously at Murph.

"Long story, bad ending. Trust me and don't ask her, but I'll tell you the whole story when you come back here next time," Murph said.

"I'll hold you to that. But I better be going. Not as much wind today as yesterday, and it's coming from the north. That's the thing about big cats, they don't like pointing into the wind, so I'm going to be tacking back and forth a lot to get there."

Lindsay asked, "Why not use your diesels? You could be there in two hours, easy."

JC shook his head. "It's not about the 'getting there' for me now as much as it is about the journey. I've spent too much of my life trying to get somewhere fast, and I never took the time to relax and enjoy the trip. While it has gotten me to a comfortable place, I got here alone. I envy the four of you, enjoying the here and now together. One day I may get back to that, but if I do, it'll only be with someone who enjoys the journey as much as I do."

ALL FOUR OF us walked to *Wanderer* with Johnny and stood on the dock as he cranked the engines. We passed the shore power cord up to him, then untied his dock lines. We watched as he motored out through the breakwater, looking back, and waving at us one final time before he made the turn and unfurled his sails. Our view of him and the boat was now blocked by the breakwater, but we could still see the mast and the sails moving steadily westward above the rocks.

"It's funny, I don't remember being this sad when he and I went our separate ways over a decade ago," I said.

Murph said, "I just met him, and I'm sad to see him go, too. Though it'll be a blast to see him again at your wedding, and then back down here."

"I've been thinking about his summer plans. What do you think about taking *Why Knot* up to Annapolis and watching the F50 races this summer, Kari? I'd love to see those boats in action, and we could meet up with Johnny there," I said.

"That would be a blast! You guys want to come with us?"

Murph looked at Lindsay, who obviously liked the idea. "We're in! Sounds like a fun weekend. And speaking of fun weekends, the mackerel and ribbonfish are running off Virginia Beach, what say we run over there this morning in *Irish Luck* and catch a few. I wouldn't mind smoking some and making fish dip."

"Let's go."

On Thursday morning Murph came over to my office looking concerned.

"Hey Marlin, I just talked to Casey, I asked him to keep an eye out for Johnny. He had a slip prepaid for Tuesday through tonight, but he never showed. Have you heard from him since he left?"

I shook my head. "No. I'll give him a call and see what's up." I dialed his cell phone which went straight to voicemail.

Murph said, "Well?"

"Voicemail." I thought this was strange, there was decent cell from Mallard Cove to Bayside. I looked up the number for the Cape Charles Harbor Marina and called them to see if he was still there. The dockmaster told me that Johnny had arrived on Sunday afternoon, and prepaid his slip for two nights. He asked the dockmaster about a good restaurant and then walked in that direction. The place he sent him to, the *Fish House,* was a bar and grill that was right next door. This was the last time the dockmaster had seen him since the marina office closed early on Sundays. And despite having prepaid for the second night, when the dockmaster returned to work on Monday morning, *Wanderer's* slip was empty. He hadn't seen either the catamaran or Johnny since.

I looked up at Murph, "I'm sure he's all right. The Chesapeake hasn't been that rough, and we know he got to Cape Charles okay. Maybe he met some woman who wanted to go see Baltimore or St.

Michael's or somewhere other than Bayside, and he's... distracted. He'd want some privacy so he probably turned his phone off. I bet he just forgot to call and cancel his second night at Cape Charles and the slip at Bayside."

Murph agreed. "You're probably right. I think that it would be easy for the right woman to 'distract' him. Maybe even the wrong woman!" He grinned as he left, reassured that Johnny had gotten hooked up with some gal and was now off on an adventure to who knew where. That's the theory I was leaning toward too, I just hope that it's someone nice this time. If he was still in the same frame of mind like he was when he left here, confident and laid back instead of insecure and covering up with a false bravado like he had when he arrived, this is a definite possibility. Maybe more like a probability. I remembered right before he left he said that he was planning on "living life day by day," and playing things "by ear." He's probably carrying out that plan.

My cell phone rang, interrupting my thoughts, but I was really happy to see the name on the caller ID. "Smitty! How the heck are you?"

"I'm good, and about five minutes out, single-handing my way down the coast. Can you and Kari break away for a minute and help me tie up? Thor and I have, uh, *something* for you guys."

Smitty used to be the most popular and highest-paid cast member on *Tuna Hunters* until Baloney joined the cast and barely edged him out on both those points. He's a great guy and a very imposing figure, at six and a half feet tall and almost four-hundred-pounds. His biracial heritage makes him look like a plump version of "The Rock" crossed with "Tyrus," but with a longer beard than Tyrus and a few more tribal tattoos on his arms than both he and The Rock two put together. As imposing as he first appears, the guy is really just a teddy bear and a great friend.

"I'll see if she can break away and we'll meet you down there. But you shouldn't have brought us anything."

I heard the big man's amused tone, "Yeah I should've, Shaker. You're getting married in a few weeks, remember? This is a combination wedding gift and also a thank you for saving Thor's life last fall." Thor was his equally gargantuan yellow Labrador retriever. Well, technically he's a "yellow" lab, but really he's closer to chalk white in color, much like the English Labradors.

Thor almost perished in a fire on Smitty's old boat last November, but I was able to squeeze through a hatch and lift him out. This, just seconds before fire engulfed the vee-berths where he had collapsed from smoke inhalation. Burning fiberglass emits some very toxic and nasty fumes, and he couldn't have taken much more of them and lived, not to mention surviving the fire that followed. Kari and I both loved that dog, and he is smarter than a lot of humans I know.

"I was just glad that we could get him out of there before it was too late. Anyway, let me try to round up Kari and we'll meet you down at the dock."

Since he was already going to be here for the wedding, Smitty had decided to forego the rest of this summer's tuna season up north to fish a few tournaments for white marlin and yellowfin tuna off ESVA instead. His forty-two-foot Pete Jones deadrise boat, *Sea Quest*, had replaced his Downeaster design that had been lost to the fire. With no time to build a new boat before the beginning of tuna season and filming commencing, I helped him find a great deal on a one-year-old Jones boat built up in Maryland. I think he was put off by the maroon hull color at first, but like the rest of us, he grew to like it. She added even more color to the Mallard Cove charter fleet which includes white, yellow, orange, light green, and now maroon hulls. They're all backed in at the dock behind the *Cove*'s deck. Very eye-catching, to say the least.

Kari and I watched from the floating dock as the sleek deadrise came through the breakwater then turned and idled in our direction. Right before reaching the dock, Smitty spun the single-screw boat in a very fluid motion, using his bow thruster and rudder to line her up straight with the slip. He backed in slowly, stopping perfectly when his aft cleat was opposite one on the dock.

How someone docks can really show the difference between a truly professional captain and some hotshot who wants attention. I saw one of the latter back in a multi-million-dollar sportfisherman once, his very last day on that boat. Showing off for the crowd on the dock, this guy was moving so fast in reverse he was pushing a wake with the stern. He went to shift into forward gear with both engines, but one transmission's linkage stuck. He backed right into the concrete dock with what had a second before been a beautifully varnished teak transom, which ended up becoming a lifetime supply of toothpicks. That's not something that will ever happen to Smitty, he's a good and cautious captain.

Kari exclaimed, "Thor!" The huge dog had his front paws up on the gunwale, now getting his coconut sized head petted by her, his tail going a mile a minute. That's when I saw the Labrador puppy coming across the deck and who was now trying like heck to grab and bite that wagging tail. He looked to be at most about three months old. The little guy's coat was the same color as Thor's, but he had a brown nose instead of the black one like his much larger counterpart.

Smitty emerged from the deckhouse, a huge grin on his face. "It's great to be back here. You know, the place looks and feels even nicer in the spring. It's warmer, too!" We film *Tuna Hunters* in December and January, the two coldest months on ESVA outside of February.

Smitty hugged Kari across the gunwale and held out his island sized hand to me to shake. My hand almost disappeared in his palm.

Kari said, "We missed you guys! And who's the new addition?"

Smitty scooped up the pup and handed him to Kari, who instantly got a wet tongued face wash from the little guy that was now cradled in her arms.

"He's not a new addition, at least not exactly. More like a hitch-hiker. I've been calling him T2. Kinda like Bobby is B2. But that's not the pup's real name."

She looked confused, and I wasn't really clear on things either. I asked, "So then, what's his name?"

His smile got even wider. "Whatever name you two give him. He's your wedding present, one of Thor's pups. That's where the T2 came from, Thor 2."

It's funny, Kari is one of the most mature-beyond-her-years

people I've ever known. Except when she is around her dad that is, and then she becomes the epitome of a "daddy's girl," and it's like she's a little kid again. I've never seen that happen to her in any other situation. Until now. The young executive who manages and develops multi-million-dollar properties and who can hold her own in arguments with the toughest contractors around has now been reduced to a pre-teen girl, laughing, and squealing with delight.

"Stop! Your little tongue tickles. And you have puppy breath. Thank you, Smitty, and thank you, Thor! He's so precious."

Smitty replied, "I was worried that you two might not want a puppy. But having seen you both so upset when we all thought we'd lost Thor, I figured it was a good gamble. I took the pick of his last litter instead of a stud fee. This guy had the biggest paws of the bunch, and he's a smart little bugger."

I said, "Tank."

Kari looked at me questioningly. "Tank?"

"Yeah, because when he was walking across the deck and chasing Thor's tail, I saw he has this really wide stance and he's built like a tank. But it's really short for Piankatank."

"The Piankatank river! I loved that trip," Kari said.

The Piankatank twists and turns its way up what's called Virginia's Middle Peninsula on the western side of the Chesapeake. When we got my vintage forty-two-foot Chris Craft back after it was repaired following an explosion that severely damaged it, Kari and I had taken an overnight cruise across the bay and up that particular river. It was our first trip together on the Chris, so the Piankatank has very special memories for the two of us.

I replied, "Me too. But speaking of rivers, I bet these two might like to take a walk."

Smitty said, "I can guarantee Thor would. Though the little guy has his spot on the deck over near the scupper that he's been using en route. But it would be good to keep him using the grass. Like I said, he's really smart for a pup, and already 'cabin broken.' He used that one deck spot on longer legs of the trip coming down here when we couldn't stop."

As Kari headed off with Thor and Tank, we heard a commotion from up by the marina's inlet. There was no mistaking the voice, even before spotting the light green hull. Baloney was furious, yelling at someone behind him. As *My Mahi* cleared the inlet, *Zopilote* then came into view, with an equally furious Marco Vazquez returning verbal fire in extremely rapid and loud Spanish.

"What the heck? A *junk*?" Smitty was as taken aback as I had been when I first spotted it.

"Yeah, Baloney and the owner don't see eye to eye on nautical rights-of-way. Or, much of anything else for that matter. Good thing we have the new *Catamaran* beach bar, because that guy Marco Vazquez likes hanging there, and Baloney still prefers the *Cove Beach Bar*. It has kept this war from getting hotter than it already is."

Baloney spun his boat around and backed it into the slip while continually barking orders at his new mate, Sammy Collins. Not that Sammy needed any direction since he was one of the best mates on ESVA, but Bill has always given his mates loud and unnecessary orders. That includes Sammy's predecessor, B2, right up until the day he took over as captain on the *Golden Dolphin.* Both B2 and Sammy can do the job in their sleep, but this is just Baloney's way. The truth is the sympathy it generates with their charter clients probably is also reflected in larger tips for Baloney's mate.

As Sammy tied them off to the dock, Baloney spotted Smitty and yelled, "Hey, stranger! Welcome back! You're just in time to buy me that beer you owe me from this winter."

Smitty retorted, "I see you've been busy making a new friend since I left."

Baloney scowled, "Just for that remark, you can make it a six-pack."

"Hah! I missed you too, Baloney! Yeah, I think I will let you buy me a beer at the new bar."

"What, you're a blowboater now? I stay on the other side, the one with all the fishermen and the real boaters. You know, the place where you can buy me and Betty's dinner, too. Or, right there on the *Cove's* deck. Your choice."

Smitty shook his head slightly. "Sounds like I don't really have a choice."

"Now you're catchin' on. Hey, Thor! Who's that with you," Baloney asked as Kari and the labs returned from their walk.

Kari replied, "It's Tank, our new 'fur child' who's also Thor's son. Tank, that's your uncle Baloney."

The puppy stopped, cocked his head looking up at her, then looked over at Baloney and barked in his biggest voice, which was more like a squeak than a bark.

Smitty laughed, "Atta boy, Tank! You're a great judge of character. Way to bark at the bad man."

"Just for that, I want dessert with dinner, too," said Baloney.

Tank walked out on the finger pier to me, plopped down across my right foot, and started chewing on the leather lace of my other deck shoe. Kari took note of that and said, "I think he should go back to work with you this afternoon. He can stay in my office after we get him some chew toys."

I pretended to glare at her as she hid a smile. We now had a run to make a pet store run over to VA Beach after work if I want to be able to keep wearing this pair of shoes.

11

WEDDING FLU

The three of us missed the Beer Thirty meeting because of our pet store adventure. We unloaded our haul onto *Tied Knot*, then headed to the "*Cat*" for dinner since it was a little late in the day to start cooking. Besides, both beach bars, as well as the *Cove*'s deck, are all pet friendly. And despite his earlier protest, that's where we found Baloney, Betty, and Smitty just finishing up dinner with Thor lying next to them. We took an adjoining table, and Tank plopped down between Kari's and my feet. He had a big rawhide bone, the kind that's knotted at both ends. He had insisted on carrying it around himself, even though it was almost half as big as he is. But it kept him happily occupied, and away from my shoelaces.

Smitty said, "Got him all set, I see."

Kari said, "Oh, that's just a down payment. He has a pile of chew stuff back at the boat, but that's his favorite so far. We also bought a bed, collars, leashes, and bowls."

Smitty said, "Collars and leashes as in more than one? You know he's going to grow like a weed, and he'll need bigger stuff soon, right?"

"One does need a complete wardrobe with a nice selection of

colors you know," I said in my best condescending voice, rolling my eyes and taking a shot in the arm from Kari because of it.

"Hey! He's the first 'fur kid' we've ever had, and I'm going to spoil him rotten if I want to," she said.

And I thought getting married would be the biggest change in my life. Apparently not.

"What are jou doing in my bar, channel hog?" An agitated Marco Vazquez walked into the *Cat* and spotted Baloney. He started across the room toward the table when Tank saw him. The little guy started growling but didn't take his teeth away from the rawhide bone. However it was enough to get Thor's attention, and he issued a warning bark, stopping Vazquez in his tracks when he saw the big dog.

Baloney said, "It ain't 'your bar' and I've been here a helluva lot longer than both these bars and way before you ever even heard of the place. I'll eat and drink anywhere I damn please, and if you don't like it, you can crawl back into that hunka junk and set sail, or whatever ya call what you do with it. But get lost, we're havin' a nice conversation, and you ain't invited to join it, Marco Polo."

Still eyeing Thor, Vazquez retreated toward the bar, muttering a string of what sounded like both curses and threats in Spanish.

Bill said, "Good boy, Thor." Then, turning around and looking at Tank, "You, too, little guy." He picked up an uneaten French fry from his plate then passed it to Tank, and it quickly vanished.

Kari scolded, "Tell me you didn't just feed my dog 'people food' and right at the table, Baloney!" It wasn't a habit she wanted Tank to learn.

"Just a reward for bein' such a good watchdog. We already know that Thor goes after bad guys, and now his kid is learning, too. This was just a little positive reinforcement as part of the lesson." Baloney grinned, then glared over in Vazquez's direction. When another cast member of *Tuna Hunters* was attacked some months ago, Thor had taken a chunk out of the assailant's leg.

I said, "No more people food, and no treats from the table."

Tank had now stopped working on the bone and was looking up at Baloney.

I said, "See what you've done? He's begging."

"Calm down, Shaker. He's just takin' a break from that rawhide, and sayin' hi to his uncle Baloney. C'mere, pal."

Tank got up and walked a few steps over to Baloney who petted him, much to the pup's delight. Baloney looked over at me and smirked, his hand stopping at the same time. But Tank wasn't through wanting attention or looking for food. He grabbed Bill's finger like a chew toy, causing him to yelp in pain.

"Baloney! I thought I told you not to feed him at the table! That includes finger food as well." Everybody laughed. Everybody but Baloney that is.

"Needle toothed lil' buggar." He carefully inspected his finger for punctures.

"Don't blame him, he couldn't help it. Your finger probably smells like French fries. You started him on those," Kari reminded him.

"I won't be doing that again, or actin' like a pin cushion either. His name shoulda been cactus instead of Tank. But he's still a good boy for growling at that butthead, Marco Polo."

BACK AT OUR houseboat after dinner, we roughhoused with Tank until he finally started losing interest and let out a huge yawn. We piled both him and his rawhide bone on his bed, and he was soon completely out. I had been afraid that he'd cry all night, his first one away from his littermates or Thor, but it was almost like he was already used to living with us. It was going to be easy to have him around.

FRIDAY WAS Tank's first full day with us, or actually, with me. Kari had her day all laid out up at Bayside, going over wedding stuff. With only two weeks left before the big day, she was starting to be all about the details. Fortunately, she was working with the very best, the crew up at Bayside Club. All I was responsible for was the rehearsal dinner, which would be at the *Rooftops* restaurant at Bayside. Again, those folks are all pros who work there, so we are all set. The reservation for our honeymoon hotel in Bermuda was also made and reconfirmed. As a wedding present, Casey and Dawn are lending us their Cessna Citation jet to go out to that island nation and back. So, all I have to do is keep out of Kari and her mom's hair for the next two weeks and keep taking our new four-pawed kid outside for walks. I'll be really glad when he gets a little bigger and can go a little longer between "trips to the fire hydrant." I brought him with me to *Tuna Hunter Productions* today, where there is no shortage of people who are fawning over him and volunteering to take him for walks. But I want him to get used to going everywhere with Kari and me, including on walks. Oh, and no, he won't be going to Bermuda with us. "Uncle" Smitty and Thor will be "Tank sitting" while we're gone since he's already used to them.

KARI STILL WASN'T BACK by the time I was finished at work. I had missed the Beer Thirty Bunch again so I headed over to the beach to check on the catamaran rental fleet and to let Tank play in the water. I saw the eight-meter on its way back in with Dickie and Murph aboard. Tank spotted the catamaran when it was a couple hundred yards out and he froze, completely mesmerized. He watched it the rest of the way up to the beach, and while they loaded it onto its motorized cradle.

Dickie was telling Murph, "Yeah, like I said, these handle just like the other foils, but in really heavy air they can jam at different angles and twist the frame, causing it to become unstable and crash. So make sure you don't take them out if we have really high winds forecast. I should get the others back to you in a week or so, after I finish the new modifications. Then we'll have to start the patent process all over again, but with the increased adjustment speed and range it will be well worth it. That, and the larger water intake which isn't affected like this smaller one when you pick up grasses or other floating junk in them."

Tank and I had been walking over to them during their conversation. Dickie spotted me as I walked up. "Oh, hey Marlin! How's the fleet working out?"

"Hey, Dickie. Great, thanks. This will be our second weekend, and we're completely booked again. Our only problem so far was that Chris had to chase one guy down because he was having so much fun he didn't want to bring it back in. I think Chris said the guy was going to talk to you about buying one."

Dickie laughed. "I did sell him one, and I hope you don't mind, but I just gave Chris a commission on the sale, too. He had the guy primed, all I had to do was collect the money and build the boat."

"I don't mind a bit. That'll take some of the sting out of the little hassles that go with this business like having to chase after that guy."

"Perfect! It's like having a store display without my needing more employees."

Our arrangement is working out almost as good for Dickie as it is for Kari and me.

Murph was bending over and roughhousing with Tank. "So, you're the little guy I've heard so much about! Well, your new pal Murph is going to get you a Frisbee and I'll teach you how to play with it."

Tank play-barked at Murph, approving the plan. Or, he was barking because it's what puppies do when they have fun. You can choose whichever one you want to believe, and you'll probably be right in either case.

With the eight-meter now safely back above the high tide line on the beach Dickie said, "Well, I'm going to take off, guys. I've got the newer foils in the truck. Remember Murph, just be careful not to use these others in high winds."

Murph replied, "Got it, Dickie. I'll put them back in *On Coastal Time*'s dock box, and you have that combination and a key card to the security gate. So, we're good to go."

After Dickie took off I asked Murph, "Flying solo?"

He replied, "Linds went up to meet with your bride and your

future mother-in-law a little before noon. I'm kind of expecting them to grab a wine or two before they head back. Didn't Kari tell you?"

I shook my head. "No. But I've been trying to keep out of all that as much as possible. You know Kari, she's the organizer and planner. Letting her do it all ensures she'll get the wedding she wants. Or, the one her mom wants. I've got the rehearsal dinner and the honeymoon plans all set, and that's all I want to have to deal with."

"Yeah, and I've got the bachelor party all set too, so we're good," he grinned.

I didn't want to know what those plans were, not that he'd tell me anyway. It's just less I had to worry about. Actually, Tank had come along at a great time, keeping my mind off things and my nerves under control. His comic relief is a welcome distraction. Speaking of which, while Murph and I had been talking, Tank had been exploring, and was now headed back to us with a heavy stick about twice as long as he is. His head was at a ninety-degree-angle to his body as he dragged it over between Murph and me, then plopped down and started chewing on it.

"Hi, guys." We turned and saw Kari and Lindsay headed in our direction, each holding a glass of wine in each hand. Murph had been right about the wine, but wrong about the where.

Tank spotted his new "mom" and tore off across the sand to meet her. I was starting to get a glimpse of the new pecking order around here, and I wasn't at the top of it. Wait, four glasses of wine. Not at the bottom of it, either. When Kari walked up I took both glasses from her so she could pick up Tank and get another face washing.

"You'd think he hadn't seen you in a week."

"You're just jealous," she teased.

"Maybe," I answered.

"Tell you what, you'll have my full attention in Bermuda. How about that?"

"That'll work."

Tank started squirming around in her arms, finally wanting to be put down. He raced around her, pawing at the sand and barking. No doubt about it, I was on the second string with him. I looked at the two of them, trying to envision what they would look like together in five years. I liked what I saw. If he turned out to be half the dog Thor is, he'll be a great protector and pal for her. We'd already gotten a glimpse of how he had a sense for people with bad intentions last night when he growled at Marco Vazquez. But as for him having Kari as his favorite, I'd be lying if I said I wasn't a little bummed over it.

I saw Lindsay looking first at me, then at Kari and Tank. She nodded slightly, then reached over and squeezed my bicep. It was that whole "being like a sister" thing again, and she knew exactly what I was thinking.

"Hey, there's going to be no getting a table anywhere here tonight, and I just bought four big steaks. How about coming over to *OCT* for drinks and dinner?"

"We'd love to," Kari answered for the both of us. Make that the *three* of us.

As the women relaxed down below in the salon with Tank, Murph and I grilled out on his upper deck, giving us a little time to talk. He asked, "Have you tried Johnny again today?"

Johnny. I'd forgotten all about him after Smitty and Thor showed up with Tank. The pup had been that much of a life change.

"No, I'll try him again right now." I dialed his number, with the same result. "Voicemail again. Now I'm starting to get worried."

Murph looked concerned, but the reason wasn't what I was thinking about. "Mar, have you thought that maybe he's ducking you?"

I was completely taken aback, "No! Why would he be trying to duck me?"

"Well, first off, if he is, he's not 'trying,' he's being successful. You saw how screwed up his divorce made him; it's not all about being a shy geek. I know the symptoms, and that man has the 'female flu' and he's nowhere near being over it. Did you see the way he looked when he talked about his ex and her 'boy toy' down in the Keys? I know you might not have seen this part either, but I could tell he wasn't all that crazy about coming to your wedding. And if I were him, I wouldn't be up for going to anybody's wedding right now. I'm just saying..."

I still wasn't buying it. "Then why not just come out and tell me that?"

"Because then you'd see him as being more damaged than you already do, and closer to the point where he really is. You said he got off the boat all pumped up, putting on a good front. Kari sure saw it. Do you think that guy would want you to see that going to a wedding would make him just about as uncomfortable as he could be? Especially right after reconnecting with his childhood best friend? Not happening, bubba."

I had to admit, Murph had a point. I hadn't really looked at it from this angle. Hadn't even begun to consider this angle. If he were right, Johnny would be feeling as awkward as hell, and ducking me now would kind of make sense. He could come up with some cocka-mamie story later about some wild woman he met, and how they had taken off together. It would build up the front he was trying to project. Wild and crazy single guy meets an even wilder woman, takes off on a coastal cruise until things burn out and they go their separate ways. He comes back to Mallard Cove looking like the stud he wants everyone to think he could be. For the sake of his ego and our friendship, we forgive him for ducking out and missing the wedding. Life goes on.

But Murph wasn't through, and I wasn't prepared for what he was about to say next.

12

MISERY & COMPANY

Murph suddenly looked sad. "Johnny isn't the only one that's a little uncomfortable about weddings, and especially your wedding." He turned back toward the grill, now silently focusing on the steaks.

I waited to see if he was going to say any more, or if I was going to have to prod him. I wanted, no, I *needed* to know what he meant by this. That last statement sounded like it might easily be something that could end a friendship. I could see he was already mentally kicking himself for having said anything, so if I was going to find out, it was going to be up to me.

I asked quietly, "Why?"

Murph shut the lid on the grill. "Because of the effect it's having on Lindsay and me."

I shook my head. "We've been through this already. Women get weird around weddings. It's not something we guys understand, nor are we meant to. The only part we understand is that some single women can get crazy and loose around weddings. They made a whole movie about guys who crash weddings because of this, and it was even filmed on the Eastern Shore. I think weddings trigger certain hormones or something."

Murph added, "That was up at the Eastern Shore of Maryland. Filmed in Easton and St. Michaels. But this has nothing to do with that, though you're probably right about it having to do with a hormonal something or other. All I know is she gets really grouchy with me every time those two get into the details of your wedding. It got better after we got back and got into the catamaran business with Dickie, but now it's gotten rough again."

I asked, "What changed?"

"Lindsay's changed."

LINDSAY WAS COMING up the outside steps, on her way to ask about when the steaks would be done so that she and Kari could time the sides so it all came out together. But she stopped when she overheard a serious conversation going on between Murph and Marlin. She started to turn and go back down, not wanting to interrupt, but then she heard Murph mention her name. She stopped again, staying out of sight but just within earshot.

"OKAY, so what changed with Lindsay, Murph?"

"She just changed, okay? She hasn't come out and said it, but I know she wants to get married now."

"Gee, I can't see why she'd want to rush into something like that. I mean, you guys have only been living together on boats for what, two or three years? Close quarters, working together, and yet you still haven't killed each other. You've reinvested together everything you both have made. You had to scrape to get by at first, but now you two are really successful and can take life a little easier. You share everything, you love each other, and you're pretty much joined at the hip from business to your daily lives. Gee, how silly for her to want to marry you."

"You don't get it, Marlin, I don't want to screw up her life."

"How would you marrying her screw up her life?"

"I screwed up Dawn's by just getting engaged to her, then I realized that I wasn't the marrying type and broke it off. She took it hard."

"Newsflash, Murph, Dawn got what she wanted. Who she really wanted. Sorry if that's an ego bruiser, but so did you. Though you're being too pig-headed to admit it to yourself. Dawn and Casey getting together was probably going to happen no matter what as soon as his way-too-quick marriage to Sally was over. If you hadn't broken up with Dawn, she probably would have busted up with you because it turned out she wanted Casey instead. Yeah, he and I had some long talks when we went down south to save your butt. Where I went swimming with the sharks to save your butt. Maybe you remember, that time Casey, Linds, and I saved your butt?"

Murph totally ignored the part about how Casey, Lindsay, and I pulled out all the stops, risking our lives to get him back after he was abducted. Instead, he was getting angry. "I warned Casey over and over about Sally, but he wouldn't listen to me. When she decided she wanted me out of Bayside, that was it, I was doomed. He listened to Sally over me, even though I'd been working for and with him for fifteen years by then. Do you know how much getting forced out of that place cost me?"

"No, Murph, and I don't care. Because I know what it would have cost you if you hadn't left there and hadn't left Dawn. Something that you can't put a number on. Something a lot of guys never get lucky enough to find when they settle for the Sallys of the world. If you haven't figured it out yet it's called happiness, pal. And a big part of yours is due to a certain blonde who is as beautiful on the inside as she is on the outside. A lot of guys would call you pretty darn lucky. A lot of guys would want to make sure they didn't lose her."

"You just think I should get married because you are, Marlin. Misery loves company, isn't that it?"

"I really ought to hit you for saying that. You're supposed to be my best man, standing up for me. Standing up for Kari and me, together. If you can't do that, if you don't believe in that, then you should do what Johnny's doing and not even bother to show up.

"Misery, huh? You think Kari and I are going to be miserable? I'm looking forward to every day from now on with her, and I know that she is too. Maybe you don't have a good grasp of what marriage really is, Murph. It isn't the slip of paper, it's the commitment in front of your friends and your God. Meaning you were willing to take that leap, that she was worth it to you. Worth more than just sharing an address and a bed without any real strings attached. Meaning that when sexy French chicks like that Danielle come around, Linds knows you'll look, hell you'll even stare, but she also knows that's all you'll do. Meaning when you're eighty and staring is all you can still do without big pharma's help, that you came home every night for the last forty-some years just because she was there. And that wherever you call home is just that because she is there.

"Let me ask you something, Murph. Can you picture a life without Lindsay in it? A happy life with just you? If you can, then you're right, you're not the 'marrying kind.' But if you can't, then you still have a lot of questions to ask yourself, even though you already know a lot of the answers, too."

Murph gave me a stern look. "I'm not going to get engaged because I'm being pushed into it. I got pushed into it with Dawn, and that isn't going to happen now. I'm not going through that again. If I ask Lindsay it's not going to be because I'm being pressured, it's because I want to. Because I need to."

"I'm not going to pressure you. Hell, I'm never, ever, going to mention it again. I've said all I'm going to say on the subject. You brought it up, and now you know how I feel. Murph, you were smart enough to see what Mallard Cove was, and what it could be. Now hopefully you're smart enough to realize who she is, and who you can be together."

I hoisted my glass, nodded my head slightly, then headed to the stairs. A chagrinned Lindsay was waiting for me at the bottom, her eyes welling up. She silently hugged me harder and longer than she ever had before, then let me go, but not before first kissing me on the cheek.

She said quietly, "That was for me, and for Kari."

I smiled at my friend, not knowing what was in store for her and

Murph, but silently hoping it would all work out. It wasn't my call, and I'd said too much already that she had apparently overheard. Not that I had any choice but to answer after Murph lobbed that bomb at me. You always want the best for those you love, no matter what that turns out to be. Only time will tell what that is in their case.

LATER, Kari and I were lying in bed in our darkened stateroom. The only faint light was coming in from between the window curtains from the low light fixtures on the dock. It was just enough illumination to see that Tank was asleep over in his bed. He had started softly snoring after he rolled onto his back with all four paws in the air. Seeing his faint outline caused Kari to chuckle.

"That's something new."

I replied, "I hope it's not a trend. He'll get louder as he gets bigger, just like that squeaky little bark of his."

"It's sweet that he feels secure enough around us to sleep on his back because that's as vulnerable as he can be," she said.

"Secure enough? Are you kidding me? He adores you, and he has already started guarding you. You're his now, like it or not."

"I get the feeling you don't." She sounded worried.

"Kari, you know how you can look at a vacant piece of property and envision the highest and best use for it? Like you did here at Mallard Cove, and you have done with your Lynnhaven project? Well, I saw a bit of the future myself today on the beach, kind of like a snapshot into the future. It was you and Tank, five years from now. He was right by your side like he's supposed to be."

"And where were you, Marlin?"

"Who do you think was holding the camera?"

She laughed again. "I feel like I'm stealing your dog."

"He's not my dog, he's our dog, and both of us are responsible for him. But it's his job to watch over you. You can't change that and neither can I, not that I'd want to. People can choose the dogs they are responsible for, but left to their own devices, dogs will choose their people, too. Even if two people share feeding duty, most dogs will still pick one of them as a favorite. Apparently Tank and I feel the same way about you. We both want to protect you, and we both want you to keep feeding us." I grinned.

Kari snuggled in closer to me in response. "What happened tonight?"

"Nothing yet, but I'm still hopeful."

She pulled back and slugged me in the shoulder then moved back in close. "I'm serious. Something must've happened between you and Murph. After you both came back down below when he had finished grilling, you hardly said two words to each other."

I tensed up, knowing I'd have to tell her everything. She felt this, backed away a few inches and propped herself up on an elbow, leaving me some breathing room. Kari and I make it a point not to have any secrets from each other, though this subject is not one that I would have volunteered to discuss. But since she brought it up I can't avoid it now, either. And I trust her to use her best judgment on what I'm about to say.

I related my conversation with Murph, from his theory about Johnny to his comments about marriage, and the fact that Lindsay heard most of it. Even in the low light, I could see that Kari was now pensively biting her lower lip, a habit of hers when she's not yet sure of something. Indecision doesn't usually last long with her, and tonight was no exception to that rule.

"I can see why you were so quiet."

I nodded. "I had already said all that I was going to by then. Casual conversation wasn't something I was up for; I didn't want to accidentally say something to set him off again in front of Lindsay this time. He has yet to apologize for that 'misery loves company' crack. This is something he has to figure out on his own, rather than the two of them having to figure it out together. He's right about one thing though, he shouldn't get engaged just because of peer pressure."

Kari sighed. "I'm worried now. I thought things were getting better between the two of them. Why do weddings always have to be so damned stressful?"

I was surprised since she always seemed to have everything totally under control. "You're stressed? Wait, you don't think you're making a mistake with me, right?"

"What? No! First, it's dealing with all the details with my mom. This is her last chance at a big wedding, one she's always wanted for her girls. But my little sister eloped, and my middle sister wanted a small, simple wedding. Ours though is a bigger wedding than mom even dreamed of. But it had to be big since half the guests are business-related, the other half are family, our mutual friends, and friends I grew up with. You only have a few old friends, and you don't have any family. Oh, I'm sorry about how that came out, Marlin."

"Don't be, it's the truth. At least not many family members who don't want to kill me." This was one of those stories for another time.

She nodded. "And now to top it off, there's Lindsay and Murph having issues because of the wedding."

I said, "I don't think our wedding caused their issues, it just helped bring them to the surface. I don't blame Linds though, it's been almost three years. They've been through hell together, and a lot of it we were dragged into the middle of with them, too. Yeah, I know he and Dawn had a tough breakup, but she's not Dawn. She was partly the reason he broke it off with Dawn. No, he's got to decide what he wants, and I get the feeling there's a timer counting down, so he better not take too much time to do it."

She said, "You did what you could, and said what needed to be said. Not much more either of us can or should do."

"Except hope for the best." I pulled her in tight against me, needing to be close to her right now. As it turned out, she wanted to be even closer, and I was fine with that idea.

13

SAILING PALS

Tank and I were over at the beach again this morning pretty early, watching several of our catamarans take off. But the first cat we saw was already out on the water by the time we got there, it was the *ESVACat 18* demo boat sailing away with just Murph aboard, no Lindsay. I tried not to read too much into that, but I couldn't help it.

I let Tank off the leash I'd had him on for our walk over here, and he quickly started scouring the beach for sticks that floated up overnight. He found one that was the perfect size for him and brought it over, plopping down on the sand with it next to where I was standing. He sank his needle-sharp teeth into the water softened bark and started pulling it off in strips. Better the stick getting the "Tank treatment" than my deck shoes.

I heard Kari's voice behind us, "I thought I might find you two over here."

Tank jumped to his feet and scurried over to Kari with a big bark of welcome. At least, as big a bark as he could muster. She bent down and picked him up, getting her usual face wash in the process.

I said, "You know, in another month or so he's going to be too big to do that."

"I'll worry about it then. Meanwhile, I'll enjoy it while I can."

She set him back down and he came running back over to me. Not to visit and get petted, but to pick up his stick to take it back over to Kari.

"Traitor," I said.

"Hey! I thought you said you didn't mind him being partial to me."

"Normally. But that was our stick, and now he has given it to you. I'm very protective of my sticks."

Kari shook her head. "It's not a competition."

"Yeah, I can see that. But you owe me a stick. A good one, too."

She came over and looped her arm through mine. "You can have half of every stick I own. Consider it my dowry."

"Good because I'm fresh out."

We watched as Tank played with the stick, placing it on the sand so that he could paw and dig on either side of it, barking and dancing around it simultaneously as if daring the wood to fight back or even to move.

"The demo boat is out," Kari observed.

"Murph was already on the water when Tank and I got here. We saw him sailing off by himself. The water is such a great place to go and think when something is bugging you," I said.

"I hope he gets things worked out; that they get things worked out."

I nodded somewhat sadly. "I don't like to think about what it will be like around here if they don't."

We lapsed into silence, watching Tank play, and listening to the morning's small waves lap along the shoreline, and laughing gulls "talk" as they flew over the shallows, looking for their first meal of the day.

Directly overhead, descending through ten thousand feet on its way to Dulles International Airport in northern Virginia was a

Boeing 757. Two of its passengers were returning to the US after the conclusion of a successful and very lucrative business deal. One that had now put them on a collision course with several of the people on ESVA, including some at Mallard Cove. These two were ruthless, lacking any morals or empathy, with their eyes only on their goal. They'd kill any and all who got in their way. Pirates, by any definition. And one of them had a boat to catch as soon as they landed.

TANK WAS LYING at our feet at the *Cove*'s deck on his best behavior, probably because he was asleep after playing so hard on the beach. We had just ordered breakfast when Lindsay joined us, motioning to our server for coffee. She sat down, looking solemn.

"Hey, I'm sorry about last night, guys. That you two got dragged into the middle of Murph and me, I mean."

Kari replied, "Don't worry about it. Are you all right?"

"I'll let you know later because frankly, I don't know myself." She paused, then continued, "I really envy you two. You want the same things, and you want to go after them together, as a team. I used to think Murph and I had that too, but now I just don't know."

I said, "You're just having a bump in the road. You guys will figure it out, just like we did. We didn't always realize that we wanted the same things. Her dad did his best to get her to dump me, remember? And she almost did."

Kari's dad, Sam Albury, didn't like me much at first. It had taken quite a while for him to come around, and it was very difficult for Kari, his firstborn daughter. He had wanted her to marry a doctor, a lawyer, or some other professional. His other two daughters married a waterman and a sportfishing mate, two very tough and not well-paying professions. Sam was less than pleased.

Kari and I had started dating before I created the *Mid Atlantic Fishing Foundation* and before it bought *Tuna Hunters Productions*. Back then I was a fishing guide who wrote occasional articles for national fishing magazines for a living. In Sam's eyes, I was just another waterman who wouldn't be able to provide well for his daughter. He still doesn't know much about our combined finances; just enough to know that we aren't worried about where our next meal will be coming from. Though he also knows Kari's job with M&S is a very lucrative one, and originally thought I was freeloading off of her instead of carrying my share of the bills. But we're hiding a secret from him and the rest of her family. Kari and I had been targets of members of my family that had wanted me dead. Very wealthy members of my family. Let's just say that they aren't as wealthy now as they used to be, and we are financially set if we never work another day in our lives. But we love what we're doing, so why quit?

So now I'm the only man Sam has ever given his blessing to marry one of his daughters. He is a tough, successful contractor, and I'm proud to have him think well of me, though I didn't like him much at first, either. That had been a really tough time for Kari, who had always been the apple of her father's eye. She'd never gone against his wishes before. So while we're happy now, it hadn't always been this way.

Linds sighed, "It's more than just a bump. After you guys left we really got into it. Then he grabbed some clothes and moved over onto *Irish Luck* late last night, and I haven't seen or heard from him since. I was kind of hoping to find him here."

I said, "He took off by himself on the *ESVACat 18* earlier. He had launched it by the time I got there, I don't know that he even saw me when I walked up."

Linds looked even sadder now than she had when she sat down. I didn't know what I should say, so I stayed quiet. Fortunately, Kari knew exactly what to do.

"Would you give me a hand after breakfast, Linds? I need to pick out bridesmaid gifts, and I thought I'd head over to Virginia Beach."

"Sure, but it feels funny giving you input on my own gift."

Kari replied, "Nope, I already have my Maid of Honor gift picked out. I just need help with the rest."

"Okay. I guess it would be good to get away for a bit."

Kari winked at me when Lindsay glanced down at her menu. She had this handled.

SINCE TANK and I were a pair of bachelors for the rest of the morning, I picked out his rawhide bone and brought it along with us to the office to keep him occupied. Having an office is something still relatively new to me since up until two years ago mine was the salon of my vintage Chris Craft, which was also my home at the time. I had a laptop and an aging printer that I used when writing my articles, and that was about the extent of it. Then Kari came along, and she helped get me organized.

Actually, "helped" isn't the right word. She completely organized my mess, singlehandedly. Thinking back, that must've been right about the time that she decided I was worthy of becoming a lifelong project. Up until that point the only thing I knew about clouds was which ones to look out for when I was out on the water. You should have seen the look of horror on her face when she found out that all my contacts, records, and photos were only saved on my laptop. The one that didn't even have a password installed. The one that had only a half-century-old wooden hull and a couple of plastic bilge pumps between it and King Neptune's living room. Up to the cloud it all went, just before my phone and computer were destroyed in an explosion. It would have all been gone forever, if not for her. So would I, but that's another of those stories for another time.

Anyway, while I like having a real office, I also like it when it's quiet, as it is right now and most other Saturday mornings, when I'm the sole person here. It's only busy on weekends during filming season in December and January. Kari is often in her office one floor above mine on Saturday mornings, too, so it works out for both of us.

I heard Tank's tail thumping on the floor as he wagged it when Thor came in. Smitty poked his head in the door at the same time.

"Want to join me for a late lunch, Marlin?"

I glanced at the clock; I didn't realize that I'd already been working for over five hours. "Sure, thanks. Didn't even realize what time it was."

"I figured. I saw you two headed here this morning and hadn't seen y'all come out, so I thought I'd check on you."

"Yeah, time for us to clock out, and it's past time for somebody's walk. Let's go."

The *Cove* deck and the *Cat* were both slammed, but there was a four top with a great view of the beach available in the *Beach Bar's* far corner. All the *Pelican Fleet* catamarans were out, but Murph's demo unit was back on the beach. Now it was the eight-meter's turn to be missing. Maybe Dickie took it out with someone or with Murph.

Mimi came over to check on us after our food arrived.

"Everything good, gentlemen?"

We both nodded in agreement. Mimi had timed it perfectly, arriving tableside when both our mouths were full. I think they teach this in restaurant management school, that managers and servers must always time their inquiries to when the patrons are unable to speak.

"Marlin, um, is everything good between Murph and Lindsay?"

I almost choked on a hunk of hamburger. "Why do you ask, Meems?"

She saw I dodged the question, so she knew the answer and wasn't going to ask anything more. She's a friend of all of ours as well as being the head of restaurant operations here. Mimi's no gossip, just a very sharp operator. If there were problems between the partners, she was smart to find out about it as soon as possible and not get caught in between them. But Lindsay was out shopping with Kari, and Murph wasn't around. How did she know?

"It's nothing Marlin. Forget I asked. Please?"

I nodded. "No worries, Meems." But I was worried. Something made her ask. As she walked away, Smitty spoke up.

"It was probably about that hot little number he took out on the sailboat with him. She showed up here in an outboard probably fifteen minutes before I came to get you. She ran into Murph just as he was starting down the dock toward *Irish Luck*. I saw them two minutes later coming back with a bunch of weird shaped carbon fiber stuff. I was curious about what it was so I followed him and watched them fit it all on that big catamaran and take off. I didn't know that it was a hydrofoil."

My heart was sinking. "What did this girl look like?"

"About thirtyish, maybe five-foot, petite, short blonde hair, kinda curly, and hotter than a twenty-dollar pistol in a pawn shop. Wearing a bright yellow microkini, one of that kind that screams 'Hey, look at me, and how much I'm not wearing!' European looking, both the swimsuit and the woman."

It sounded like the French girl from the other day. And that didn't sound like Murph wanted to reconcile with Lindsay. Dumb, dumb, dumb move pal, though I'm prejudiced when it comes to my "little sister." We all knew that he had a reputation back in Florida as quite a "player" a few years back, at least up until he met Dawn. Before her, his longest relationship had lasted only a few days. Theirs survived a few months, but his and Lindsay's was going on its third year. Now it sounded like it too might have come to its end. I was sick, knowing how this would crush Linds when she found out, and I was really pissed at Murph. It's one thing to break up with your girlfriend, but another thing entirely if you parade around with another girl twelve hours later.

Now I realized it was not only going to hurt Lindsay and put the final nail in their relationship's coffin, but it was going to reach even farther. He was pulling this crap two weeks before my wedding where his potentially now ex-girlfriend is the Maid of Honor, and he is the Best Man. In his case, a real contradiction in terms. It meant they would have to walk down the aisle together on the way out of the church and even dance together at the reception. Yeah, this is just great. You think I'm upset? Kari's gonna kill him.

Smitty saw the look on my face, and I guess it told much or most of the story. He said quietly, "Sorry, man."

"Me too, Smitty. Me too."

We ate the rest of our lunch mostly in silence. I'm going to owe Smitty a few lunches after this one turned out to be such a bummer.

But I made a down payment on all that starting with a vodka after lunch, or so I figured. As upset as I was right now, I would be completely useless this afternoon, so I decided I'd make doubly sure of that.

I had reached the bottom of my vodka when Kari and Linds walked up. Smitty was still nursing his. I knew he had only stayed to babysit me rather than leave me to get drunk alone. One look at Linds and I was really ashamed of myself. I had been getting madder at Murph because of how their issues would complicate my life. It was selfish as hell of me because the second most important woman in my life was about to be going through probably the toughest time in hers.

Kari said, "I figured we might find you here Marlin. Hey, Smitty."

"I'm getting too predictable. This is twice in one day," I replied.

Smitty gave Kari a half-wave and stood up as she and Lindsay pulled out chairs to sit down. "I hate to part good company, but I have engine oil that isn't going to change itself."

He started to reach for the check, but I grabbed it first. "This one's on me, pal. Thanks for getting me out of the office."

"Glad to." He worriedly scanned the water before leaving with Thor in tow.

Lindsay looked over at the empty cradle, "Murph take out the eight-meter?"

"It was gone when I got here." I know, it wasn't the whole story, but it was the truth.

"I wonder who he went out with? That's too much boat for only one person."

I shrugged and grabbed my glass. If I were drinking, I couldn't be expected to answer questions. That's when I remembered that it was empty. Seeing me looking at the empty glass, our server came over.

"Another one, Marlin?"

I debated for a second too long and Lindsay said, "Yeah, another one for him, and one for Kari and me, too."

I had wanted to get her out of here before Murph showed back up with that woman, but I guess I already missed my chance. Maybe it was better that she was here and knew about it rather than be the last one on the docks to know. Marinas can be big rumor mills, and being the last to find out things like this really sucks.

Over by the bar I saw Mimi glance our way then look out over the ocean, obviously worried about the same thing. I shrugged gently at her, which Lindsay missed. Kari didn't, and looked over to see who I was passing signals to, and why. The "who" part was obvious, and unfortunately the "why" was about to be answered soon enough.

A few minutes later Lindsay pointed and said, "I think that's the eight coming back in."

It was indeed their catamaran, coming into sight from the southeast side of Smith Island, still far enough out that the occupants weren't yet recognizable. Fortunately, our drinks arrived at that point, giving us a needed distraction.

"To my real friends. Thanks for being here for me," Linds said, holding her glass up for us to clink ours against.

Kari knocked hers lightly against it, but I couldn't do it since I was currently feeling like a heel for chickening out by not telling and preparing her for what was coming. Lindsay looked at me quizzically, then followed my gaze back out over the water to the eight-meter. "That son of a bitch."

Kari looked out at the boat then back at me. I grimaced and shrugged again.

Lindsay looked at me, the hurt showing on her face. "You knew about this?"

"I only heard after I got here. Last time I saw him was this morning, heading out by himself on the eighteen."

"Why didn't you tell me when you heard about it, Mar?"

I looked down, and shook my head, not knowing what to say.

The three of us sat there in silence, now watching as the boat approached with the woman at the tiller. Right before they reached the cradle we could tell that it was indeed Danielle, that French woman from a week ago. And Smitty hadn't exaggerated about her microkini; it left little to the imagination. The two of them maneuvered the boat onto the dolly, then Murph motored it back up to its parking spot. He gathered up the foils and headed for the covered breezeway between the bars along with Danielle.

Murph was halfway to the breezeway when he spotted the three of us at our table. He stopped in his tracks, causing Danielle to look over at him. She followed his gaze and obviously recognized Lindsay. She smirked at her, then said something to Murph and laughed. Lindsay could only take so much. But if you thought she was the type of woman who would fall apart and run away when something like that happens, you couldn't be more off base.

Lindsay stood up and said, "I'll be right back. Please stay here, guys."

We watched as she went out to intercept Danielle and Murph. On seeing her approach, Danielle reached over and put her hand on Murph's arm. I couldn't see her face, but from my angle, it looked like Linds didn't even flinch. Instead, when she reached them she said something to Danielle, who bristled. Then Murph turned to the scantily clad woman and said something that had her pulling back her hand from his arm like it was radioactive, and then she stomped off toward the *Catamaran* bar.

Lindsay held a brief but quiet conversation with Murph who looked defiant at first, but then more like a scolded schoolboy toward the end, shuffling his feet and lowering his head a bit. She turned toward us, walking back to the table, chin held high. Murph watched her walk away, and I'm not totally sure but I think the look on his face might have been regret. It sure as hell should be.

When Lindsay sat down, I didn't know exactly what to expect. But whatever that was, this wasn't it. No tears, just a stoic look with her lips pursed tightly in a straight line. Neither Kari nor I said a word, knowing she would talk whenever she was ready. We didn't have long to wait.

"I told him that he might as well go ahead and sleep with her since she's already gotten what she wanted, so he might as well get what he wants, too. She played him so perfectly that he believed she came back here because of him. What the hell is it about you guys that when some slut shows up in a thong you quit thinking with your big head and let your little head take charge?"

I guess I deserved that for not telling her earlier when I had the chance. But it doesn't matter, I don't even care if she aims all her barbs specifically at me. If she wants to vent, I'll be happy to take the brunt of it if it'll make her feel better. I'd do anything to make her feel better right now.

She continued, "I mean it's bad enough that he broke my heart, but now he's going to break my wallet, too? I get it that he doesn't want to spend the rest of his life with me, he made that pretty clear last night. But then he gives that bitch an up-close look and demonstration of the most valuable breakthrough in sailing that we don't even have patented yet? She just happens to know all about eight-meters, and he believes it's only a funny coincidence that she shows up here? Then when she comes back she's all but gift-wrapped herself for him. She talks Murph into letting her take the helm of the demo boat so she can put it through the paces so now she knows exactly what its capabilities are? God, you guys can be so dumb!" She sat back in her chair and took a long sip of her drink.

I didn't know what to say or do, but fortunately, the sounds of a heated argument came from the breezeway, distracting us. Murph and Danielle were going at it, loudly. And it sounded like only one of them would be getting what they wanted today. A few minutes after the shouting ended we saw a small center console outboard come shooting out of the marina and into the path of Vazquez's junk, forcing him to steer wide. As the outboard passed us just offshore we saw that it was Danielle, headed west into the Chesapeake.

"Good riddance," Lindsay said. While it might have made her happy that Danielle left, if she was as involved in the sailing community as Linds was afraid she was, the damage had indeed already been done.

Kari said hopefully, "Maybe she won't know what to do with the information. Besides, it's not like she has a blueprint for the devices. Anyone can dream up the idea, but it takes someone like Dickie to build and refine it. The news of it was bound to get out sooner or later anyway."

"Later would have been better," Lindsay said. "Now I need to contact Dickie and let him know what happened because I know Murph won't. You two want to come back to the houseboat with me? I've got plenty of vodka there, and I could really use the company right now."

14

AUSSIE RULES

Instead of going to her houseboat, we talked Lindsay into coming back to ours. For one thing, our entertainment deck was one deck higher than on hers, giving us more privacy from the dock to be able to talk openly. Plus, we are two boats out beyond Murph's Merritt. At her boat, he would have to pass by every time he came and went. So, she quickly agreed. She made her call to Dickie from our boat. He was completely unaware of what had transpired, Murph hadn't contacted him, and he was not a happy camper. By the end of her call, I had made each of us a drink and we all settled in on the couch across from the bar.

"I like being out beyond the *Irish Luck*. If I end up staying here on the houseboat, I might move it down a few slips. Of course, I'm just assuming that he'll live on the Merritt."

I glanced over at Kari, who was on the other side of Lindsay. I saw that we both had been caught off guard by the thought that she might possibly move off the houseboat or even away from Mallard Cove.

Kari spoke up, "You might want to move slowly, Linds, maybe this whole thing with Murph will blow over and you guys can mend fences. Not to bring up a bad subject two weeks before we get married, but Marlin and I had our issues at first over the idea of getting married, too. I almost let my dad talk me into breaking up with him."

Lindsay replied, "Yeah, but he didn't show up the next day with a butt-flossed bimbo now did he? Mar's not that kind of guy. No, I should've known that Murph would want to go back to being a player and never settle down. The thing is, when our relationship was good it was so damn good, you know what I mean? I guess I just wanted that to last a lot more than he did. But he's made it crystal clear that nobody is going to push him into anything, especially not an engagement and marriage. And I'm through pushing, except when he puts an investment of mine at risk over some cheap French piece of ass. How could he have been so stupid!"

SUPPORTIVE AND QUIET, that's what I was over the next two hours as I executed my duties as newly appointed chief bartender and steward. This was penance for not telling Linds the whole story before Murph hit the beach with Danielle, as well as for just being a guy, since guys are not high on Lindsay's list right now. I'm not blaming her; I'm giving her some latitude as well as space. Fortunately, Kari is here to commiserate with her and she even shared some stories about an old boyfriend of hers that I really could've gone without overhearing.

As the sun sank lower and their glasses got refilled, they both opened up to each other farther than they had before, their friendship having been cemented long ago but reinforced so much more this afternoon. Want to find out who your friends are? Just look around when life is at its lowest point.

I had just refilled everyone's glasses when we heard loud angry voices from all the way over on charter boat row. Baloney and Vazquez were at full volume.

Lindsay stood up and said, "Wrong day for them to start this crap again. I've got to go take care of it, once and for all."

Kari asked, "You need a hand?"

"Nah, I've got this." She stood up, more steady on her feet than I thought she'd be after a few hours' worth of cocktails.

As she disappeared down the stairway I worried about where this could be going. After all, I needed Baloney to keep his slip here at least during the filming season. But since I didn't own any part of Mallard Cove, it wasn't my business to butt in. Kari reached over and put a reassuring hand on my arm.

"She'll handle it well."

"I know, but I wouldn't want to be either of those guys right now."

BALONEY AND VAZQUEZ were both face to face in the cockpit of *My Mahi*. A small crowd had gathered on the Cove's already crowded deck to watch. It wasn't every day you got to see a reality show star get into a verbal altercation with a guy who looks like a short pirate. Lindsay arrived on the dock behind the stern, put two fingers in her mouth and blew a very loud and shrill whistle that stopped both of them as they turned toward the source of the ear punishing sound.

"Front and center, both of you!" She pointed at a spot by her on the dock. Neither moved, still frozen and staring. "Okay, let's try this again. You two can get your asses up here right now, or you can get your gear together and cast off, it's your choice."

This time both of them reluctantly climbed out of the boat and onto the dock, but not without glaring at each other first.

Lindsay continued, quiet enough for the two of them to hear, but not loud enough to be overheard from the deck. "Boys, this can't continue, which means we have to settle this, and right now."

Vazquez and Baloney both started to speak, each intending on blaming the other. Lindsay held up a hand, not in any mood to hear it. "Nope, shut it, both of you. I need you two to follow me."

She led them to the same four top corner table in the *Cove Beach Bar* where she had been sitting when she spotted Murph with Danielle. It was the only open table, but it didn't put her in a better frame of mind. She sat in one of the chairs and pointed to the two on either side of hers.

"Sit!"

They both sat, and started to talk again, but she held up her hands again to shush them. Their server arrived to take their order and Lindsay said, "Vodka rocks and lemon for me, and these two will have the most expensive beer we have on draught and put it on Baloney's tab. Make sure nobody pays it but him. Plus, we'll have the seafood nachos, and put them on Vazquez's tab."

As the idea of having to pay not just for his beer, but for Marco Vazquez's sunk in, Baloney looked ill. And Vazquez was none too happy about buying food that Baloney would have any part of. But a quick glance at Lindsay's serious face was enough to keep them both quiet.

"So boys, here's the deal. You two have caused trouble here for the last time. There's no more 'get out of jail free' cards left in the deck. I 'get' that you don't like each other. I could care less about that. What I do care about is making sure that this is a place people think about as being fun and peaceful, which is not something that you two have been helping with.

"I get it. He's a stinkboater, and you're a blowboater, and you're never going to like each other, but you know what? I don't care! What you two need to decide is whether or not you like being here more than you dislike the other guy. Because if one of you goes, so does the other. And this is really stupid when you think about it, arguing over what kind of propulsion each one of you uses."

"Es not jus' about propulsion, chica. Es much more than that. These charter guys tink dey own the sea."

Baloney exploded, "Oh, an' you don't? Pushin' your way into the channel, whether you got the right-of-way or not? When you've got that motor runnin' it doesn't matter if you've got that sail up, you're a 'stinkboater'. And like it or not, you have to follow the same rules as me!"

Fortunately, the drinks arrived at that point, and they all took long sips.

Lindsay said, "Why don't we focus on what you both have in common. You both like being out on the water, you both like boats and Mallard Cove, you both like having the right of way when you're coming or going. And..." She paused for effect, "You both have egos the size of damn cruise ships!"

Each looked angry at first, but then the one corner of Baloney's mouth curved up as he tried to suppress a grin. Vazquez wasn't as successful at hiding his.

She continued, "Look, the last thing I want to do is ban you guys from here. But if this happens again, that's exactly what I'm going to do. I don't care if you're not friends, but you have to be civil to each other. If you'll each do me a favor, I think it'll go a long way to making sure that'll happen. Marco, please don't come through the breakwater and into the marina with your sails up again and take it easy when you dock. No more hot-rodding. And Bill, anytime you are near Marco outside of the marina and he has his sails up, even if his engine is running go ahead give him the benefit of the doubt and treat him like he's only under sail. I'm asking nicely here you two, because I really, really don't want to toss you guys out of here. And that would mean being banned from the whole property, permanently. Restaurants, bars, all of it."

The men glared at each other across the table but their concentration was broken as the seafood nachos arrived. Before they answered they each dug into the tower of chips, both wanting to get at least their share of the seafood part.

"Chica, these are good! An' for jou, I'll leave my canvas down in da marina. But only for jou. An' I wanna say haim sorry to hear 'bout your troubles, I don' wanna add to them."

"Me too, Lindsay. Wish that you and Murph coulda worked things out. And I'll do what you ask. You got enough on your plate; you don't need the two of us actin' like dogs at a fire hydrant markin' our territory. Whaddaya say, Marco Polo, truce?" He held out his hand across the table above the nachos.

"Jes, Baloney, truce for the sake of Chica. But it don' mean I like you." Both shook hands quickly, then hit the nachos again.

"Yeah, well, I don't like you either. But you're easier to get along with when you ante up for the nachos."

Marco grinned. "Jou is okay when jou buy beers, too." He had heard about Baloney's reputation as a suds mooch.

"Don't get used to it, this is a once in a lifetime thing."

Lindsay sat back and smiled, enjoying her drink, and watching the two verbally jousting and trying to "one-up" each other with their redirected machismo. They were telling boating stories that were no doubt designed to both impress as well as cheer her up. She sighed as she realized that the news about Murph and her must be all over the marina now. Then their server brought over another vodka and two more beers.

Baloney explained, "You needed another so we could each pay for one of them, and we wouldn't have to argue about who did it. But now if you'll excuse me, I've got to see a man about a horse."

"I gotta go wit jou so jou don' get lost. Be right back, chica."

As soon as they were out of sight, a very attractive sandy-haired man in his thirties wearing fishing shorts and a polo shirt got up from the bar and made a beeline for the table. He had a game show host smile, a South Beach tan, and a mouth filled with overbleached teeth. He addressed Lindsay in a deep Australian accent as he pulled out Baloney's chair and sat down uninvited.

"G'day, Lindsay. Jeremy Campbell's the name, but you can call me Jez." He stuck out his hand, which she didn't take. Undeterred he withdrew his hand but continued speaking without giving her a chance to interrupt, "And now that we both know each other's names we probably should get to know even a bit more about each other, and I'll go first. I'm the best eight-meter sailor on the Chesa-peake, and I hear you just lost your sailing mate. I'm available for that, and anything else you might have in mind." The smile got even wider.

She paused a minute, pretending to look him up and down, but really stalling for time. It worried her that she'd never seen him before but he seemingly already knew a lot about her. Too much, in fact. When she saw Baloney headed back she answered, "Well Bruce, I've met a few fig jams in my life, but you are by far the most up your-self of all. So, why don't you just rack off and get on ya bike."

His smile faded quickly. "You don't give a bloke much of a chance, do ya? Give it a little time, we can get on just fine."

From behind him he heard, "Jou ain't got no more time, 'cause jou is in my frien's chair, and dat means jou is leaving now." Marco and Baloney had returned and were flanking Jez on either side of the chair.

"Why don't you ruddy bogans bugger off, I'm flat out with the lady here."

Baloney said, "Yeah, well, you're gonna be 'flat out' if youse don't bugger off yourself. You're in my chair, and you need to be somewhere else. Like maybe Delaware. Now, shove off."

Jaz replied, "An' you two don't have a clue who you're dealin' with. I can make you two pull a Harry and you will."

"That's enough! Tell your story walkin' or to the cops, it's your choice. One way or another mongrel, you're outta here, and I mean off the property, and don't ever come back." Lindsay's eyes had narrowed and her voice was just above a growl.

Jez slowly got up while staring daggers at Lindsay. "You're a feisty Shelia, ain't you? This won't be the last you'll see of me, mark my words about that. Coulda worked out well for both of us, but you just made yourself the wrong choice."

He jostled both of the shorter men on his way past them, earning a "puta madre" from Marco. They both stared at him as he made his way through the crowd by the bar and out into the breezeway then out of sight. Reclaiming their chairs, Baloney looked very surprised before addressing Lindsay.

"That was kinda harsh, Lindsay."

She shook her head. "He threatened both of your lives. We don't need business from people like him, or as Marco said, 'puta madres.'"

"What the hell does that mean?"

Marco chuckled, "It means he sleeps with his mother. You know, a motherf..."

Baloney interrupted, "I get it! But whatta ya mean he threatened our lives?"

"Pulling a Harry means disappearing, or as he put it, making you two pull a Harry. The Harry was Prime Minister Harry Holt, who disappeared on a swim back in 1967."

Marko asked, "How do jou know all this stuff, and that slang jou use on him?"

"I used to date an Australian a few years back, and they never really lose the slang. It's easy to pick up on. So, I just insulted Jez about six different ways, and almost as strongly as Marco did." She smiled.

Baloney looked shocked as he realized something. "Hey, Marco Polo, did you just tell that jerk I was your friend?"

"No! It was a number of speech, I don' mean nothin' by it."

"Good. Don't make a habit of that either. And it's a figure of speech, not number," Bill replied.

"Oh, jou gonna correk me when nobody can unnerstan' jou through that Jersey accent of jours."

Lindsay rolled her eyes. "Cool it! I know that you two aren't happy unless you're at each other's throats but keep it civil or you'll make me toss you both!"

Baloney held his hands up in surrender. "We're just talkin' not fighting."

"Good, keep it that way." She upended her glass and stood up slowly and somewhat unsteadily. An afternoon of vodka had taken its toll. After a trip to the ladies' room, she continued toward the security gate. Standing in front of it she fumbled for her keycard when suddenly she was grabbed from behind by the neck and shoved violently. She was pinned against the metal gate by a man's body against her back, his fingers choking off her airway. She grabbed his hands and tried prying them away from her throat, but he had a vice-like grip.

"I told you it coulda worked out good for both of us, but no, you gotta be a big butch Shelia. Well, it's still gonna work out good for one of us, and I mean me...whaaaa?"

Lindsay felt the pressure of his body disappear and was able to then pry his hands away from her neck. She spun around to find Baloney and Marco taking on Jez. Though Jez had a height advantage of several inches, he couldn't overcome the two against one advantage, especially since Baloney had him by his long sandy hair from behind with both of his hands. Jez was busy trying to deflect blows from Marco. After receiving several well-placed punches from him, Jez broke free of Baloney, spinning sideways but losing some shaggy locks in the process. With both men now on a full-frontal assault he stumbled backward and with a little more "help" from Marco in the form of a kick he lost his balance and fell backward into the chilly water. Rather than try to get up onto the private dock he swam across the basin to the tee on B Dock, pulling himself up on the concrete surface right behind *Coastal Dreamer*.

"Are jou all right, chica?"

"I am now, thanks to you guys. I never even knew he was behind me. He was squeezing so hard; I couldn't even breathe enough to scream. And nobody could see what was happening from the restaurant deck because of all the charter boats between me and them. If you two hadn't come along and looked this way when you did, it would have been another story. Thank you again, guys."

They heard then saw a small center console outboard shoot out from between B and C Docks, it's motor winding up to wide-open throttle and earning a few shouted curses from boaters that were now subject to its wake at their slips. Jez was at the wheel and making straight for the breakwater's inlet.

"We should call the cops." Baloney was still worried.

Lindsay shook her head. "No, we don't need the bad publicity. I'm all right, and he knows better than to show his face around here again. Now we know how he got here, and to look out for that boat."

"Jou sure jou all right?"

"Yes. You guys go on home, I'm okay. Thanks."

Baloney replied, "Alright, but any sign of trouble just yell and we'll both come running."

"I will."

The men watched as she went through the gate and it latched

behind her. She smiled as she heard Marco tell Baloney, "I still don' like jou."

Baloney replied, "Good. I still don't like you either. But we're gonna look out for her together."

"Jes, that we gonna do togeder."

15

TRUTH SERUM

I was in the hot tub all intertwined with Kari, her legs wrapped around my hips when we heard Linds coming up and out of the stairwell. Kari let out a small squeak of surprise and then hugged me tightly, pulling our chests together.

Lindsay crossed the deck and over to the bar without really looking in our direction. "You guys are never going to believe what just happened. I'm going to make myself another drink. Are these your glasses? I'll make refills for you two as well. I'll be right there; I really need to sit down to tell you all this. Hey, what was that chain doing across the stair landing? I figured you wanted it there so I hooked it back after I came through."

Kari chuckled in my ear as she watched our friend approach and it dawned on her that our clothes had been hastily strewn in a line that ended at the hot tub. All of our clothes. Two oversized fluffy towels sat on a chaise. That's when she looked over into the tub.

"Oh... were you guys... so, that's what that chain was about. Oh well, sorry, I'm already here now and so are your drinks. Carry on." She sat in one of the chaises that faced the tub as Tank went over to her with his rawhide bone. He lay down next to her chair, drawing a pat on his head.

Kari laughed, her arms around my neck still holding our chests tightly together. Then as Lindsay began telling us what happened, we were shocked and concerned.

"I'm just glad you're okay, Linds. We should be able to get a picture of him from one of the security cameras to pass around to the crew. Are you sure you don't want to call the cops," Kari asked?

"I'm positive, Kari. We don't need to get the reputation as being an unsafe place, and chances are he won't come back since he knows we'll all be on the lookout for him now. Plus, we don't know if his name is really Jez Campbell, and we have no idea where he lives. All we do know for sure is he's Australian, and he gets around at least some of the time in that outboard." She leaned back on the chaise and took another sip of vodka.

"I had a perfectly good buzz on before the adrenaline rush wiped it out. Damn, you should have seen Baloney's face when I told him that he wasn't just paying for his beer, but Marco Vazquez's too. I thought he was going to have a stroke." She grinned at the memory.

That she was smiling so soon after everything that happened to her in the last twenty-four hours showed what an incredibly strong person she is. I know that inside she is in emotional pain, but her wanting to be around us now instead of locking herself in her houseboat alone I'm taking as a very good sign.

I said, "Nice going! Wish I had been there to see that. Speaking of 'seeing that' how about handing us each a towel?"

She grinned slyly, "What, and miss the floor show? Not a chance. Besides, there's nothing here that I haven't seen before. I've been to the spa with Kari, and if you'll remember, Mar, you gave me the 'full Monty' that night you locked yourself out when you thought Dave the security guy was an intruder. You came out on deck with nothing but your gun. Then Murph and I popped up wearing just a couple of pairs of his boxers so you got a good look at my 'girls', too."

At first, she grinned at the recollection, but after mentioning Murph's name that smile quickly faded. Kari and I both knew we needed to keep her mind off of him. She climbed out of the tub and retrieved her oversized towel, wrapping herself up tightly like a cigar.

I held my hand out for her to pass me mine, but instead, she smirked, taking her drink along and reclining in the chaise next to Lindsay.

"So, there's a floor show in this bar, I like it," she said.

"Kari, please gimme a towel!"

"No way dear. Because if I recall correctly, in the shower later that day you compared my 'girls' to Lindsay's and said hers were bigger. Now you'll have to pay the added 'cover charge' for that!" She held her glass out toward Lindsay, who clicked hers lightly against it as they shared a laugh.

Lindsay teased, "Did you shut off the heater, Mar? From here it looks like your 'braille thermometer' is saying the water's getting cold."

I was willing to go along with this gag to a point if it kept Lindsay's spirits up. "The water temperature is just fine, thank you. It's just that my water aerobics class instructor suddenly bailed on me."

"Well if the water temperature is still good and you won't get out, maybe I'll just come over and join you."

As she started unbuttoning her blouse, I'd now reached that point I was talking about.

"No! Er, no, I'll join you two, you win."

Before I could stand up, they both started mimicking a famous old-time striptease tune. I stood, and as I turned away from them and toward the chaise where my towel lay, they both whistled. I climbed out and wrapped the towel around my waist before bringing my drink over with me and claiming the chaise on the other side of Lindsay.

"No, now we've won. But I hate it when I'm the only one at a party that's overdressed," Lindsay quipped.

"Funny lady," I said as I reclined in the chaise. I started going over her conversation with that Jez creep in my head. There were a couple of things that didn't add up.

"Hey, you said this guy claimed to be 'the best eight-meter sailor on the Chesapeake', and that he knew you and Murph had hit a rough patch."

She nodded. "You mean we broke up. Although the way he put it was 'lost your sailing mate'. What about it?"

I said, "The eight-meter has been on the beach for long enough now for the word to get out about it, and about you two buying into Dickie's operation. So, it's not surprising that he might've heard about it, no matter where he's from if he's around boats. But your dust-up with Murph just happened, yet he knew all about it? While that news has gotten around the marina over the past few hours, nobody knows this guy. How the hell did he hear about it? Why would he care enough to find out?

"The one common denominator that sticks out in my head is that woman, Danielle. What if he's in with her as some kind of industrial spy or something, trying to learn as much as they can about your automatic foil thingamabobs. She targets Murph, comes over this morning and gets lucky enough to find him in the middle of a spat with you. It was the perfect opportunity to drive a wedge between the two of you and push you even further apart. Then after she leaves this Australian jerkoff comes sniffing around to see if he can find you, figuring you might show up at the *Cove* or maybe even catch you taking out the eight-meter."

I continued, "I'm having a hard time believing that two separate people who either know or claim to know a lot about a small sailboat class that's still in its infancy in the USA both just happen to show up here. Then they target the two people outside of Dickie's crew who know the most about these new foil devices, in a beach environment where you don't usually think twice about strangers walking up and asking questions about your boat. Except you picked up right away on Danielle's vibe because she wanted to show off her knowledge a little too hard to impress you two. And at Dickie's shop, another eight-meter expert showing up there would have sounded even louder warning bells to them. Come to think of it, we need to check and see if Dickie might know of this Australian dude."

Lindsay looked thoughtful, "So, what you're saying is that maybe this chick came after Murph, not the other way around? That the whole thing is a setup to find out more about those foils?"

"I'm saying it's possible. From what I saw at a distance, you didn't give him much of a chance to explain this afternoon," I said.

Kari added, "Maybe you should give him a chance to tell his side of the story. If he was the one being chased, that does change things quite a bit."

"As far as that French slut goes, maybe. But about him leaving last night, it doesn't. And if he was so innocent, why hasn't he tried to explain? I haven't heard anything from him," Lindsay said.

I took the easy question, "Because I've seen you mad at me, and I know enough to let you cool down first before attempting to reason with you. I swear you must've been born a redhead because you have a temper like one."

"Funny guy, Mar. So now I'm a hothead."

"On occasion, yes. Though even then I still love you like a sister."

She scowled. "I thought you were an only child. Oh, oh, I'm sorry, I didn't mean to..."

My heredity is, well, complicated. Technically, I'm a bastard. Though I like to think of myself as a kind and loveable one. Another of those stories for another day. Like I said, a complicated one.

I reached across and patted her arm. "Don't worry about it, Linds, I know what you meant. But this does go to show that things aren't always as they seem. Maybe they aren't with Murph, either."

"Maybe," she conceded. "The problem is, even if they aren't, everyone else already thinks they are. I'd like to say that I don't care what anyone else says or thinks, but that's not true." She looked down into her glass. "What'd you put in that vodka bottle anyway, truth serum?"

"Oh, just think of the questions I can ask you now that you have to answer." I gave her my best evil leer.

"Uh, let's not. I've had all the truth I can handle for one day."

LINDSAY MAY HAVE HAD ALL the truth she could handle, but not all the conversation, which continued as the sun slipped lower in the sky. Only the subject had now switched over to the wedding, and as you might've guessed, I didn't have a lot to add. So, after listening for a while I started following our line of clothing in reverse, getting dressed while also gathering up Kari's clothes and taking them over to her. Then I headed down to the galley to find some thing or things to throw on the grill for the three of us.

As I was digging through the 'fridge, my cell phone vibrated, it had been in my pants pocket on the deck all this time. I discovered I had four texts from Murph, which had all arrived during the last three hours. The first one started with "How much trouble am I in?" and each got progressively more anxious. This last one pleaded for me to text him back. I called instead.

"Marlin, thanks for calling me." He sounded even more anxious than his texts.

"Sorry, I just saw your texts. Kari and I were in the hot tub, so I didn't have the phone with me."

"Oh. I thought maybe you were dodging me."

"Nope."

"So, do you know where Lindsay is?"

"Yep. Up on the top deck, talking with Kari."

"How much trouble am I in? She was pretty hot over at the bar, I figured I'd let her cool down a bit before I called her."

I said, "Smart man. Except the part about humiliating her in front of a crowd of people with that French bimbo. But why would you even want to talk to her after you left her?"

Murph said, "I didn't leave her like permanently, I just needed some space to think. So I went next door to sleep on the Merritt."

"And you thought just calling her on the phone would be a good idea instead of facing her? But first you decided to take some chick in a thong out on a date?"

"It wasn't a date! And it wasn't my idea, it was hers! She talked me into it after she saw me come back in the eighteen. She hit me up on the beach about the eight-meter and said that she'd never sailed one herself, but she'd seen them in magazines. I guess I was feeling kinda lonely, and she was really nice and interesting, and I said okay I'd take her out for a spin. That's all it was, I swear. I wasn't trying to get anywhere with her, and we were just taking the foils back to the dock box when Lindsay went ballistic. Wouldn't let me say anything."

"You blame her? The whole friggin' marina is talking about how you dumped her for some beach slut in a thong."

"That's not what happened!"

I said, "Perception is reality, Murph, at least in marinas. You know that. She's totally humiliated, and now she's talking about leaving Mallard Cove. Then she was attacked by this Aussie dude..."

"She was what?"

"Yeah, Baloney and Vazquez saved her from the guy..." But he had hung up. Twenty seconds later I heard him jump aboard *Tied Knot*, then fall heavily on the outside stairs. I had come down the inside stairs and hadn't unhooked the small chain on the outside steps yet. Five seconds later I heard him continue pounding his way up the stairs.

By the time I got up to the top deck he was already standing next to Lindsay's chaise checking on her, but mostly pleading his case. I kind of came in somewhere in the middle. By that point, it was obvious what he was trying to sell, she wasn't interested in buying.

"...you made yourself perfectly clear last night. And I don't even care whose idea it was to go sailing. If you were really thinking of me, you wouldn't have taken her. Hell, you shouldn't have even been talking to her after what I told you when we met her. And the three of us are now pretty sure that guy Jez was working with her to try and get information by putting the moves on me. He attacked me after that didn't work. See, that's the difference between us Murph; you jumped at the first thong that came along, oblivious to her real intentions. And I told that smooth talker to take a hike. So, you were right last night; we don't have a future together."

"That wasn't what I said, Lindsay, I only said I wasn't ready to get engaged again right now, I didn't say that I never would be."

"Right, I had almost forgotten, thanks for reminding me. You were engaged when we started dating, though you had neglected to mention that little detail before we were rolling around in the sack. Now I know how Dawn must've felt. Almost. At least we weren't engaged when you took up with that French bitch. We've only been living together for three years, so it's not like we were in any kind of a serious relationship," she said sarcastically. "Three years, Murph, years I won't get back. Years I threw away on you, wasting my time with you. I really thought we had something together. But I guess you knew what you were doing last night after all. Maybe I ought to thank you for not letting it drag out to four years."

"I didn't 'take up' with Danielle! She conned me into a ride on the eight-meter. That's all, I swear! And we might still have a future, but I need to be sure before I commit to that."

"Well Murph, I'm sure of a few things. The first is that if you aren't sure of a future with somebody after three years, you never will be. And the second is that if you've screwed up my part of the ESVACat investment, you're going to pay me back, and I mean every single cent I put in. By the way, Dickie is furious with you, too. And the third thing I'm sure of is that I'm going to have a nice dinner here with my two friends tonight, and you aren't going to be part of it."

Murph stood there silently for a few seconds, processing everything that Lindsay had said. With a very downcast look he turned and left without a word. It had been awkward for Kari and me to witness, but Murph had brought it on himself right then by barging in. Even though our conversation had started with him being concerned about his own troubles, he *had* shown up immediately after hearing about Lindsay's attack.

"I was right, Mar, this stuff is truth serum. It felt good to get that off my chest," Lindsay said as she held out her empty glass.

I gathered both hers and Kari's glasses and took them over to the bar for refills. With tomorrow being Sunday and none of us working, I figured it wouldn't be a bad idea for an evening of "truth serum" to let Linds vent as much as she wanted or needed. As I added the lemon wedges, my phone vibrated again, Murph had texted me.

MURPH: *"Can we meet for breakfast, just you and me?"*
Me: *"Sure. When and where?"*

Murph: "*Cove @ 6:30?*"
Me: "*C U there.*"

MY "TRUTH SERUM" intake would now have to be curtailed somewhat this evening if I were going to make it to the *Cove* that early. But since I was acting as this evening's bartender, that was easily accomplished. Though I planned to keep both women's glasses topped off.

If Lindsay wanted a chance to rant, rail, and howl at the moon, she was going to get that. And it would be accomplished safely, in the company of friends, with no vehicles involved. Judging from what I was overhearing now in her conversation with Kari, the evening was headed in that direction. The talk was centering around "guys" and not in a very positive light. No offense taken by me, I get it, and can't blame her. She had been unbelievably stoic all day despite having been humiliated, physically attacked, and then confronting someone who she was sure had every intention of betraying her. Now it was time to purge those repressed feelings with a close female friend of the non-offending sex. Kari was the perfect choice for that.

Kari looked up at me as I handed her a full glass, and I winked. I could see the relief on her face as well as a hint of a wry smile. She was reassured, knowing that I understood what was happening and that I wouldn't hold anything against either of them, no matter what I might overhear. A lot of communication from only a wink and a smile, but I'm marrying the right woman.

Okay, confession time, on this round of drinks I started cutting Kari's refills with tonic, something that she of course picked up on after her first sip. She looked back up at me and subtly nodded in agreement with what I'd done.

I was like a one-man catering crew tonight, mostly silent and in the background. I wanted the two of them to keep up their conversation, which was as I had hoped, mostly one-sided with Kari doing a lot of listening. So, I fed all of us and Tank, cleaned up the upper galley and bar while keeping the glasses full, as well as keeping the pup walked and empty. Finally, a little after midnight a very wrung out and inebriated Lindsay started to wane. I had anticipated this and had prepped one of the guest rooms for her since we didn't want her being alone over on her houseboat tonight after so much had happened.

Kari and Tank headed for our stateroom, leaving me to make sure Lindsay got to her room okay. She was good until we reached the top of the stairs, then I was glad we had the forethought to install the elevator, too. As it was, I had to keep an arm around her waist to steady her while she walked from the elevator to her room. I had a lined trashcan beside her bed, just in case dinner decided to come back up after all that vodka. I tucked her in after getting her shoes off and pointing out the can.

She slurred, "You're a good annoying older brother, Mar, you know that?"

I smiled, "Sleep well, sis." As I turned out the light and closed the door, I heard her starting to softly snore.

16

THE MORNING AFTER

Tank was waiting just inside the door to our stateroom, so I took the little guy out for one final walk before turning in myself. As we hit the dock, he looked down toward the gate and started growling. That was when I saw a hooded figure in dark clothing leaning over the big dock box behind Lindsay's houseboat. I couldn't make out any of the person's features in the dark, the dock lights are only there to provide safe footing at night so they're aimed low. But one thing for certain is that it wasn't Murph, and that meant they were not supposed to be in that box.

"Hey you! What are you doing in there?" Tank and I started running down the dock toward the person, about fifty feet away. The figure grabbed some things from the box then leapt into a small center console outboard that was waiting in the empty slip next to the houseboat. Another person was at the helm and quickly pegged the throttle. The boat was planing by the time it reached the end of the long slip and banked hard right, heading for the breakwater's inlet without any running lights.

"What the hell is going on out here?" A shirtless Murph came out of *Irish Luck*'s salon, the light from the widescreen tv backlighting him.

"It's Marlin. Somebody just broke into your dock box."

Murph hurried over to the box. "Damn it, the foils are gone." He picked up the open combination padlock from the dock. "And they knew the combination."

I asked, "Who else besides you and Lindsay knows it?"

"Dickie. Though he wouldn't need to take them in the middle of the night."

I shook my head, "No, this wasn't Dickie, he's bigger than this guy, and Dickie wouldn't have run when I yelled."

"The only other person who might have seen me enter the combination is Danielle when I went to pick up the foils before our sail yesterday."

I replied, "This person was definitely not Danielle, they were at least six or eight inches taller. I only got a brief glimpse of the boat driver, but that person may have been about Danielle's height. If she was the one running the boat, then it's possible this might've been that Jez guy."

Murph said, "We better call the Sheriff."

I thought a minute then said, "Lindsay didn't want them called today after her attack because of the negative publicity it could bring. And a unique theft like this will surely hit the local paper, they read all the incident reports and this could bring a lot of unwanted attention to Dickie's foils before he's ready for it." I could see Murph thinking it over. "It's not like they're going to pawn or sell them, they only fit your eight-meter. And there are no fingerprints, the guy had on dark gloves, I could see that much. If it was those two, they're probably going to take them apart to see what makes 'em work."

"Maybe you're right, Marlin. We can always call the law in the morning. I'll sleep on it and decide then." He grimaced as a thought hit him, "Lindsay is going to kill me over this."

"Don't worry about that now. Go back and get some sleep, and I'll meet you for breakfast at the *Cove*."

. . .

KARI WAS STILL SLEEPING SOUNDLY as I got dressed just after six, trying to be as quiet as possible. Tank looked at me, and I motioned to him with my hand to follow me. He stood up and followed silently, one very bright fur kid. I fed him then put on a light jacket on our way out, it was still in the fifties in mid-May, and the sun was just starting to peek above the horizon. We took a long walk, ending up at the *Cove* where Murph was already waiting, his coffee mug already drained. It was obvious he'd been there for a while, even though I was five minutes early.

He said, "Hey."

"Good morning." I sat in the chair across from him, and Tank lay down under the table. Technically, he was only allowed on the restaurant's deck (Tank, not Murph), but I doubted that any inspectors were out this early to be able to catch him. Plus, I knew the staff loved him, and they wouldn't mind.

"I don't know how good it is. Seems like I keep shoveling more crap on myself. It was bad enough arguing over an engagement, but then I blew it by taking Danielle for a ride. Now the foils. I've got to call Dickie and tell him later, but that's the least of my worries. How bad was Lindsay after I left?"

"She needed girl time. I played the invisible bartender as she talked to Kari all night."

He winced. "Sorry, Marlin. I didn't mean for you to get caught in the downdraft."

"Comes with the territory. I'll live."

"Yeah, about that, do you think there's any chance of my mending things with her?"

"Last night I overheard all the details of the story about you spending the weekend with her while you were still engaged to Dawn. And how she didn't find out about Dawn until she showed up at the office at Bayside to surprise you and Dawn happened to be the one she asked to help her find you. Then how she drove back to northern Virginia in tears. She said you were relentless after that, and your breakup with Dawn. Even though she never wanted to see you again, you finally wore her down until she eventually agreed to go out with you again. I'd heard the gist of it before this, but I really got the nitty-gritty last night."

Just then our server arrived with coffee for me, a refill for Murph, and then she took our order. I was grateful for the interruption; it had giving me a chance to think. After she left I looked at Murph and continued.

"If I hadn't heard that entire story last night I'd tell you that you have absolutely no chance in hell. None. But you two have a few things going for you that you didn't even have back then. You've gone through hell together on more than one occasion, living through bullets and even bombs over the last few years. And you've built a great future together with this place, your shares in the Lynnhaven deal, both becoming paid board members on the *Fishing Foundation*, now investing in ESVACats, all of it happening in just a few years. And all of it happening because you were together."

I stopped to put together the right words because they would probably be the most important words and the most heartfelt sentiment that I'll ever give Murph. Plus, my head was hurting and the day was fuzzy from last night's drinking, even though I had gone easy on myself. But I desperately needed to get this right.

"You two are my friends. Actually, you're both Kari and my best friends. However, if I hadn't heard your explanation last night there's no way that I'd be sitting here this morning having any part of you trying to patch things up with Linds. That just wouldn't be happening. But last night I heard her tell the story about when you met, which is still a bit gut-wrenching for her, and understandably so. However, I also heard something in her voice as she told how you just wouldn't give up, despite all the calls she refused, all the texts she didn't return, and the hundreds of flowers, none of which she threw out, by the way. Even through that hurt and humiliation, she saw something in you then, and she's seen that something even more in you over these past three years. I don't think that's anything that can evaporate overnight.

"I'm going to tell you something, Murph, and you need to listen very closely. If you don't have any intention of ever asking her to marry you, if that's something you don't think you'll ever be able to bring yourself to do because you still feel a strong attraction to other women, then you need to let her go. She's a good woman who deserves a good life with someone who will promise to be there with her for it, for the whole thing. From listening to her last night I know she's reached the point in her life where she wants that.

"You know I love you like a brother, and we've been there for each other when it has counted. But she's like a little sister to me too, and now's my time to be there for her to protect her. If you think about what I've said and you know in your heart that getting back together is the right thing to do, think about everything I just said, you'll find something in there that'll help. But if you don't think you should, then don't. You'll be doing both of y'all a big favor by getting it over with now. But you'll need to get completely clear of each other, or the hurt will linger longer."

My timing was perfect, as our food arrived. Murph's was a big breakfast platter, and mine was in a bag, to go. I grabbed the bag and stood up.

Murph asked, "Are you going to tell her about the foils? She should help decide if we call the cops or not."

I shook my head. "Nope, that's your job. And you need to do it in person, not over the phone. I'm going back to cook breakfast for everyone. Give them time to wake up and eat, then come over."

I HAD the galley cranked up with a dozen pieces of bacon frying on a hot griddle. A pitcher of pancake batter sat ready to pour as soon as those beautiful strips of cured, smoked, pork were done and out of the way. My mantra of "carbs are our friends" for the morning after one of *those* nights was in full force today. While it didn't really apply to the bacon, I didn't care. It's *bacon*.

Two arms wrapped around me from behind, and I felt Kari's body press against mine, her face against my left shoulder blade.

"You are one very desirable man."

"Because I'm making pancakes."

"Of course! What else would I be talking about?"

I said, "Well, there's the bacon, too."

"No carbs in bacon."

"I cut your last few drinks with tonic. You shouldn't be in that rough a shape this morning."

"I'm grateful for that, and no, I'm not. I'm only slightly hurting," she said.

"There's a pitcher of fresh-squeezed orange juice in the 'fridge, and that'll start taking the edge off until the pancakes are ready."

"I knew there was a darned good reason I was marrying you."

"You just love me for my culinary talents."

"Those too." She hugged me tighter before letting me go and heading for the OJ. She poured two glasses and handed me one. That's when I saw she hadn't gotten dressed yet and was only wearing a robe. This was her usual signal that she planned on having a slow-paced and casual Sunday, my favorite kind.

"Anyone get the license of the truck that hit me last night?" Lindsay emerged from the stairwell, looking rough.

Kari said, "The galley fairy squeezed OJ, there's bacon cooking, and pancakes right behind it."

I put on my best indignant voice, "Galley fairy? Really? Now I don't know if I should tell you that I brought back not just one but *two* of the *Cove's* sticky buns. They're in the warming drawer."

These are a signature weekend offering at the restaurant and have become especially popular with those who might have indulged a bit too much the night before. Kari quickly retrieved both pastries, handing one to Linds who immediately took a bite, her eyes rolling back in her head right before they closed.

Lindsay said, "If you ever dump Marlin, I'm marrying him myself. Not only can he cook, but he gives great take-out."

Kari and I shared a glance and a smile. It was a really good sign if Lindsay could joke about marriage this morning. I am really dreading when Murph comes over to tell her about the theft of the foils. The two women sat down at the counter.

Lindsay asked, "You went up to the *Cove* this morning just for these?"

"Well, no, I had to meet someone for coffee. Speaking of which…" I poured three mugs and placed them on the counter.

Lindsay's face turned sour. "I can guess who you were meeting, and hopefully they weren't wearing a thong."

"Thankfully not." That's a mental image I want no part of, especially right before breakfast.

"Don't tell me, let me guess what the topic of conversation was."

I said, "Linds, being caught in the middle between our two best friends isn't a place I like to be. From now on if y'all want to know things about each other, you need to talk to each other directly, not through either Kari or me."

"I guess that's my cue," said Murph, who had just walked in. Lindsay glared at him. His showing up right now wasn't helping her headache.

"Murph, I don't want to talk to you right now, I'm not in the mood."

He sighed. "We do need to talk now, and this can't wait, it's business." He stood at the end of the counter, looking very uncomfortable as he related the story of last night's theft.

Lindsay said to me, "You were right not to call the sheriff. It's not like they're going to assign anyone to this case for follow up, they'd only do a case report so we can make an insurance claim, which we aren't going to do. And yes, that would've surely made the paper, but not in a good way." She turned back to Murph, who looked like he had been summoned to the principal's office. "You need to go call Dickie and tell him what happened. Ask him if he knows that Jez guy. And tell him that you'll be paying the company back for those foils out of your pocket. Not that you can pay him back for the loss of the technology."

Murph nodded and pulled out his phone.

"I said you needed to *go* and do that. As in, *leave*." If there had been any doubt in Murph's mind about how mad Lindsay was over this, her tone completely erased it.

Murph gave me an apologetic look, then turned and left.

"I'm sorry, Marlin, but I'm glad you didn't get hurt. If it was that Jez guy, things could have gotten rough."

I said, "Whoever it was wanted the foils and to get away. I think it's a pretty safe assumption that Danielle had something to do with it, and I'd say there's a really good chance she was running the outboard. Beyond that, I don't know."

"This is making my head hurt worse," she said.

I gave her some aspirin along with a stack of pancakes. We all three ate mostly in silence. I'd love to say that it was because of my aforementioned culinary talents, but there was a lot of thinking going on too. And of course the aftereffects of being overserved last night.

Linds excused herself after breakfast, saying that since she was feeling halfway human again, she wanted to finish her recharge with a long nap in her own bed.

"She has a great idea, you know," Kari said.

"Hmmm?"

"We don't have anywhere to be today, right?"

"Not that I know of," I replied.

"Starting next week things are going to get very busy with wedding stuff. This will probably be the last day we can completely relax before our honeymoon."

I didn't want to think about it. All the wedding stuff that is, not the honeymoon.

"Un huh."

"Why don't you walk Tank, then come back to bed?"

Like I said, I love casual Sundays.

17

DECISIONS

The tiny boatyard had recently been purchased from the estate of a waterman on the Virginia Middle Peninsula. Located off the Severn River on the west side of the Chesapeake, it was a few mostly wooded acres with a small collection of various sized old wooden work sheds. The rails from the single boat hauling ways led up into one of the sheds. Other than the rough concrete boat ramp next to it for trailers, this was the only way to haul and launch boats.

While far less than the ideal setup for a modern commercial boat-yard, it suited the purposes of the new owners perfectly. The long wooden dock that extended out into the river was a big plus, and their small center console outboard was tied up at one of the slips at the end. An eight-meter catamaran rested on a trailer at the head of the ramp.

Jez carefully disassembled the automatic foil adjusters in the largest workshop while Danielle looked on.

"Bloody ingenious. The whole thing is hydraulic, articulated according to the water pressure, which varies by the speed. Simple, and foolproof." Jez said.

"Oui, but how fast can you make another set so that zey match our boat and so we can patent and sell the technology?"

He smiled slyly, "Fast enough, Danny, fast enough."

~

THE WEEK STARTED EXACTLY as Kari had warned, with wedding-related craziness starting to ramp up. Tuxedos needed fitting, groomsmen and Best Man gifts had to be purchased, lists and honeymoon reservations needed rechecking. That was in addition to my normal workload, which was ramping up even further as we got into pre-production on the new show at *Tuna Hunter Productions*.

And that's not to say it's all stressful and boring, actually far from it. For instance, take our field trip to the tuxedo shop that included Mutt and Jeff, aka, Baloney and Smitty. They were on complete opposite ends of the fitting spectrum, a challenge for even the most competent tailor. Then add in the banter you'd expect from these two fishing opponents and friends, and you would be close to picturing the experience. Yet you still wouldn't have it all.

Smitty was the first into the shop, taking up the entire doorframe as he passed through. Baloney was right behind him, his usual unlit cigar in his mouth, prompting a quick warning from the tailor about this being a no smoking shop. Baloney bristled and was about to let loose on the tailor but I quickly assured the man that Bill never lights up except out on the water. I said the cigar was merely an oral fixation the doctors said is symptomatic of his psychosis. And that it may or may not be protected under various national disability laws, so it's best not to mention it. Baloney's triumphant look faded as he realized what I had said to the man. It didn't help when the tailor checked his inseam a few minutes later, taking longer with the measurement than Bill was comfortable with, and he let the man know it.

Casey and Murph had come in for their fittings earlier, and I wasn't sure if they'd be sorry or relieved that they hadn't come with us when I tell them this story.

. . .

"THAT'S HILARIOUS! Moe, Larry, and Curly get fitted for tuxedos," Lindsay laughed. She had met Kari and me for dinner on the deck at the *Fin and Steak*, the slightly more upscale restaurant at Mallard Cove over by the dockmaster's office.

"Soitanly porcupine," I said in my best Curly Howard voice. It was good to see Linds laughing again. It was Wednesday, and her demeanor had been slowly improving with each passing day.

She became serious, "So, Murph has been pestering me to death. Texting and calling repeatedly."

Kari asked, "So, what did he say?"

"I didn't take his calls, but his texts said he wants to get back together. At least he's smart enough not to just barge in at the houseboat. I didn't reply to any of the texts nor the calls. Then to top it off, he sent not one but three large floral arrangements today."

"Did you send them back?" Kari asked.

"I couldn't bring myself to do that, and I couldn't throw them out, so I kept them. You know how I love flowers."

Kari glanced at me, trying as hard as I was to hide a smile. I'd told her about my whole conversation with Murph, of course.

Lindsay sighed. "I just don't know what to do, guys. I mean, I know what I want. But he made it pretty clear that night it wasn't what he wants, at least not any time soon, if ever. He told me that he felt a lot of pressure when he got engaged to Dawn. She had been pushing him and so had Sally. He felt that if he didn't cave, Sally would make his friendship with Casey suffer. Which she did anyway to suit her own agenda. It was a regular soap opera, and that's what I'm trying to avoid here."

I said, "I think he's trying to send you a signal, by saying he wants to talk. You know him better than anyone, would he do that if he wasn't at least a little bit open to changing his thoughts on the subject? Sounds like if you want to find out, you'll need to communicate with him.

"The last few times you guys talked you've each been pretty emotional. Maybe if you can both put emotions aside for a bit you can find out where each of you are right now, and that would be a start. If you pack it in for good, don't do it on a sudden emotional whim like that. Do it because you've talked it over with calm cool heads and decided that you really don't want the same things out of life. But don't take the chance to throw away what really could be because you let emotions get in the way. And I'm not saying that love should be guided totally by logic, that doesn't work either. I'm just saying it shouldn't be completely blocked by emotions or pride."

WHEN I WAS GUIDING I tried to avoid fishing on the weekends unless it was the only time my clients could go. If the "weekend warriors" know that you're a pro, they'll follow you to find your best spots. Nothing will make you madder than to return to a spot the next day only to find that your previous day's "shadow" is now squatting on your prime territory. The exception was for migrating schools of fish that move up and down the beach, that never stay in one spot for long.

Today being Saturday, there were a lot of boats cruising up and down the coast. But since Murph and I were after mackerel, it didn't matter, there were enough schools of the silver sided torpedoes for everyone to be happy. We were in *Marlinspike*, my twenty-six-foot Gold Line center console, running north along the beaches of the barrier islands. Kari and Lindsay were together up at Bayside, going over the final wedding details. Kari was the one who suggested I wet a hook with my Best Man. She knew that if I went with her, I'd be bored in no time and would just get in her way. I told you I was marrying the right woman.

"Birds, eleven o'clock," Murph said.

I squinted and saw what he was talking about, a flock of seagulls diving in one location. The mackerel follow schools of baitfish, in this case, glass minnows, and go tearing through the bunched up bait. Mackerel's mouths are full of razor-sharp teeth that rip apart the minnows, inhaling most of them but leaving enough floating bits and pieces to send the seagulls into a feeding frenzy. I adjusted our course slightly, then made a big circle as I slowed to trolling speed.

Murph picked up a light spinning rod then dropped back a Clark spoon lure and was quickly rewarded with a hookup. We'd only keep a few of the oily fish for eating; I like mine broiled with a lot of lemon and butter or smoked for fish dip. But we'll also keep some for bait if they haven't already gorged on the minnows. They make great tuna and blue marlin bait only if they haven't fattened up too much; it makes their bellies soft, and they'll wash out quickly when trolled. Murph landed this first one, being careful to avoid the teeth.

"Good belly on this one, you may want to tell Spud," Murph said.

I called Timmy O'Shea on my phone, "Hey Spud, we're on some hard bellied mackerel, about three miles north off Smith Island."

"You're a good man, Shaker! I'll see you there in ten."

Spud was on the hunt for as many good mackerel as he could get to brine and rig for bait. His baits were highly sought after because he was extremely picky about both his fish and his rigging. Many of the top tournament crews swear by his product.

"So, Lindsay is going to ride up to Bayside with me on *Irish Luck* on Friday morning."

They were still living separately but had agreed to sit down and have a conversation after the wedding since both would be busy with Kari and me until then.

I said, "Nothing like a couple hours on a boat to make her realize why she fell for you in the first place. You two were such a dynamite duo in the tournaments, and you used to love it all: the travel, the excitement, and the fishing."

"I still like the fishing, it's just the travel part that really got old. I like being around Mallard Cove and ESVA now."

I nodded. "Getting more settled."

Murph scowled, "Trying to tell me something again?"

"No, Murph, I told you I'm finished with that subject; I think you're telling yourself. There's nothing I can say to either of you that you don't already know. Here's the deal: you guys will either sort things out, or you won't. Kari and I will still be close friends with both of you no matter what, so there's no pressure from us in either direction."

Murph thought about that. "I appreciate that. But can I ask you something?"

"You know you can."

"Are you scared about the whole marriage thing, maybe making a mistake?"

I shook my head. "Scared? No. Nervous? I'm always nervous about being in front of big crowds, and I think most people are nervous about getting married. If not then they probably aren't taking it as seriously as they should. It's the biggest decision you'll ever make in your life, at least it ought to be. But if you're asking me if I'm specifically worried about marrying Kari, I'm not. I've known for a long time that my future is with her."

"But how do you *know* that?"

"Simple. I try to visualize my life without her. That's an image that scares the hell out of me."

18

WANDERER

2 00 miles off the Virginia coastline on May 27th...

MY WIFE of the last five hours was looking over at me from across the narrow aisle in the Citation, illuminated only by the low cabin lights. We were hurtling through the night at over forty-thousand-feet, above a black ocean. We had departed Accomack airport thirty minutes ago, bound for Bermuda. She reached for my hand, as she leaned over to kiss me, the luckiest guy in the world.

The preceding week had been mostly a blur. I had met more of Kari's relatives than I had ever known existed, many at our rehearsal dinner. It had been the largest dinner party that I'd ever had anything to do with, much less host. I had even managed to survive a Murph organized, alcohol-fueled bachelor party tour of some of the more "exotic" bars in VA Beach and Norfolk; all of us safely transported by stretch Hummer limousine and sober driver. This morning at a brunch I gave for all my groomsmen at the Bayside Club, I noted that somehow I looked less the worse for wear of any of us. How I managed that I have no clue, but I was thankful for small miracles.

Surreal images kept floating around in my brain as we streaked across the night sky. One especially stuck out: Kari, looking the most beautiful I'd ever seen her, in that magnificent wedding dress and uttering those two words that made me the happiest man in the world: "I do."

Then there was Baloney in a tuxedo, hungover and without his cigar. In fact, I never saw him with a stogie all day, which was a new record. As dashing as he looked, it just felt, well, kinda wrong.

One of the wildest memories was Spud, out on the floor dancing with two beautiful women at once. Come to think of it, I never saw him without both of them on his arms from that point on through the rest of the evening.

Oh, then there was Lindsay catching the bouquet, and Murph with his "deer in the headlights" look watching from the sidelines. But the image that was second only to my one of Kari was also one of Murph, picking his jaw up off the floor at his first sight of Lindsay in her bridesmaid's dress. She looked spectacular. Baloney, Casey, and I all managed to get dances in with her before Murph monopolized the rest of her evening.

Everything happened as planned and was exactly as you'd have expected with Kari organizing it. I have to admit, the groomsmen brunch was her idea as well, as I'm not all that thoughtful.

Kari's mom was happy the way that everything turned out, she finally got the wedding she always wanted to give her daughters. I even got taken out to the side patio by her dad for a first drink with him as his son-in-law. It meant a lot to me since my own dad was gone, and I think he knew that. I'd have given anything to have had my mom and dad there with me tonight. But it also was a testament to how far I'd moved up in his opinion, and I was really happy about it.

No, there was only one thing that was a disappointment to me about the whole day. Just as Murph had predicted, Johnny never showed up. If it really was about him being uncomfortable around weddings right now, I'll understand. And I guess I need to be ready for the "I met up with this wild woman" story sometime after we get back. But that'll be in the future, and the whole idea was soon out of my mind.

ON ARRIVAL, we breezed through Customs and grabbed a taxi to our destination. I had originally booked us into a hotel, but Eric Clarke had heard about our Bermuda plans and insisted that we stay at his place on Riddell's Bay in Southampton Parish. Eric's a partner in all of the M&S and Shaw properties including Bayside, and he built the first home in Bayside Club Estates. He's a sharp guy in his early forties who has already built a ten-figure net worth, and he's one of Kari's biggest fans. No way that he'd let us stay in a hotel when his Bermuda house would be sitting empty for that week.

Eric, his fifteen-year-old daughter Missy, along with his girlfriend, retired Congresswoman Candi Ryan, had all come to Bayside for the weekend to attend our wedding, the reception, as well as the rehearsal dinner. I like Eric, he's unpretentious and fun to be around. He and Missy are on my list of favorite fishing partners, though we don't get the opportunity to get out on the water together nearly as often as any of us like.

The taxi ride was almost but not quite as long as it gets on Bermuda. The house was located on the opposite end from the airport, on another island almost twenty miles away. Bermuda isn't a single landmass, it's a combined group of over a hundred islands and islets, the larger ones linked by roads.

Eric's place turned out to be a sprawling six-thousand square foot waterfront mini-estate with a pool, several verandas, a sauna, and a spa, all situated on over an acre. Here in fully developed Bermuda, that's a heck of a lot of waterfront property for one home. Parts of the newly renovated main house date back to the mid sixteen hundreds. A full-time gardener keeps the lawn and landscaping well-manicured, while a maid along with a very accomplished cook named Alice take care of everything else inside the house.

For the next week we planned to take advantage of everything that both the home and the island have to offer. Lying out by the pool, checking out the nearby pink sand beaches, taking a water taxi to a few of the highly-rated restaurants in Bermuda's historic capital of Hamilton, as well as doing some shopping. But mostly, just spending time alone together. No cell phones, no work, just the two of us completely unplugged from our daily lives. Our offices have the landline number for the house, but they also have strict instructions not to call except in an extreme emergency.

We never even ventured off the property for the first two days; Alice kept us well fed and pampered. Then slowly we started exploring the nearby beaches and sights. Tourists are forbidden from driving cars on the narrow and twisting roads, many of which started as horse paths hundreds of years ago. Instead, most get around using motor scooters, and Eric had a small fleet of them at the house. We could have ridden them into Hamilton but opted for getting picked up at our dock by a water taxi instead. It was faster, safer, and easier to do some sightseeing along the way.

On our last full day in Bermuda I had a special surprise for Kari. We were picked up at the dock early by the country's best inshore fishing guide and whisked off in pursuit of two species that I knew she'd never caught before, bonefish, and hogfish. While she's a very accomplished mid-Atlantic angler, these fish were both usually found in more tropical waters like down in Florida, though "hogs" do range all the way up through the Carolinas. But Bermuda is bathed in the warmth of the Gulfstream year 'round, and these two species thrive here.

Kari was excited to learn what our targets of the day would be, and ecstatic to find out that this was strictly a fly rod trip. We had watched a few videos together on bonefishing, and I had originally planned on us taking a bonefish trip down to the Florida Keys, but when I read about the bonefishing here, it was the perfect opportunity. But I'd never before heard of anyone catching a hogfish on a fly rod.

Our guide lived up to his reputation as the best on the island. Kari ended up throwing at half a dozen big "bones," hooking up with four of the six, a good ratio for these gray ghosts of the flats. She brought all four alongside the boat for pictures and quick releases. Late in the day she also had some luck with hogfish, bringing in a huge eighteen pounder that took over twenty minutes to boat. Instead of releasing him, he had a date with Alice's skillet. And while I really wanted this to be Kari's fishing day, she insisted that I take a shot at catching a "hog" on fly. I ended up catching a big one about twenty inches long, which I released since we already had our larger dinner fish. With that, our guide headed us back to the barn while Kari and I enjoyed two well-deserved beers on the ride in.

We rode past the old Royal Naval Dockyard at the point of Ireland Island. Its silent cannons have stood guard for centuries over the North Lagoon on the route to Hamilton. Kicked back in the small flats boat, we were enjoying the scenery until we spotted something that neither of us expected to see right now.

Kari pointed and said, "Look over there, isn't that Johnny's boat?"

I followed her gaze and spied the catamaran, tied up at a small marina in the first slip inside the vacant tee end. I nodded. There was no mistaking that unique window line which was more at home on a sportfisherman than a cruising cat. I thought about asking our guide to run us over there but figured this visit might easily turn into a long one. It would be best to get our fish to Alice and let our captain get home as well.

"Up for a scooter ride when we get to the house?" I asked Kari. I figured it would take us twenty minutes to reach the marina.

"Yes, and some answers as well."

We paid our guide and added a big tip, then dropped the hogfish off with Alice. We asked her to prepare our portion but divide the rest up between her and the rest of the house staff, earning us each a big smile. Hogfish is a delicacy in Bermuda, and rightfully so. Then we hurried to the small garage and sped off on a pair of scooters.

As big a surprise as it had been to see *Wanderer* here in Bermuda, we were in for an even larger surprise when we arrived at the marina. *Wanderer* was backed into her slip, her name facing the dock. Only her transom now read *Mistral*, with a home port listed as *Cannes*, and her green bottom paint had been changed to black. But there was no mistaking this custom boat for any other, it was definitely the one that Johnny had built in Virginia. And somehow I doubted the short blonde woman in the cockpit who looked to be roughly twenty years older than Johnny had lured him away from his plans to attend our wedding. Then again, you never know.

From the dock I addressed her, "Excuse me, I'm looking for the man that owns this boat."

She looked confused and shook her head, turning toward the cabin. "Phillipe?"

A man about her age came out into the cockpit. In a heavy French accent he said, "My wife does not speak English. What can I do for you?"

"We are looking for our friend who owns this boat, Johnny Knowles. Is he aboard?" Kari asked.

"You are mistaken. My wife and I own *Mistral*, and I have never heard of this Johnny Knowles person."

Originally he had sounded cordial, but his tone had suddenly changed when he heard that our friend owned the boat.

I said, "This is a very unique boat, and quite new, so I'm positive this is the one that he had custom built. In fact, we've both sailed her. Where did you get it?"

"I bought *Mistral* from a broker in Virginia who delivered it to us here, and I have all the paperwork to prove the sale. The previous owner was a woman, so this is obviously not the boat that you think it is." He turned to his wife and said something in French. She disappeared into the cabin. "We are leaving for France now and have no further time to waste with you."

Even though we didn't have cell service in Bermuda Kari had been carrying her phone everywhere with her for the camera app. She started taking pictures of the boat and managed to get one of the man before he put a hand up in front of his face. He exploded.

"I do not grant you permission to take pictures of either my boat or me. You must stop immediately!"

I'd had enough of this guy, who was obviously lying. "I don't care who or what you grant, we'll take pictures of whatever we want. And I want to know where my friend is, and you're going to tell me."

"I told you, I do not know your friend, this is my boat which I have bought legally from a woman, not a man."

Before I could board the boat his wife came out of the cabin holding a short-barreled pump shotgun, and she was bringing it up to bear on us, or at least she was trying to. Instead of holding the butt up against her shoulder and sighting down the barrel, she had the nylon stock tucked up under her armpit. She was clearly someone who was at the very least uncomfortable if not completely unfamiliar with firearms. She'd be lucky to be able to hang onto the shotgun if she fired it, much less hit either of us with it. But even a blind squirrel finds an acorn once in a while, and I wasn't ruling out beginner's luck. Especially the way she was waving it around with her finger already on the trigger.

A quick glance up and down the dock revealed there was no one else in sight, so we were on our own. Kari and I held our hands out at chest level as we started backing away and up the dock. I saw Kari still had her phone loosely gripped in one hand, the camera lens facing toward the boat. We retreated up to the base of the small dock and watched helplessly as Philippe and his wife cast off and motored out of their slip, taking any answers they might have had along with them.

The dockmaster's office was locked, so we had no choice but to return to Eric's house to call the Bermuda police. I used the phone in the kitchen and Alice overheard my conversation. After I hung up she addressed me.

"Marlin, you shouldn't get your hopes up too high with the police."

"Why is that?"

She sighed, "Because no one was hurt, and it was a conflict between tourists. Remember, in this country three things make up most of our economy: tourism, international insurance companies, and rum. They don't want trouble with any of those three, especially tourism. So, they like to keep our crime numbers low, if you know what I mean."

Kari said, "That woman pointed a shotgun at us!"

Alice nodded. "Which might be the only thing that gets them to write it up, but they probably won't want to. If she had shot it off and hurt one of you or damaged property, they'd have no choice but to file a report."

It was over a half-hour later before the small blue and safety-yellow police SUV pulled into the drive. The young officer was dressed in the requisite dark blue Bermuda shorts with a white short-sleeve shirt. The whole outfit was highly starched with knife-edge creases. The officer was nice and polite, but we quickly found out that Alice had been right. He came in and sat down at the dining table, taking his time interviewing us, then finally getting around to reviewing Kari's pictures and the video she took of the woman with the gun. She had switched her camera over to record video right before we put our hands up. He frowned as he watched the somewhat shaky clandestinely shot video.

"And what time was this video taken?"

Kari replied, "A little over an hour ago."

He looked thoughtful. "And they said they claimed they were headed back to France?"

I said, "Yes. And who takes off on a trans-Atlantic crossing last thing in the afternoon? They left prematurely, no doubt because they're hiding something and they're lying about having bought the boat from a woman. It's clearly Johnny's boat, and now it seems that he's disappeared."

"But you have nothing to lead you to think that he disappeared here in Bermuda."

He said it as statement, not a question, and I was beyond irritated now. "I don't know anything concrete, but he might be bound and gagged and still aboard that boat for all we know! Are you going to go after it or what?"

"Mr. Denton, please calm down. First of all, you have no proof of a disappearance, since as of yet no one has reported him missing in the United States, correct?"

"No! We all just assumed that he was still aboard his boat, cruising the Chesapeake."

"Right, sir. Without his having been reported missing in the US, we have no cause to detain and search the boat since there's no evidence that a crime has happened in Bermuda, and it might not be your friend's boat."

I lost it. "I'm telling you; we sailed that boat ourselves. I know that boat! And what about the crazy woman who pointed that shotgun at us? Aren't you going to go after her for that?"

"We indeed have very strict civilian firearms laws here in Bermuda, among the strictest in the world, and possession of a weapon such as this would be a severe infraction. But because of our strict laws, many of the so-called firearms incidents that get reported turn out to involve fake weapons, as criminals try more and more to bluff their victims with replicas. Guns are hard to get even on the black market here and are extremely expensive when they are available. Replicas, on the other hand, are usually highly detailed and sell for a fraction of what real firearms do. From your video it's impossible to positively determine if that is a real weapon or a fake. In addition, with their stated destination being France, they have had more than ample time to travel beyond the twelve-mile boundary limit of our territorial waters. And if that was a real firearm, it's probably on the bottom of the ocean by now. There's nothing we can do, I'm sorry sir."

He stood up, but Kari and I did not. We would have walked him out if we believed that there really hadn't been anything he could have done, but he wasn't even willing to try.

Alice let the officer out then came back over and told us on her way back to the kitchen, "It wasn't his fault; he's just doing what he's been told. Unless there's an injury involved or a substantial theft of property from a non-resident, they won't make a record of it."

Kari said, "I don't think Johnny's still on the boat. His cell phone started going to voicemail over three weeks ago, right about the time he left Cape Charles. I think that's when he disappeared, and probably where his boat was taken from him. No way he'd have ever sold it since it was the centerpiece of his plans for his future, he loved that boat."

I knew what she was telling me, but I just didn't want to admit to myself that there is a good possibility that Johnny might be dead. I was still somewhere between frustrated and furious with the Bermuda police and their refusal to even attempt to intercept *Wanderer/Mistral*. Those two that are aboard her are hiding something, and yet they were willing to risk arrest by dragging out a weapon that could've landed them in a foreign jail for years because of it. And yes, I'm positive it was a real shotgun and that they are now on the run. Unfortunately, I don't fancy taking them on in France even if and when we might be able to locate them there.

I started thinking aloud. "If those two had been the ones who took *Wanderer* from Johnny, why be so bold as to stop here in Bermuda, mere weeks after he disappeared, and in a place that was on his list to visit? Why not make it a straight shot from the Chesapeake to Cannes or wherever the hell they are headed and put some distance between them and the US?"

"This just backs up their statement that they picked the boat up here. They were probably doing small day trips, learning the boat before heading 'across the pond.' The thief, or more likely thieves, might not have known about Johnny's plan to winter here in Bermuda. It's the closest foreign country to the United States mid-Atlantic, and easy for Europeans to fly here. They'd be anxious to get it out of Virginia where it might be recognized. Moving it to another country makes it that much harder to track and detain, and a good place to finish their sale," Kari said.

I had to concede her points. "Okay, let's say you're right. One or two others steal the boat and arrange to sell it to Philippe and his wife. Maybe they have a past connection with each other or maybe there's a network for buying and selling hot catamarans around the world. These two were really hinky, and his whole manner changed when we said we knew the owner of the boat. So, they know more than they are admitting, or they at least suspect a lot about the boat's ownership history. He was too quick to say that he had the paperwork to prove it was a legit sale. So, they knew the boat was hot, probably bought it at a real discount because of it, and that's what they're hiding."

Kari nodded. "If you were coming to buy a yacht to sail back to France, you'd probably get here on a one-way airline ticket. And if you were dropping off a hot boat, unless you left the States in tandem with a second boat and sailed it back, chances are you would be leaving as fast as possible on the airlines, also on a one-way ticket back to the States. You wouldn't want to hang around and take a chance on being spotted with the boat; you'd want some distance between you and it, and fast. Probably time it so that as soon as Philippe and his wife arrived, you conduct your business and hop on the next plane. Spend as little time as possible here."

I said, "I agree. And the one or ones that have the answers we need are now probably back in the States. But I'd like to swing back by that marina on our way out tomorrow, talk to the dockmaster and maybe find out more about this Philippe guy and his wife. I know it's in the opposite direction of the airport, but I have to know more if we're going to find Johnny." What I really meant but was afraid to say was *if we're going to find out what happened to Johnny.*

19

JOE & JANE BLOGGS

It wasn't really how I anticipated spending our last evening in Bermuda, theorizing what might have happened to our friend. But in yet another sign that I had married the right woman, Kari was just as focused and as determined as me to figure out what happened and find Johnny. The next morning our taxi driver was happy to add to the fare by running us back to the small marina before reversing course and heading to the airport. Since we were on a private plane, there was no rush, it wouldn't leave until we were ready to go.

The dockmaster didn't seem all that surprised to find out that Kari and I had questions about Philippe and his wife. "The whole thing was a little strange. Broussard called from France, gave me a credit card number to reserve his slip, which is normal. He said his new boat would be arriving from the US, and he would pick it up here. But I never saw it arrive; it was here when I got to work that Saturday three weeks ago.

"What was not normal is that no one was around the boat until the Broussards arrived later that morning. Sometimes foreign boats change hands here in Bermuda to avoid paying taxes in their home countries. But when they do, the ferrying crew always takes their time going over the boat with the new owners in detail and gets them to sign off that it is in the proper condition with no damage. That didn't happen in this case; I never saw the ferrying crew at all, and that's highly unusual."

Kari asked, "You said that their last name was Broussard? Did you happen to catch the wife's first name?"

"Ella. They seemed nice, though they were gone for a couple of weeks, said they were going to anchor out at St. George's then slowly making their way around Bermuda while learning the boat. They stopped back here to provision yesterday, but they had prepaid through tonight. I thought they weren't leaving until tomorrow morning."

I thanked the man and we got back in the taxi for the hour-long ride to the airport.

Kari was biting her lower lip again, so I waited to hear what she was thinking. "They hung around for three weeks, going from one end of Bermuda to the other before heading to France. That doesn't sound like they were too worried about being spotted."

I nodded. "I agree. Sounds more like buyers who thought they could defend their possession of that boat to the authorities, instead of the thieves who had stolen it. I think we rattled them when we said the actual owner was a friend of ours. They hadn't counted on the boat being recognized, and they panicked."

"So, the last place and time that we know Johnny was aboard was that Sunday at Cape Charles. Then six days later it arrives in Bermuda with its name and bottom paint color changed. Just enough time to get that all accomplished and sail it here if it was stolen Sunday night at Cape Charles," I said.

Kari said, "So, if you were the thief or thieves, you moved pretty fast, and kept a very low profile once you got it here. Do you live in Bermuda?"

"No," I said. "I'd live somewhere close to where I stole the boat, in an area I'm familiar with. I'd need a boatyard where they didn't ask any questions, and where they didn't get a lot of traffic."

"Exactly. And there are more than a few of those around the Chesapeake. They would be in a hurry to get the work done and the sailboat out of US waters. Then, once they got here, they'd want to get themselves out of this country as fast as they could to avoid being connected in any way with *Wanderer*. I want to know where they went, where they are, and who they are."

"I agree. The fastest way out of here would be on the airlines. If we can find which flight the Broussards arrived on, then that's our starting time," I said. "There should be at least two of them, and they'll have one-way tickets out of Bermuda to the US. Shouldn't be that many others with one-way tickets on that day, if any."

Kari frowned. "The airlines aren't going to want to give us passenger information."

"I'm not planning on asking them. This is a job for Rikki Jenkin's group. And she's got some pull with the FBI; we'll see if she can get them to start looking into Johnny's disappearance from their end. If we try to get them involved, since we aren't related to him, it'll be a hard sell. Especially since we know he went missing weeks ago, and we can't prove that he didn't just change his mind, decide to sell *Wanderer,* and move ashore somewhere. The boat's not overdue or missing since we know where it is, or rather where it was. But something happened to Johnny, and I want to find out what it was, and where he is."

WE LANDED at Norfolk International to clear US Customs before heading back to Accomack Airport. I called Rikki from the tarmac and told her the whole story, and what we were thinking about the boat crew returning. She was waiting at Accomack when we landed twenty minutes later. While it is only four-minute car ride from Bayside, I suspected her being here wasn't a good sign. She hugged each of us as we got off the plane but had a very serious look on her face. Now I was certain her news wasn't good.

"Welcome back, you two. I'd ask you how your trip was if I didn't already know how it ended."

"It was incredible up until we found Johnny's boat with no Johnny in sight," Kari replied.

"Well, I wish I had better news for your return. My friend from the FBI said that officially they can only do so much since we don't have a lot of facts. However, off the record, he said that they and the Coast Guard are investigating a rash of high dollar catamaran disappearances from the Chesapeake up to Delaware. Seven in the last year and a half. Usually with just a couple of people on board at most. The only common denominator besides the boats being catamarans is that many of the owners or crews are known to be swingers."

I snorted. "Johnny is about as far from being a swinger as you can get."

"Except he got off the boat trying to put on a real party-guy vibe until he started to relax around everybody," Kari reminded me.

Rikki said, "First impressions usually stick with strangers. If that was his normal routine, it could've made him a target. Easier for a stranger to approach."

"So, what are they going to do about Johnny," I asked.

"My friend said they'll open a missing person file on him and look into Phillipe and Ella Broussard. He'll call if they turn up anything. But he didn't sound optimistic." Her tone softened and she put a hand on my arm. "Marlin, you know that since he hasn't turned up in three weeks, if this really was a boat hijacking, the chances are very slim that he might still be alive. These modern pirates don't like leaving witnesses or clues."

I couldn't blame Rikki; she was just putting into words what we all were thinking. "I know. But I can't give up when there is that chance, no matter how slim it is, that he's alive. Even if he's not, I want to know what happened, and I want whoever did it to pay."

Rikki squeezed my arm before letting go. "I'm with you on that. Any help you need from my group, you'll have."

That was a pretty broad and powerful statement coming from Rikki, since her security company does a lot more than just protect wealthy people and secure their property. The biggest part of their business is taking care of things for the government, situations that are too messy for politicians to be near. Elected officials love the term, "plausible deniability," and Rikki's group is expert at providing it clandestinely, for a price. This offer was backed up by a lot of expertise, manpower, hardware, and occasional law-bending. But she is our friend, as well as a foundation board member, so this offer was based on that friendship, and not dollars.

Rikki's girlfriend, Cindy Crenshaw, is also a partner in Bayside and runs all of their hospitality-related businesses as well as the hotel at Mallard Cove. The two live together aboard their Hatteras, *Hibiscus*, at Bayside. Though Rikki doesn't know Johnny, she and Cindy are an integral part of the waterfront community at Bayside and have a vested interest in wanting to make it more secure.

At first glance, you might think that Rikki is a model or maybe an actress. She's about five-foot-nine with ice-blue eyes and short, naturally platinum-blonde hair. She's also a professional badass. I once saw her shoot and kill a murderer without hesitation, and she never had so much as a hand tremor afterward. I was there because I got drafted to be her backup when there wasn't anyone else available. It was definitely not because I'm a badass, which isn't part of my job description. I shook like a leaf for half an hour after that, and I didn't even shoot the guy. I was there for Rikki; completely out of my element but watching her back, and she's never forgotten that. I know I can count on her to help me find Johnny.

On our way back to Mallard Cove, Kari and I decided to stop by the *Fish House* bar and grill at Cape Charles. After we explained what we wanted, the manager was happy to cooperate by letting us show his staff a picture of Johnny and me that I have on my phone. One of the bartenders remembered Johnny even though it had been three weeks since he had been there. It had been a slow afternoon that day and Johnny had left a huge tip.

"Probably also because he was doing so well with this little brunette. She was hot, and he was almost a foot taller than her. She had on a trucker's cap, and I love it when women wear those. I was bummed when they left together, I was kind of hoping he'd blow it and she'd stick around 'till the end of my shift. One thing I remember about her that was a little off was her hair. It was really straight and cut kind of uneven, but it was a dull black. Not like yours, which looks natural." He motioned to Kari, who smiled at him. She noticed he was staring at her eyebrows.

"That's another thing I just remembered; her eyebrows weren't black like yours; they were really blonde. It was kinda funny, 'cause I used to date this chick that had blonde hair, but her eyebrows were dark. But her hair color came out of a bottle, so maybe this gal's did too."

I asked, "Have you seen her around here before or since?"

"I wish. Nah, she's not a local, if that's what you mean. If she is, she's not a regular."

I gave the guy twenty bucks, and we thanked the manager on our way out.

BACK IN THE car I said to Kari, "Well, we knew it was a long shot."

"Wait, Marlin, while we're here, let's go talk to that dockmaster again."

We found him in a tiny office in the marina parking lot. After we gave him the description of the woman he scratched his forehead.

"Might've been in that day in an outboard buying gas, but I can't be sure it was the same gal. Lots of short gals in trucker's caps around, though this one was all by herself. Come to think of it, she might've gone next door to the restaurant after she fueled up, too."

Kari asked, "Do you remember what kind of boat it was?"

"Maybe a little center console outboard, an older one, but I'm not sure. Lots of them like that gas up here too, so it's easy to confuse 'em. Not even sure if it was that same day or not."

I thanked him and started toward the car when I saw Kari staring at the big vacant waterfront parcel next door. She turned back to the dockmaster and asked, "Do you know who owns that piece of land?"

He nodded and said, "Oh, that? The town. Used to be the railroad yard where the cars got loaded onto barges back before the CBBT got put in. That killed off the rail traffic."

"What are they going to do with it?"

He laughed. "Argue over it, mostly. Damn politicians'll probably end up stealing it, and we'll be the ones who'll end up paying for it."

ONCE WE WERE BACK in the car again I smiled at her.

Kari asked, "What?"

"You. And waterfront land."

"Hey, it has possibilities, and I'm good at my job. Be glad, since you own half my shares in the M&S properties now."

"I what?"

"Remember when you asked me about buying those six catamarans? You said you weren't just asking for advice; you were asking me because that was *our* business. Well, if that's true, then half of *our* investment in Mallard Cove and Lynnhaven is yours as well. Turnabout is fair play, like they say."

I shook my head. "Half of the *Pelican Fleet* is hardly worth half your stake in those properties."

"Marlin, what difference does it make? It's not so much that I have half and you have half, it's that we own it together. That was part of the whole, 'I do' thing you know."

I had always thought of half the *Pelican Fleet* as being hers, but I never really thought about her M&S investments before this. The idea that I might now have a stake in my favorite place in the world along with my favorite person in the world was really cool. It helped take the sting out of not finding more information about Johnny.

AFTER WE PARKED at *Mallard Cove*, I had to find two dock carts to load all our luggage and the pile of presents we brought back from our trip. As we passed the charter dock we noticed that all of our friends' boats were in, but nobody was at home for us to drop off their gifts. It's just as well since I wouldn't mind a little peace and quiet for the rest of the day before we both get back to work in the morning, but I had been really looking forward to collecting Tank from Smitty.

We pulled the carts up to *Tied Knot*, and Kari started to load up with luggage to take in with us.

"Put that stuff down, we have something to do first," I said.

"What?"

"Seeing as how this is the first time we'll be on our now aptly named boat together since our wedding, I have to carry you across the threshold."

"No, you don't."

"Yes, I do. It's a law somewhere."

"I don't think it is."

"Well, it's a tradition, and I'm not about to start breaking those, either."

"Oh, like you didn't break a few laws this morning by smuggling those Cuban cigars back?"

"That doesn't count. Half of 'em are gifts," I replied. Bermuda isn't exactly a smuggler's haven these days, and I figured we wouldn't be scrutinized that much when we returned. I was right; I don't think they gave the cabin much more than a cursory glance and didn't discover the two boxes of contraband tobacco.

I unlocked the door, picked up my protesting bride and carried her in.

"Well, that's the first load, now you have to help me with the rest. Fortunately, it's all lighter."

I got shoulder punched for that, as I expected, but she was giggling and smiling as she did it. We quickly unloaded our carts and I returned them. I ran into Smitty on the way back to his boat, he had taken Thor and Tank for a long walk. Tank was really happy to see me, play bow barking and attacking my leather shoelaces again. Maybe he wasn't going to be such a mama's boy after all.

We stopped by Smitty's boat to collect his bone, then all of us headed over to *Tied Knot* so that Kari and I could give Smitty the present we brought back for him. Of course, as soon as we walked in the door, I instantly became "Dad, who?" as Tank took off running to Kari. While those two were busy, I dug out Smitty's dog sitting gift.

"Gosling's Black Seal rum? I didn't even know they made this! Thanks, guys!"

I beamed, glad that he appreciated the rare fifteen-year-old single-barrel rum. "Thanks for taking care of her pup." I frowned in Kari's direction, who scowled in return.

He chuckled, "Well, we can't pick who a dog chooses. Have you ever thought about getting a cat, Marlin?"

"Have you ever thought about giving me back that rum, Smitty?"

He chuckled louder and longer this time, while simultaneously tucking the bottle back into the safety of the crook of his arm. "C'mon, Thor, let's go home and let them unpack in peace."

As the two of them left I saw that Tank and Kari were now rough-housing. If any unpacking was going to get done anytime soon, I guess I was the one who would be doing it. I hauled the luggage back to our bedroom over Kari's weak protests. I knew she'd been looking forward to playing with Tank, so I waved her off.

I had just finished unpacking when Murph and Lindsay arrived. Together. Linds hugged me, then sat on the floor with Kari and Tank while Murph and I fetched beers for all of us then pulled two dining chairs up close to them for ourselves. Kari recapped a lot of what we'd done on our trip and showed them the pictures she'd taken on her phone. Then she brought in a bottle of Black Seal for Murph, and a unique bracelet packed with vintage and antique charms she'd found in a little shop there for Lindsay. I was left to break the news about *Wanderer*. They both went from ecstatic to somber.

"Not good," Murph said.

"No," I agreed. "But Rikki is on it, so hopefully we will have some answers soon."

I saw Murph and Lindsay exchange looks. It was a double-edged sword; the look they gave each other was one of sadness and resigna-tion, but the good thing about it was they felt the need to silently communicate together. The same type of communication that Kari and I share on occasion, which you wouldn't do with someone with whom you are totally on the "outs." Neither Kari nor I were going to ask, just observe, but it was an encouraging sign for their future.

"I talked to Dickie while you were gone. He's heard of that Jez guy. Supposedly he just bought a small boatyard somewhere over on the Severn River, he didn't know exactly where." Murph said. "He's heard rumblings that he's going into the catamaran building business, too."

Kari spoke up, "So, we were dead on about him sneaking around over here, trying to steal ideas. And all the more reason to believe he's the one who stole the foils."

"Looks that way, yeah."

I said, "Maybe we need to return the favor and do a little snooping around ourselves this week."

Murph nodded. "I think so."

At that point my phone interrupted us. Rikki was calling. "Hey, Rikki."

"Marlin, it looks like your thinking was right about the cat's crew returning to the USA. An hour and a half after the Broussards landed in Bermuda, a Joe and Jane Bloggs boarded a flight for Dulles Airport. One way with no return scheduled, which wasn't that surprising since they were traveling on fake US passports. Whoever they were, they snuck into Bermuda, because there's no record of them at all on the Bermuda Customs computer, at least not under those names."

I told you her cyber crew was good. Fortunately, they were on the team that wear the white hats. I said, "Sounds about right, then."

She continued, "These guys are pros. Those passports say they were issued four years ago, and at first glance they come up on the Customs computers as being legit. But do a deep dive on them and it turns out that those four-year-old passports both had their info uploaded only two months ago. Whoever did it has some real skills. We're trying to get some airport security video of this pair returning, but I'm not expecting much. Anyone that's this slick would surely be smart enough to be disguised and won't be caught looking directly at cameras. Oh, and they're real smartasses too, by the way. Joe and Jane Bloggs is the UK equivalent of John and Jane Doe here in the US.

"Their trail runs cold at Dulles, no one using those names have boarded any flights since. Even more reason to believe these are our thieves. They must've either been picked up, or they had a car parked and waiting. But this, combined with where we think *Wanderer* disappeared, is a good indication they're from the Chesapeake Bay area."

"Where do we go from here, Rikki? The only way I'm going to find my friend, either alive or dead, is by finding this pair." Even though we had more information, it didn't seem like it was going to help that much, and now I am as frustrated as ever.

"My FBI friend has promised to keep me looped in on what they find out. Meanwhile, just keep your eyes peeled for suspicious acting catamarans or ones that are in suspicious places. It's about all we can do."

I thanked Rikki, hung up and related her side of the conversation to everyone.

"There must be hundreds of those big cats that cruise the Chesapeake every summer, between the ones that are based here and the tourists who are passing through." Lindsay saw it as I did, a Herculean task to watch for suspicious catamarans. "I mean, define 'suspicious.' That could mean anything from someone acting paranoid because they have their personal stash of weed aboard to some guy trying too hard to be as low key as possible because he's cheating on his girlfriend," she said, making a point to avoid glancing at Murph.

I said, "I know, it would be like winning the lottery. But someone does win it, almost every week. And you know what they say: you have to play to win." I didn't know what else to tell her; I know this'll be a long shot. "But it's still better than doing nothing, even if it's only keeping us busy."

Murph spoke up, "Speaking of being busy, I know you just got back, but you want to take a ride over to the Severn River with me? I'd love to find Jez's boatyard, poke around and see what we can find. If he was the one that stole those foils, I'd love nothing more than to get them back."

I knew that this was only partially about Jez, and mostly just to get my mind off of Johnny. But I appreciated Murph's attempt to deflect my attention. I nodded. "Give me two days to get things settled after having been away last week. We can take my Gold Line; it should only be about an hour's run from here."

"I was hoping you'd offer to 'drive,' since Irish Luck would be kind of conspicuous poking around over there. Not many sixty-foot Merritts running around in that river."

"Or anywhere else, for that matter. She's such a beauty." I loved the lines of that iconic Florida built sportfisherman. "My Gold Line won't even rate a second look, there are so many center consoles on the bay these days." The last thing we wanted to do was draw attention to ourselves, though I'd give us about the same odds of finding those foils as we'd have of stumbling onto a hijacked catamaran. However, like I said, it was better than doing nothing.

20

PARTNERS IN CRIME

The thing about having great people working for you is they can take the stress out of your job if you leave them alone and let them do theirs. I've always been a fan of that principle, and because of it, I came back to a nearly empty desk. Between the Foundation's Chief Staff Member, Sharon Dee Albury, (another of Kari's cousins) keeping MAFF on track, and Carrington Stuart, who has been the Senior Producer on *Tuna Hunters*, I was good to go with Murph on Wednesday morning.

I cranked up my outboards on *Marlinspike* to let them warm up while I waited on Murph. He showed up with a pair of box lunches and a small cooler, apparently anticipating a long day. We idled out, hanging a right just past the marina's breakwater. It was a beautiful, sunny day, just barely above seventy on its way to almost eighty. I headed for the channel at Fisherman Inlet bridge as I brought our speed up to a fast cruise. After we passed under the bridge, I set a northwesterly course toward the mouth of Mobjack Bay. I quickly altered it a bit to the south, to bring us below the bow of a big sailing cat that we spotted in the main shipping channel.

The captain of that cat was taking advantage of a leisurely downwind "dead run" by setting his twin headsails in a "wing on wing" configuration. This meant the wind was coming straight down the channel from behind them, and they set one sail out to starboard and the other to port. It wasn't the fastest scenario, but it didn't require the constant attention that flying a huge spinnaker would. Today was the perfect day for this since the wind was light, only about seven knots out of the north, and there was little if any roll to the surface of the Chesapeake. Easy sailing, making way without having to work your tail off by constantly needing to adjust a spinnaker. My kind of sailing.

As we got closer to the boat, we could see two women sitting on the hard foredeck, using the angled front edge of the cabin as a backrest. They waved casually with their free hands, their others each clutching coffee mugs. The man at the helm gave us a curt return wave, like he was tired of having to acknowledge other boaters. I readjusted my course again for Mobjack.

Murph asked me, "So, does that look suspicious? The guy looked grumpy, but the women seemed happy and relaxed. Seems about normal to me. So, how are we supposed to tell what suspicious looks like? For all we know the three of them are hijackers, and the real owner of the boat is down below, tied up or dead. I mean, how are we supposed to figure this out from a distance?"

I wondered about the grumpy looking man being "normal" remark. We hadn't had time to ourselves since I got back to be able to have a private chat. Which was part of why I wanted to make this trip with Murph. "Nobody really expects us to spot the hijackers out in the open. It's more about us being around the water, the docks, and different marinas where we could possibly run across something. We only need to keep our eyes and ears open and keep aware of our surroundings. In Virginia alone, we have over seven-thousand-miles of Chesapeake tidal shoreline. Add in Maryland, and there are another forty-five-hundred miles. That's more than the entire west coast of the United States. And thousands of private marinas and docks. They could be working out of anywhere. So, we'll keep on our toes as we move around. And speaking of 'normal,'

I noticed you moved back aboard the houseboat since we've been gone."

He nodded. "I wouldn't exactly call things 'normal;' more like retesting the waters."

"Remember what I told you before I left, Murph," I warned.

"I wouldn't be back there if I thought we would be less than long term, Marlin. I don't want to hurt her any more than you want to see her hurt. If I thought that was where this would end, I'd have stayed on the Merritt."

"And she's good with this?"

"Let's just say that I got into more detail about what I had originally tried to get across to her. After she thought about it, she decided to be a bit more patient. Especially after I told her what you had said. She knows I'm serious, I'm not interested in being the guy I was down in Florida, and that's what matters now."

I hopped up on the Birdsall-built lean seat and rested a foot on the wheel to make any minor course corrections that might be needed as we crossed the bay. Since it's midweek, there's not a lot of traffic to deal with, only some deadrise crab boats and a few freighters in sight. As we glided across the bay's surface, we saw occasional bird activity. A group of seagulls and pelicans were floating together on the surface, obviously resting after having already fed on schools of baitfish. A few minutes later we saw what appeared to be bluefish and rockfish tearing up a small school of menhaden on the surface with another flock of seagulls wheeling overhead.

As much as we wanted to stop, since we did bring some rods with us, our primary goal today was to find Jez's boatyard, and we had a ton of shoreline to search along the Severn River. The fish would have to wait for our return leg, depending on what time that would be. Hopefully, they will still be around and in the mood to eat. All we knew was that it was a small boatyard and that he was focusing on catamarans, we didn't even have a name to put with it. Hopefully, there would be several cats tied up at the docks, if they even have docks.

Mobjack Bay is just north of the mouth of the York River. It's about six or so miles across, and the East, North, Ware, and Severn rivers all empty into it. The Severn is the nearest to the mouth of Mobjack, only in a couple of miles or so on the left. Instead of what you might picture as a typical river, it opens up into more of a bay with numerous jagged looking tidal tributary offshoots of varying sizes. Though it's only a couple of miles from the mouth of the Severn to its far end, when you include all of the branches and tributaries, there are dozens of miles of shoreline in the combined area.

If you're picturing maybe downtown Hampton or even Miami with concrete seawalls or riprap, you'd be disappointed. Much of this area around the Chesapeake is made up of farmland, woods, or marsh with natural grass, sand, or mud shorelines. In addition to a few mid-sized boatyards and marinas, there are hundreds of properties with private ramps, docks, and slips, not to mention tiny coves with "shade tree mechanics" and small boat repair operations that cater to the boats of local watermen. Any one of these might be Jez's boatyard. All Dickie knew was that it was "small." At least that ruled out the few larger set-ups on the Severn that I already knew about. My guess is it might be one of the older family-sized operations.

We entered the mouth of the bay and headed for the Severn. We saw an angler on a boat just outside of the Severn boat a monster-sized flounder, and I made a mental note of the location. It's an occupational "hazard," but one that helps put fish in my boat.

As we turned into the Severn and passed Caucus Bay, I didn't see anything that resembled a boatyard. Murph had his binoculars out and was scanning the shoreline. I was resigned to the fact that this could take most of the day or even longer, if we even found it at all. We decided to give it a little while, then when we came up on one of the handful of larger boatyards we'd stop and ask if they might know of Jez.

Following along the right side shoreline, we passed a large manor house that looked like it might have been there for centuries. Knowing some of the history of this part of the Chesapeake, it probably had been. Just beyond the next point was Whittaker Creek, a wide and deep tributary that looked on the chart to be over a mile long. I idled down and followed it back a quarter mile to the first little bend, which actually turned out to be a "Y". The left arm turned back to the tributary's original direction while the other narrowed and headed back into an area of thick woods. At the dead end of that part of the fork was a long wooden dock. At its base on one side was a wide, rough, concrete ramp for boat trailers, and on the other side was a ways. This was an angled ramp with a set of railroad tracks that allows a dolly to ride down into the water and haul larger boats.

Judging by all the new wooden timbers making up the dolly frame and the swath of fresh concrete under the steel rail tracks, it had recently been expanded and rebuilt to hold wider vessels. As in catamarans. If that wasn't enough of a hint that we had gotten unbelievably lucky, the sign on the end of the dock read *"AussieCat Boat Works."* Well hello, Jez.

I took *Marlinspike* in as close to the shoreline as I dared before turning and laying her up alongside the dock, bow facing out. I'm expecting trouble when we run into Jez, and even though both Murph and I are carrying our pistols under our shirts, I want to be able to get out of there in a hurry if necessary.

The place looked completely devoid of people, not exactly what I expected during the usual midweek work hours. To the left was a long open metal roofed pole shed. A wide gravel yard separated it from a line of wooden buildings on the right. Apparently business wasn't booming here just yet. The cradle on the ways was also empty, and the big doors on all the wooden buildings were closed. We looked through the filthy windows of the big building the dolly rails ran into, and it was as empty as the ways. Murph took out his phone and took several pictures of the boatyard, the ways, and the dock. We continued down past the first building and made a stunning discovery. Between it and the next workshop was a catamaran that was undoubtedly an eight-meter. Murph began snapping away with his camera-phone, especially at the foil attachment points that had obviously been recently modified. They looked identical to those on the ESVACat, and these modifications had yet to be painted to match the rest of the hull.

"That son-of-a-bitch," Murph exclaimed. "He's even copied Dickie's foil attachment design. You can see where this has just been added. There's only one reason to do that, he must have the foils, too."

Murph marched over to the next building first checking the smaller door alongside a large rollup garage-style one. Both were locked. While he did that, I peered in through a set of windows that overlooked the gravel yard. These were almost as filthy as the first building's. Inside, just beyond the window was a long wooden workbench. Lying on top of it was a set of foils almost identical to the ones stolen from Murph's dock box.

"Murph," I said, calling him over.

One look through the window and he was off on another cursing tirade. As he calmed down, he started snapping photos through the dirty glass, then he turned to me. "We have to steal them back."

"They aren't yours," I said.

"What do you mean? That's Dickie's design!"

"It sure looks like it. Except for the housing around the actuator, it's shaped slightly different and is a different color."

Murph looked back through the window. "You're right. Don't know how I missed that. But it's still Dickie's design, Jez just copied it! He definitely stole the ones from Mallard Cove."

"True enough. But since we never filed a police report we'd have a hard time proving that ever happened."

"So what do we do? We can't just leave them here!"

I shook my head, "Unfortunately, we don't have much choice unless you are willing to do time for burglary."

Murph looked back through the window again. "He's got several hull molds and a fiberglass setup with drums of polyester resin and epoxy. There are rolls of fiberglass, Kevlar, and carbon fiber cloth, too. From the looks of those molds there's no doubt about it; he intends to go into production on that eight-meter."

I said, "Time to get out of here and go talk to Dickie and Lindsay."

No sooner had those words left my mouth than we heard the sound of a car approaching on the gravel driveway leading to the boatyard. Murph started out toward the gravel yard, but I grabbed his arm. "What are you doing? We need to hide!"

"Why? He's a thieving son-of-a-bitch. I want to call him out on it."

"No! You need to talk with your partners first. He doesn't even know that we know where he is and what he's up to, which is to our advantage right now. Plus, we don't even know that it's him that's coming. C'mon." I dragged him by his arm over past the eight-meter to the first building and around the corner closest to the woods line. There was a cleared area about five feet wide that led back alongside the building running down to the ways area. From here we can see who is arriving by peering around the corner, hopefully without being seen ourselves.

We didn't have long to wait as a shiny new BMW parked under the pole shed across the gravel yard. Danielle got out and walked directly to the door of the fiberglass workshop, unlocked it and went inside. That just confirmed another theory, that she and Jez were definitely working together, if they weren't outright partners. I motioned to Murph that we needed to go, and he reluctantly turned and led the way. We made our way back along the cleared area down to the ways and then over to the dock.

Back on the boat, I was thankful for how quiet the four-stroke engines were. The fiberglass workshop was over a hundred yards away, and their low volume shouldn't carry that far and alert Danielle. I idled out to the end of the dock then hit the throttles bringing *Marlinspike* up to her fastest cruising speed.

Murph said, "I should have seen it, that those two were working together. I guess some part of my ego didn't want to accept that I got played and that it almost cost me Lindsay as well as my partnership with Dickie. I'm not looking forward to telling him all this, but at least we have found some concrete answers."

He called Lindsay and outlined what we'd found out and told her we'd pick her up at the dock in an hour. He looked disgusted with himself after he hung up.

"Quit beating yourself up. What's happened is just water past the stern," I said. "Besides, beating you up is Lindsay's job." I grinned in his direction and saw him nod and chuckle.

"Lately she's been really good at her job."

"Well, you *have* given her a lot of reasons."

Murph didn't reply, meaning he accepted what I had said. I kind of wished I hadn't.

21

CHALLENGE...ACCEPTED

J ez was in his outboard, returning from a parts run over to another boatyard farther upriver when he spotted Marlin and Murph leaving Whittaker Creek in *Marlinspike*. He quickly ran to his dock and tied up his boat then hurried to the shop. He spotted Danielle as he walked in.

"What did they say?" Jez was a combination of angry and worried.
Danielle asked, "Who?"

"Those two blokes from Mallard Cove, Murphy and his pal."

"I do not know. I have not seen them."

"They were right bloody here! I just saw them leave in their boat."

"I just arrived and came in here. I saw no one."

"Well then, we have to figure they saw you, and maybe the foils, too. This moves our timeline up a wee bit. We need to launch our press release today, and the posts on those social media sailing sites. It's a bit early, but oh well, she's gotta get done now."

SAYING Dickie wasn't happy would be the understatement of the year. By the time we reached ESVACats, Jez's press release and social media posts had gone out, and several people in the sailing world that are familiar with Dickie's invention had begun contacting him. Jez was claiming that his company holds a provisional patent on the auto-adjusting foil mechanism and planned to have a press conference with an unveiling at the Potomac Maritime Museum on Friday. The timing couldn't have been worse since that was the day before the kickoff party for the F50 races in Annapolis the following week. The sailing media from around the world was already starting to arrive for it. Since Annapolis is less than an hour's drive from the museum, this announcement was sure to draw a crowd of media as well as some of the F50 design engineers.

"But you have a patent on both the old and the new mechanisms! They can't steal this away," Murph exclaimed.

Dickie was crestfallen. "I did a formal abandonment of the original non-provisional patent before it was issued but after I created the second generation, to keep there from being any confusion between the two. I had gotten that first one through one of those online legal services. Since there should only be our new design, I figured we would be covered. But I didn't realize the original design application had already been published by that point. Meaning, the diagram was right out there for anyone to view, online, anytime at the US Patent Office website. He could've used that for his provisional application."

I was confused. "So, what kind of application did you make that won't cover that one, too?"

Dickie sighed, "I did a non-provisional. That means it gets researched and carefully scrutinized, but it's the one with real teeth. It takes a lot longer to get but it is the long-term, multi-year patent. It also means that it has to be issued for a finished design, not one undergoing revisions. A provisional covers you for up to a year while you still make modifications and changes before getting the non-provisional. They don't really look at it, they just automatically grant them for that first year. Yeah, I know, lots of legal mumbo-jumbo. It's why patent lawyers are so expensive, and why I abandoned that first one so we didn't spend any additional money on it. But I swear, I thought we were covered. So, it doesn't even matter that he stole the foils; I screwed up and handed him the design. He didn't even need to have the prototype in-hand; the design was out in the open. I'm sorry Lindsay and Murph."

Lindsay said, "It's not like we didn't screw up too, by losing that first set. But I think we can turn this around to our advantage. I've got an idea about how we can meet this head-on at that 'presser' and turn the tables on Jez. Here's what we're going to do..."lk

~

POTOMAC MARITIME MUSEUM, *Friday morning...*

A CROWD of about seventy people had assembled in front of the outdoor stage at the museum near the base of their dock, much more than Jez and Danielle had dared hope for. The lure of the statement: "the greatest advancement in sailing in over a century" had been too enticing to ignore. The dismasted AussieCat-8, as Jez's boat is called, was sitting on the grass off to the waterside of the stage, one hull propped up high with its foil installed in the lowered position.

From up on the stage, Jez had just proclaimed the auto-adjusting foil as his own design. He no sooner had gotten those words out as a big sportfisherman pulled up to the end of the dock in hot rod fashion. The huge diesels pivoted the hull on its axis, sending it sliding sideways to the dock. Like me, normally Murph hated hot rods who showed off as they docked, but he hated the man on the stage even more. He couldn't think of a better way to draw the attention of a crowd of sailors away from Jez than *Irish Luck's* engines growling loudly as he got into the throttles. Better to tick 'em off and get their attention.

While the docking show initially distracted the crowd, it was Dickie jumping up on the dock with one of his new foils in hand that grabbed their attention as he strode up to the crowd's edge. In his other hand he held a sheaf of papers, and now he held them and the foil aloft.

"Jeremy Campbell is a design thief and a liar. I am the inventor of the auto-adjusting foil. What he's claiming as his is an older, less functional design of mine whose patent I abandoned after some intensive testing when I discovered serious flaws in it. This is my newer, perfected design, which is currently undergoing the patent process. I have all the paperwork to back up what I'm saying."

From up on the stage Jez shot back, "And I already have a patent on this foil, so nice try, mate. So, who's the thief now, eh? I'll be lodging a challenge against your application with the patent office, so you can kiss that one g'day."

Murph spoke up, "Not likely since this one will smoke that old design out on the water. You may have a provisional patent on that, but you'll never get a permanent one. And once people get a look at its performance versus ours, you won't be able to sell it, either."

"Says the stinkpot bloke who pulls up like a big showoff. What do you even know about sailing?" Campbell jeered.

"I know enough to whip your butt out on the water, you thief! If your design is so good, then you should welcome the chance to prove it. Say, off the beach at Mallard Cove on the Eastern Shore next Sunday morning at ten?" Murph's tone was a jeering, taunting one.

Jez glanced at Danielle, who gave him a quick nod before he turned back to Murph. "Done."

Dickie said, "And when we win, you agree not to challenge my new patent."

"Hah! Scared because you know you'll lose in court, eh bucko?"

"No, I'll win in court and we both know that. However, we both also know that the lawyers always win by raking in big fees, which is what you're trying to threaten me with, hoping I don't have enough cash to outlast you. But if you're scared of losing out on the water..."

"Hey! There's only one top eight-meter captain around the Chesapeake, and you're lookin' at him. You're still on, bucko. I'm gonna kick your butt every which way, and then after everybody gets a gander at how well my great invention works, I'll be licensing it to any interested cat builder, including you F50 blokes." He turned back to the audience, "So, you bunch, come Sunday a week to watch, but bring your checkbooks, too. You're gonna need 'em after you see my *patented* foil in action."

I WAS STANDING NEXT to Murph who was in the helm seat of *Irish Luck*, up on the flybridge. We were only a few minutes into our two-hour ride from the Potomac back to Mallard Cove. Lindsay was sitting in the navigator's seat next to Murph, and Dickie was standing next to her.

I asked Dickie, "Are you sure that your new design will beat the old one?"

He replied, "With equal crews, and especially in heavy wind, there should be no contest. I've looked up Campbell though, and he's built quite an impressive record over the last decade or so, racing catamarans in Australia. But there had started to be rumors about him cheating; different things about his designs that weren't always in line with the rules. That, and he became overly aggressive; so much so that he collided hard with another boat. One of his hulls landed on top of the other captain, crushing, and killing him. There were questions afterward about it possibly having been intentional. Enough so after that, the Australian League banned him from competing."

"You might've told me all that before I challenged him to a race, Dickie," said Murph.

"I might've. But would you have been as confident as you were if I had? We can't show this guy that we're scared of him at all. He sees any sign of weakness, and he'll use it against us. It's what he was counting on with that stupid bluff of his about going to court. But now he knows his only chance of licensing out my old foil design is to beat us on the water. We win and he's done; nobody will want that foil. Which means he's very motivated to beat us, by any means necessary."

"Lovely," Murph said.

Dickie said, "What, now you're losing your edge? It was mostly your confidence which convinced me to bring you two in as partners; the idea of you bringing that with you to the table. While I haven't seen you race yet, I've seen you handle the eight-meter, and you're damn good at it. We've got a few things going for us besides that, including my cat design. While I only got a glance at it, I did manage to snap a few photos of Jez's design. The first thing that popped out at me was the aluminum spars that connect the two hulls and frame the trampoline."

The trampoline was the strong nylon webbing material in the center that you ride on when you aren't hiked out on the trapezes. So I asked, "What's so important about that?"

"When you look at my design, Marlin, you'll see that the cross members are made of curved carbon fiber tubes that are integral with the decks on each hull. This makes the whole assembly one big extremely strong piece, instead of two hulls that are bolted together with two separate aluminum tubes. The stresses that are created by the foils, and the speed that's generated, all focus on the attachment points. Mine is spread out evenly over a couple of square feet, by being integrally molded together as part of the actual hull deck. His has two bolts per side on each spar, focusing all that stress in areas the size of quarters.

"To be honest, I started with that same design, which was the accepted way of doing things on the larger boats until just recently. In fact, the hulls your wife used as benches at the bar were the last hulls I bolted together. I wasn't kidding when I said I learned an awful lot with that boat. I saw the spars were showing signs of metal fatigue; that's what got me to switch over to the carbon fiber. It's a heck of a lot more expensive, but it's what you need if you want to keep the boat together. The variable foils exert a lot more force on the boat than the stationary type. It's a by-product of the auto-adjusting mechanism. Instead of dumping all that force by letting the boat stall and fall off the foils, it puts more strain on them when the angle increases, giving it more lift, and that strain is spread across the spars."

I kind of understood what he was saying, but not everything so I said, "I'll have to take your word on that."

Dickie chuckled. "I didn't learn it all overnight either, Marlin."

I nodded and said, "It's fun to watch people that have found exactly what it is that they're supposed to be doing in life. They make tough stuff look and sound easy. Like this foil thing. I could no more build that than a kindergartener could."

"I've been watching and helping, but it's still all Greek to me," Murph admitted.

"And I can't find fish or produce television programs, so I guess we're all even," Dickie said.

I agreed, "I guess we are. Lucky, too."

Dickie smiled, "It's been my experience, Marlin, that the harder I work, the luckier I get. It was a lucky day when you three walked into my shop. And I'd hate to be goin' up against that jerk all by myself now.

"Murph, all we have to do is two things: first we need to practice our tails off this next week because I have a bad feeling that he's going to be tough to beat. And second, we need to pray for heavy wind, because that's where these new foils really shine. You know, this race might turn out to be the best advertising we could ever hope for."

22

DICKIE'S DOWN

The Saturday before the race...

"How are dey looking," Marco Vasquez asked as he sat down at my beachside table in the *Beach Bar*. By now almost everyone around the Eastern Shore area had heard about the race. And once Vazquez found out that he and Baloney had bested a guy that had killed someone, no matter if it was by accident or on purpose, he had become determined to get the most possible mileage out of it. He had become a real fixture at both beach bars, but he had also been on his best behavior and tolerable to the point where even I let him join me as I watched Murph and Dickie practice. I handed him my binoculars. "See for yourself."

Dickie and Murph had quickly become quite a team over the past week; it was almost like they had been racing together all their lives. Their side changes as they hooked and unhooked from the trapezes and slid across the trampoline had become really fluid as they tacked and jibed their way around the practice course.

"Dat's good, dey're lookin' real smooth."

I nodded as I took back the glasses and refocused on the boat as it approached. One of the buoys was set just offshore of the two beach bars. That hopefully wouldn't change on race day, but the course direction and starting line will be dictated by where the wind is coming from at that time. The first leg of a typical triangular-shaped sailboat racing course is always the upwind one, forcing the participants to race back and forth in a zigzag pattern, and requiring the most tactical skill to advance the farthest with each tack. This was going to be a very long course, with one buoy set off of Virginia Beach, over a dozen miles away. The third was several miles offshore of the center of the mouth of the Chesapeake, forming a nice triangle course.

Right now, it looked like Dickie was going to get his wish for higher wind. A sub-tropical system had formed off Florida and had been slowly working its way north all week, with the center projected to cross onto land about at the coastal border of Virginia and North Carolina on Sunday afternoon. We might not get the rain from it until then, but what we would get in the meantime were strong southeast winds. This also meant big swells for Virginia Beach as the surge gets pushed up into the shallows next to the shore. They could very well end up racing in the highest winds that an eight-meter has ever faced to date.

Never mind that the big F50's were finishing up their event over at Annapolis; the news had gone out around the Chesapeake about the challenge and the bet. It's one thing to have highly paid professionals from everywhere else around the world competing in an event where it costs ridiculous amounts of money to attend any of the functions: that's more for the DC crowd. And the crews all pack up and leave after the race. But this race was about the pride of two local crews and boats that folks would still see sailing around here in the days after the race. This resonated with more of the locals, much like the Crisfield deadrise workboat docking contest up in Maryland. Especially since it was affordable fun for everyone and had quickly become more of a "Shore Side" versus "West Side" thing.

Mimi and Kari had quickly picked up on the growing local vibe and had started to capitalize on it. Kari had a raised stage built out on the beach west of the *Cove Beach Bar* and lined the beach with tiki torches. Mimi then called in some favors, booking the two hottest local beach bands to play through tomorrow night. A small cover charge gets you onto the beach for the bands, and to watch the race. While it wasn't quite on the scale of Antigua's Sailing Race Week, it quickly started looking like our local version of it, and a great excuse for a continuous beach party. Without a doubt, this wasn't going to be the last race of this type that was going to be held here, and there will be a lot more boats and crews involved in the future. Mimi had tee shirts made, advertising this as the Mallard Cove 1st Annual Race Week with a drawing of an eight-meter on the back. They were already on their third screen printing.

We even had to move our ESVACat rental fleet down beyond the *Catamaran Bar* to accommodate all the beach dancers that have been showing up in increasing numbers each afternoon and evening. Mimi added two huge rental tents on the beach with temporary bars to keep up with the demand. By last night parking had become all but impossible, and both the marina and hotel were booked solid. There were even a few boats anchored just off the beach in the lee side shelter of Smith island.

ONLY ONE THING was missing so far, and that would be Jez's boat. We had all anticipated that they would show up at least a few days early to practice on the course. We learned that they had spent all week up at Annapolis instead, promoting "their" foil design. They didn't even bother showing up until now, less than twenty-four hours before the race. Jez was nothing if not cocky. But we were completely caught off guard by one detail of their boat. Instead of a sail, their eight-meter was equipped with an Australian design soft wing, which is similar in shape to what the F50's have. Murph and Dickie were just pulling their boat up on the beach with a crowd of curious locals around them when Jez and Danielle swooped in close, executed a sharp turn, then headed out and over toward Virginia Beach. The crowd started watching Jez and Danielle, as were Murph and Dickie.

Murph looked worried. "What the heck is that rig? Man, that thing looks fast."

Dickie didn't sound as worried as Murph, just perplexed, "It is fast. That's a soft wing, a sail with a semi-rigid framework to give it a shape like a plane's wing. It's what I had planned to add to ours next. That damn Jez beat me to it."

"What's the advantage of having one?"

"See how high he's pointing into the wind," Dickie said. "That thing will go probably ten degrees more to windward than we can. And see how square it is at the top? A perfect triangle is the absolute worst, most inefficient sail out there. By going with the interior frames and creating almost an airplane wing, the head of the sail can be flat and about a third as long as the "foot" at the boom. This allows for a lot more square feet of sail with the same boom length. It's much more efficient in light air, but they really suck going downwind."

"Why didn't you put that rig on our boat from the start?"

"Because I wanted to keep the price down. It's more expensive to build that. Plus, these have been around for several years, but the boating public has rejected them because they didn't like the look. It wasn't until the F50's came out with them that they started to finally gain acceptance. Like I said, it was the next modification I was going to do to the eight-meter."

"How bad is this for us this weekend," Murph asked.

"It depends on the weather, Murph. If that wind doesn't increase until after the race, it might wipe out any advantage we have with the newer generation foils. But if it blows as hard as they expect it to on Sunday morning, they'll wish that they had our sail rig instead. So, pray for big wind."

DICKIE AND MURPH joined Vazquez and me at my table. I said, "Looks like you have some serious competition. That sail is wild looking."

"Can I borrow your binoculars? I want to watch them," Dickie asked.

Once again, I relinquished my glasses, and Dickie turned to face the ocean.

"Any change in the forecast," Murph asked.

"No. Jou guys are ghonna have jour hans full on Sunday," Vazquez replied.

"Good," Dickie said without lowering my field glasses. "Because we're gonna need every knot of wind we can get, that thing is faster than I thought. They just better hope there's no junk in the water."

"Why for?"

"*Why, not why for,* you bozo," said Baloney as walked up. He pulled out a chair.

"Screw jou, salami."

"That's Baloney to you, Marco Polo!" Bill glared at the Spaniard, who returned the look. "And yeah, why worry about trash in the water any more than normal?"

Flotsam and jetsam are the banes of existence for all boaters, from ropes that get caught in running gear to plastic bags which clog cooling water intakes, burning up engines and even air conditioning units in the process.

Dickie put the glasses down for a minute. "Because that foil design is really susceptible to getting small bits of junk caught in its water intakes for the actuators. It can cause them to stick in one position. If it's at the far end of the range it can make the hull stall and crash. It's part of what I changed on this latest generation of daggerboard foils; the new design doesn't clog as easily."

"Hi guys, how was practice," Lindsay asked as she and Kari took seats at the table and our ever-growing Tank plopped down next to his "mom" after first growling quietly at Vazquez. Baloney smiled at Tank.

Murph replied, "We're as ready as we'll ever be. We just need some good wind tomorrow."

"You'll have it. I just checked the latest weather, and that storm has sped up. It should make landfall an hour or so ahead of the race, which means you'll have plenty of wind," Kari said. "Is that Jez?" She pointed out to a fast-approaching sail, or in this case, wing.

"That's him," Dickie said, setting my binoculars on the table where they were quickly grabbed by Lindsay.

"Wow, a soft wing. Not the best rig for tomorrow," she said.

"How did you know about that," Murph asked.

"Homework, Murph. I read as much as I could about eights and foil catamarans before we signed our deal with Dickie. I figured this would probably be a logical next step in development."

"I guess I had the wrong partner hanging around the shop! I like the way you think, Lindsay," said Dickie.

"Chica don' just handle jour boat good, soun's like she knows how to build dem, too!" Vazquez was genuinely impressed.

"Usually the best boat builders are the biggest boat enthusiasts," said Dickie.

We watched as Jez and Danielle slowed and their hulls settled into the water, then they retracted the foils and beached their boat. Several people walked over from the *Cat* bar to help them drag it up on the beach.

Dickie remarked, "See how much wider their hulls are compared to ours? Those are similar to the old hull benches at the bar, before I narrowed and lightened our design. That's another advantage we'll have tomorrow. With as much wind as we're supposed to have, our hulls won't be in the water much, and they'll just be dragging around extra weight for nothing."

Jez and Danielle were dressed in matching long sleeve sun screening fabric shirts with their Aussie Cats logo and matching colored shorts. Apparently, they had a bit of a following from the west shore that had shown up to support them, as several of the people from the bar were wearing similar short sleeve logo shirts. We could hear the enthusiastic greeting the duo received as they walked up to the *Cat* bar. They must had made some friends during their week over at Annapolis. But Murph and Dickie had their own local fan base, so it evened out.

We all decided to watch the sunset and have dinner where we

were so we could listen to the band on the stage and just relax. We picked the right bar for the night before the race, because as the sun went down, the volume of the occupants went up over at the *Cat* to compete with the beach band. Murph and Dickie were more reserved tonight, their minds completely focused on the task ahead. We saw Danielle and Jez head out into the crowd on the beach, which had become a gyrating mass, all moving in concert with the beat and pulse of a Reggae song. There couldn't have been a bigger contrast to the two race crews.

About an hour and two beers later, Dickie left to heed the call of nature. Murph had just returned from the "head" located down the breezeway and forewarned him of a long line. He suggested Dickie try the portable heads behind the stage that Mimi had brought in for the week. We figured that there must've been a long line there as well when Dickie didn't come right back, at least until we heard the screaming above the sound of the band.

We all rushed over in the direction of the screams, finding a growing crowd around a prone figure on the sand, the scene lit only by a few flickering tiki torches. Even in the low light, I could see it was Dickie, and the back of his head was bleeding profusely where he had been hit with something.

I turned to Kari, "Go get some clean bar towels, and call 911!" I knelt next to our unconscious friend and used my hands to help staunch the bleeding until Kari came back with the towels. I used them to apply even more pressure until the paramedics arrived. They wrapped his head with pads and gauze then put Dickie in a neck brace and placed him on a backboard. Murph and I helped them carry Dickie up to the parking lot where the paramedics' van waited. A sheriff's car pulled up, its blue lights mixing with the red and white strobes of the rescue unit on the cars surrounding us.

The deputy spoke briefly with the paramedics before they closed the back doors to the van and took off, its siren wailing. Since my hands were covered with Dickie's blood, the deputy now focused on me, and I led him to where we had found Dickie. With Dickie on his way to the hospital, most of the revelers were back in front of the stage, but the damage to the crime scene had already been done. Any footprint evidence had already been obliterated by tracks from the crowd that had been there. Only the bloody spot in the sand where Dickie's head had been marked the area. The deputy did find a damp three-foot piece of two by four lumber in the sand nearby with what looked like hair on one corner. He carefully wrapped it in a pair of large plastic evidence bags.

More deputies arrived and started questioning the crowd. No one recalled seeing anything suspicious, and nobody even remembered seeing Dickie behind the stage until after the attack.

After the deputies had finished with us, we dropped Tank off at the boat, then Murph, Lindsay, Kari and I headed for the hospital. After explaining that Dickie had no family other than an ex-wife who lived in Colorado and that they were Dickie's business partners, we all camped in the surgical waiting room. Finally, after midnight the doctor who had operated on him came in and said that he was in tough shape. He had been struck so hard that his skull had fractured, and he had lost a lot of blood before he had gotten there. The next twenty-four hours would be the most crucial, and he really wouldn't know anything more until sometime tomorrow. He urged us all to go home, that there was nothing we could do here.

On the way back in my truck, Murph said what we all had been thinking. "It had to have been Jez."

"Yes, but how do we prove it? There aren't any security cameras pointed anywhere near there," Lindsay said.

He replied, "I don't need cameras to show me what I *know* happened. He tried to murder Dickie, to take out his competition."

I said, "Maybe the sheriff can lift some fingerprints off that piece of wood."

"Not likely, it was damp so it probably had just floated up on the tide. Tough for them to get anything off that with the salt water and the sand," Murph said.

We parked in the Mallard Cove marina lot, then walked past charter boat row, headed for the private dock. That's when we ran into Jez and Danielle, after they had parted with their new pals.

"Yeh, tough break, losing your mate like that. I guess you'll have to forfeit."

It was all I could do to restrain Murph, who wanted to rip Jez's throat out with his hands. I was hanging onto him with both hands.

"You son of a bitch! I know it was you that attacked Dickie!" Murph was pulling me toward Jez, who had started to back up.

"Whoa, you might wanna be careful who you go libeling there. I didn't attack nobody, I was dancin' with me gal at the time. Right Danny?"

Danielle smirked and replied, "Oui. He was with me. Dancing."

Lindsay spat out, "You lying little bitch! We know you were in it with him. And no, we aren't going to forfeit, we'll be ready to go, I'll be taking Dickie's place tomorrow. I can't wait to kick your ass out on the water before the sheriff arrests you two for attacking Dickie."

"Yeh, well, he'd need evidence to do that Sheila, and there ain't none, because I didn't do it. If he had anything on me I'd already be in jail now wouldn't I," Jez sneered.

I said, "I wouldn't get too comfortable if I were you. You'll be a guest of the Commonwealth before you know it."

"And just you stay out of this. You got no stake in this."

"That's where you're wrong. Dickie is my friend too." With that, I released Murph, who took two steps forward before landing a fist on Jez's jaw. I thought Australians are supposed to be so tough, but Jez went down on his back. Before Murph could inflict more damage, Danielle moved to block him, brandishing an icepick.

"Get back! Cheri, are you hurt?" She glanced down at a stunned and surprised Jez, who was just starting to pick himself up off the dock.

"Yeh, I'm fine, Danny. But this isn't over, bloke. Tomorrow morning I'll take you apart on the water, and then I'll finish the job on the beach."

"Don't bother to pack a lunch, it won't take long for me to take you down," Murph said.

"We'll see about that," Jez said as he stood back up, giving Murph a wide berth as he passed, despite Danielle covering him with her icepick.

The two of them hurried away in the direction of the hotel's entrance as the four of us watched them go.

"Who the heck carries an icepick," asked Murph?

Lindsay replied, "I told you that one was a snake. Never turn your back to her. Not that you ever have."

While I silently questioned the timing of her verbal jab, I didn't question whether Murph deserved it. And while I was upset that our friend was lying in the hospital fighting for his life, there was a part of me that liked the irony in the fact that Lindsay would be squaring off against Danielle.

23

STRESS TEST

The next morning the four of us plus Tank met early for breakfast on the *Cove*'s patio deck. The new canvas covering was paying off, as the rain had moved in earlier than had been forecast. The day was gray and windy, and the overcast matched our mood. Murph had called the hospital, but there had been virtually no change in Dickie's condition, and that was the good news. They said he is in a medically induced coma, and they can't assess the damage until after his brain's swelling goes down.

Tank sensed our sadness and was being exceptionally good, lying down in between Kari and me. He's one smart pup, just like his father. Speaking of which, Smitty arrived with Thor in tow. He had been out with friends last night and hadn't heard about Dickie until Murph filled him in.

"Are you sure it was that Jez guy?"

I shook my head. "Not one hundred percent. More like ninety-nine point nine percent."

"And you two are still going to race him." It was a half question, half statement from Smitty.

Lindsay said, "The deputies questioned the two of them last night, but they alibied each other, and there's no physical evidence tying them to the attack. The place was such a madhouse, nobody remembered seeing them leave the dance floor. They want us to forfeit, and we're not going to let Dickie down by doing that. So, they aren't willing to postpone, and frankly, I want a shot at them myself now."

I knew how Linds felt. Though she and Murph were closer to him, Dickie was a hard guy not to like, and kicking these two scumbag's butts out on the water would be a good start on paybacks. But only a start. Somehow, they have to be made to pay for what they've done to Dicky, and what Jez tried to do to Lindsay. But wrecking their business would certainly give us all a slight level of satisfaction. And the only sure way to do that now was to go out and prove the superiority of Dickie's designs, both his foils as well as his boat.

Smitty said, "Well, you had better check your boat over closely. Who knows what a wack job that carries an icepick for a weapon is likely to do."

Murph replied, "Trust me, I'm going over every square inch of the hull and the rigging."

AFTER BREAKFAST, Kari, Smitty, and I took our usual table down at the *Cove Beach Bar*. They are going to open early today in about an hour, though it's likely with the weather it won't be crowded, even with the race. Mimi already canceled the band for this afternoon since now she was only expecting a handful of die-hard spectators and maybe a news crew to show up. The local party people already knew that the party was over for this weekend.

The rain was now coming in waves, along with gusts a little above thirty miles an hour, and we were still an hour away from the start of the race. We had to pull our table back farther under the roof to avoid getting wet. If conditions keep deteriorating at this rate, we are going to have a tough time seeing too much farther than the starting buoy.

Kari looked worried. "This is nuts. Nobody should be going out in this."

"This is exactly the weather Dickie was counting on to take away their soft wing advantage. I wouldn't worry about Murph and Linds," I said. "If it's going to handicap anyone, it'll be Jez."

Murph and Lindsay joined us after having completed their pre-race inspection and finding nothing amiss. Their boat was launched and backed stern first partway up on the beach. They had just sat down when Jez and Danielle arrived, approaching our table slowly and cautiously. They were in their same outfits as yesterday, and while they were dressed to race, they didn't appear mentally prepared. Tank began growling at both of them.

Jez ignored our dog and addressed Murph, "I'm not sure this weather is exactly safe for racing."

Murph sneered. "Well, like you told me, I guess you'll have to forfeit then. That'll make good press for your boat: 'Can't take the weather that an ESVACat can.' I can't wait to see that in print!"

Jez recoiled a bit then said hesitantly, "We're a go, then."

Lindsay said, "We're set and ready, and that's the committee boat, heading out into position. So, if you don't want to go, you can forfeit right now. Your choice."

"Let's go, Danny."

For all her sailing bluster back when we met, Danielle looked a bit pale at the prospect of heading out into such deteriorating conditions. Can't say as I blamed her, but the look of satisfaction on Lindsay's face was great.

The committee boat, by the way, was Vazquez's junk. Murph had caught him in an inebriated moment and gotten him to agree to it before he knew what the weather was going to be. He is still trying to ingratiate himself further with our gang after his less than stellar introduction.

But there was still something about "Marco Polo" that Tank doesn't trust. He always growls quietly whenever he first sees the man, and I'm learning to trust that pup's instincts. So I never fully drop my guard around him either. In any case, he's doing penance today, having to stay out at anchor in that sloppy stuff. Not to mention, he has to come out on deck to sound the five minute and one minute horns, and both the starting and finish guns. He's going to get soaked.

The five of us watched as Jez finally convinced a few of his folks from the *Cat* to come out in the rain and help him and Danielle wrestle their eight-meter into the water. Then about ten minutes before the start, Murph and Lindsay suited up in their trapeze slings and half helmets and headed for their boat. They made a couple of runs before the five minute warning, then after the one minute horn they ran a thirty-second reach away from the starting line, reversing course and crossing the line clean, just behind the starting gun and a second or two ahead of Jez and Danielle.

Murph set their course by pointing almost as high into the wind as possible. Unfortunately, Jez was able to point about five degrees higher and still match his speed. Murph's tacking runs would need to be short, and his turns as fast as possible to keep them aloft on the foils. Jez would not need as many tacks and would be gaining more ground on each leg. Once they round the buoy off of Virginia Beach, the two boats should be pretty evenly matched on the reach, and then Murph's plan is to make up any time on the downwind leg back toward Mallard Cove.

Currently, the wind is steady around thirty miles per hour, with some higher gusts as the heavy rain bands come through. I'm estimating that the boats are making somewhere around forty miles per hour. From what Dickie had told us before, this was about the highest wind the ESVACat had ever been subjected to, but the boat was handling it well.

From my angle it was difficult to tell just how much of a lead Jez was starting to build yet, if any. They were already starting to disappear in the distance, obscured by the gray rain and the white spray coming off the foils. I knew that at the speeds they were making, it would be almost an hour before they would come back into view. And that was if, and only if, they were able to maintain their current rate of speed. A huge "if." Once they make the turn toward the offshore buoy, they would be facing more into the swells that were getting pushed in ahead of the storm. I was pretty certain neither of these cats had been in wave conditions like these before. What I did know for sure was that they would be balancing on the edge of "marginal."

"This is crazy. We shouldn't have let them go." Kari was biting her lower lip again.

I reached over and took her hand and looked down at the two rings on her finger, knowing the confidence she has in me. "The two of them have become great catamaran sailors in a really short time. And Murph knows how to 'read' the sea. If their equipment holds together, he'll get them home safe and sound."

While I meant to reassure her, when I looked up at her face I realized that I should never have said "if their equipment holds together" even though it was exactly how I felt. I had full confidence in our two friends because I knew them so well, and after spending hours with Dickie, I knew that he was a great builder and designer. The ESVACat had undergone a couple of years of testing and improvements, but today was going to be its biggest test to date. While he fought for his own life, his creation was in a fight for its life as well.

Smitty said, "I've always said it's one thing to get caught out in a storm, but it's nuts to deliberately go out in one. I mean, I know why they did it because there wasn't much choice, but that's a real washing machine out there today."

I know he is nervous and meant well, that he was just making conversation, but I shot him a look meant to shut him up. I didn't want Kari to worry any more than she already is. Heck, I didn't want *me* to worry more.

A guy in his mid-thirties wandered over to our table. He had a notebook in his hands, and as it turned out, he was a writer for a national sailing magazine. He wanted to ask us a few questions about Murph and Lindsay, and it was perfect timing. This was exactly the diversion that Kari needed to keep her mind off them being out of sight. She gave the writer all the background he wanted, without any mention of their conflict with Jez and Danielle other than saying it was a grudge match. She was the best at promotion of anyone I know, and can spin a story even better than a seasoned politician.

BY THE TIME they were halfway across the mouth of the bay Murph and Lindsay knew they and their boat were in for the workout of a lifetime. They raised the windward foil on each tack to cut down on drag, but the sound coming from the leeward foil and the two on the rudders was now up to a low roar as they sliced through the already angry water at unprecedented speeds. Spray from the forward foil now enveloped the aft part of the lee hull.

The two of them were hiked out, suspended out beyond the windward hull just feet above the water on the stainless cable trapezes. Their bodies were close to horizontal and their feet were jammed in nylon and neoprene stirrups on the side of the hulls to keep them from slipping. This was fine as they tacked up to windward in more or less in a beam sea, but it became its own special kind of torture after they rounded the buoy off the beach and faced into the swells.

The auto-adjusters were working overtime to try and keep the boat level, but the waves were over six feet and the boat galloped over the tops. As it would reach the trough in between the waves the whole boat shuddered, and spray flew as the bottom of the bows came in contact with the water. Suspended as they were, that jarring motion created an almost whiplash force on their necks, and it was wearing the two of them out as they fought against it.

The best thing about Murph and Lindsay's boat turned out to be the strength of the design. Now subjected to the most extreme conditions in its history, the ESVACat was proving her worth. By incorporating those integral carbon fiber spars to frame the trampoline frame, Dickie had created a twin-hulled boat that was as close to the strength of a monohull as you can get with today's technology. Unfortunately for Jez, his design wasn't as advanced. With the extreme stresses exerted on the boat in these conditions, the characteristics of the dissimilar materials that it was made of started to appear, even though they were going unnoticed.

The first sign that all wasn't as it should be with the boat was wet black streaks were appearing around the stainless steel bolts and washers that attached the aluminum trampoline spars to the hull. What couldn't be readily seen behind the washers was that over time salt water had seeped in under them where they were in direct contact with the aluminum spars. The result was electrolysis had started and its galvanic action was creating the black liquid as it ate away at the softer metal, turning it into a kind of sacrificial anode and weakening it at its most crucial points. A crack had formed at this point on the bottom of the spar, and it was growing with every flex of the boat as it hit the wave troughs. This kind of structural weakening was exactly the kind of thing that Dickie had feared, and why he switched to the integral carbon fiber spars.

Unfortunately, Jez and Danielle both failed to watch the boat frame, as they were focused on the sea and sails in the rough conditions. As they rounded the offshore buoy, they saw the ESVACat emerging from the rain behind them, already gaining the ground that it had lost to them on the upwind leg. Murph and Lindsay rounded the same buoy just a minute behind them.

Exactly as Dickie had predicted, the soft wing didn't perform as well on this downwind leg as the ESVACat's conventional sail when both of the center daggerboard foils are extended. Halfway through this leg Murph and Lindsay had pulled up even. As they came alongside, Jez turned to try and ram them. But having heard the story about what had happened in Australia, Murph had anticipated this and had already turned to widen the gap between the two. The result was that they escaped untouched, while Jez overshot and ended up running through a floating line of sargassum seaweed. As the auto-adjusting foils sliced through the weed, many of its small, round, floatation sacs broke off and were sucked into the water intake of the mechanism on the port side. Once in the system, it clogged the passages, locking it at its farthest forward angle.

Murph and Lindsay were determined to make the most of their lead when they reached the Mallard Cove buoy, and they made their fastest turn yet, a full thirty seconds ahead of Jez and Danielle. Once clear of the buoy, Lindsay raised the windward daggerboard foil as they set up for the first tack of their final upwind leg. They both turned to watch the other boat and try to estimate the number of seconds they were ahead. But instead, they saw the last thing they expected.

KARI, Smitty, and I were on our feet yelling our loudest against the wind for Murph and Lindsay as they rounded the mark. Beside us the writer took video while his accompanying photographer was taking rapid-fire still photos through a telephoto lens. Neither of them knew it, but they were both about to get the shots of their lives.

As Jez and Danielle rounded the mark at over thirty miles an hour and started to accelerate even more we saw that something was very wrong. Instead of a smooth acceleration as the wind hit the wing more broadside, the whole boat seemed to shudder then the hulls suddenly separated. The now tangled mass of carbon fiber and aluminum stopped within a distance of a few yards as the bow of one hull dove beneath the surface, then the wing's framework collapsed and added to the tangled wreckage that had been the trampoline. Both of them were catapulted into the middle of what had seconds before been their trampoline but was now shreds of fabric and jagged aluminum. Over the howl of the wind, we heard Danielle scream, and Jez began yelling for help.

Smitty and I joined the other two dozen hardcore spectators from both bars racing into the rough water, swimming as fast as we could into the waves toward the wreckage, now floating about a hundred-fifty yards offshore. I saw Marco Vazquez had already raised his anchor and was now motoring toward them. By the time we got to where the wreckage bobbed on the surface, Marco and one of his crew were already pulling Danielle over the side. Her face was white and slack, and her entire chest area was red with blood. Jez was climbing up a rope ladder one-handed, the other arm was obviously broken and useless, now dangling by his side. Someone grabbed him and helped him aboard. Marco hit the throttle, heading for the break-water's inlet.

Murph and Lindsay had turned around and just completed a circle of the wreck, and were now headed for shore. The wind was pushing hard against the one floating hull of the wreck, the other having been breached when it came apart and was now half submerged. Its current trajectory would take it to the beach, about opposite the stage platform.

We swam back to the beach and rejoined Kari. The three of us raced over to Vazquez's slip and got there just as the paramedics pulled up to the base of his dock. They rushed a wheeled gurney out to his boat. We stood on the dock in the rain, waiting until the para-medics and one of Vazquez's crew brought Danielle down the gangway on a backboard, placing her on the gurney. One of them was holding what looked like a bunch of white gauze on her chest, putting pressure on the source of the blood that was already turning part of that white material red. Jez was following along behind them holding his bad arm, seemingly in a daze. He loaded up into the van after the gurney, and the driver raced them out through the parking lot and onto the main road.

Vazquez came down his boat's gangway ramp, visibly shaken. "Dat little chica, she was stuck onna metal ting. Was horrible. Was bleedin' bad. Went in here." He pointed just to the right of his sternum.

Smitty said, "Stuck *on* something metal? Like impaled?"

"Das whut I said, onna metal piece. Mano, I need a drink."

Even Tank could see Vazquez was shaken. While that might have been why he didn't growl at him, he also wasn't going near him either, instead sitting at attention next to Kari's feet, on guard duty.

Kari said, "The *Beach Bar* is open. And we should go secure that wreckage and call the Coast Guard, they'll probably want to take a look at it since there were injuries."

On the way back over there we ran into Murph and Lindsay, who had been headed over to find us. Even though they hated the woman, they were understandably shaken when they heard Vazquez's account of the extent of Danielle's injuries.

"It was rough out there, but this was the smoothest part of the course. There's a lot of stress on the boat as you round the mark, but it looked like it just disintegrated," Murph said.

"It looked like they were pushing hard to try to catch up with us, and they were taking that turn really fast, but it looked like it, I don't know, stuttered? Almost like it ran aground." Lindsay was as confused as we all were as to what caused the accident.

The wreckage had already reached the beach before we arrived, and a few of the more curious spectators were braving the rain and taking pictures of it. We managed to pull it all up high enough so the outgoing tide wouldn't take it out with it.

Half an hour later four very serious looking Coasties arrived in a big Rigid Hulled Inflatable Boat and began their investigation. One of the officers began interviewing Murph and Lindsay up at the bar patio while the three other Coasties poured over the wreckage. The one interviewing Murph and Lindsay had to take a call partway into the interview, after which he looked even more serious than he had when they arrived. He made a thumbs down motion to the others, hung up and turned back to Murph.

"The female that was aboard just succumbed to her injuries at the hospital. She was impaled during the accident, and the blood loss, combined with her injuries, was not survivable."

Sorry, Danielle, I may be shocked, but I won't be shedding any tears for you since I'm sure you were involved in the attack on Dickie. And while I had yet to be interviewed, I interrupted the officer long enough to tell him about the video the writer had, as well as the stills. I didn't want the guy to get away before the Coastie had a chance to view them. The guy was still over at the *Catamaran* bar, and since we weren't going anywhere, the officer went to track him down before finishing up with Murph.

"They say if you don't have something nice to say about the dead, then don't say anything. So I think I'll just be quiet," Lindsay remarked.

Smitty replied, "It'll be really quiet around here then if we're waiting for someone to say nice things."

Yeah, we are all on the same page. This world is a lot better place without that woman walking around.

24

THE LEMON

An hour later the Coast Guard finished their investigation. With a copy of the video in hand and after a close inspection of the wreckage, they were able to determine the cause of the accident as being metal fatigue. The forward trampoline spar on the starboard side had ripped loose under the stress of the tight turn and the mismatched angles of the foils with the one still stuck in the full forward position.

The spar attachment had evidently been failing for quite a while, as had the area where the mast "stepped," and both let loose under the pressure along with the aft spar. Up by the mast, some of the hollow spar had peeled back like a banana skin leaving a jagged "U" shape of metal as it folded back on itself. This snagged Danielle in the chest like a giant fish gaff after she was catapulted forward during the sudden stop. Ironically, Jez had sealed Danielle's fate by stealing the foils with the defect, so when the one jammed, it added just enough additional stress on the spar to collapse it. Though even with stationary foils, the hidden flaws and continuing erosion of the spar would have eventually given way if it hadn't been discovered first. Today's high winds and seas had merely accelerated the timetable.

· · ·

THE RAIN HAD BEEN BLOWING in at the beach bar, and Mimi decided to close it early since the weather was supposed to get even worse before it starts getting better later tonight. It made sense to funnel what little business was left up to the *Cove* where it could help keep their staff busy. Besides, we all hated looking out at the wreck; it was an unpleasant reminder of too many things.

And as if today hadn't already been eventful enough, my phone rang while we were having lunch on the covered deck. It was Rikki.

"Hey, Rikki."

"Hey, Marlin. We may have just caught a break. My friend at the FBI said they just got a hit on that couple, Joe and Jane Bloggs. It might just be a coincidence, but a couple by that name were admitted to the hospital over by you a couple of hours ago after a boating accident. Though the woman later died during surgery."

My head started swimming as things started clicking into place.

"Marlin? Are you still there?"

"Did the man have a broken arm?"

"How did you know that?" She sounded astonished; it was the first time I can recall ever surprising her.

"Because her real first name is Danielle, and I'm sure she's a French national. The man's name is Jeremy "Jez" Campbell, an Australian, and he owns a small boatyard over off the Severn River. They probably used those aliases to duck the hospital bill.

"Damn it, I should have seen it! They've both been in and out of here several times." My heart sank. "They might have even spotted Johnny's boat when he was here. He might be missing because of me."

Rikki replied, "I'll get this info to the FBI; they might be able to nab him at the hospital. Marlin don't beat yourself up, Johnny isn't missing because of you, he's probably missing because of them. I'll let you know what I hear."

After I hung up I saw a lot of questioning looks around the table, and I quickly filled them all in. They looked as surprised as I had been that they missed all the signs, too. Murph took out his phone and scrolled through the pictures.

"Yep, there it is. That new wide cradle on the ways over at Jez's boatyard? There's only one color of bottom paint spilled on it: black. The same color you said *Wanderer's* bottom had been repainted."

I shook my head. "They've been hiding in plain sight all along. Jez knows what happened to Johnny, so hopefully the FBI can get that out of him. But after this much time, I know there's little hope he's still alive."

"I did'n know jour frien' was missing, Marlin. Haim sorry to hear dat."

"Thanks, Marco. Yes, I'd really like to know for sure what happened to him."

There was almost no further conversation at our table during lunch, with everyone lost in their own thoughts. I did call the hospital after we finished and found that Dickie had improved a bit and that they planned on starting to bring him out of the coma in the morning. The only really good news of the day so far.

The rain was continuing to drum on the canvas awning and run down the clear plastic side drops, assaulting our ears, and blurring our view out over charter boat row. Not that there was much going on over there. All the boats were in, safely tied up in their slips and waiting for the storm to pass. The whole mood was depressing, and suddenly I wanted to go home. I looked at Kari and realized she was thinking the same thing. We excused ourselves after paying our tab and went back to *Tied Knot*. I wanted to make drinks for the two of us, sit on the sofa and snuggle with my wife while we check and see what movie is playing on the Classic Flicks Channel. It was the perfect afternoon to do all these things and turn the world off for a while.

As it turned out, one of my favorite movies of all time was playing, *Key Largo*. While the weather in the movie did match what we had going on outside, I loved the old setting; the Florida Keys before they became overcrowded and overpriced. I built two Cape Charles Distillery vodkas over ice with lemon wedges and took them over to the couch and snuggled in with Kari as Tank sprawled across her feet.

We were just getting to the exciting part of the movie at the peak of the hurricane when I remembered the shootout scene on the boat and started questioning my own movie choice. I got up to make refills but realized we were out of lemons. I headed for the door.

"I'll be right back, I have to go borrow a lemon from Murph, we're out."

"Take Tank with you, he needs to go for a walk."

Sure, furball is her little buddy until he needs to go for a walk in a storm. But then he looked up at me and "chuffed" as I was attaching his leash. I guess I can take that to mean anything I want, from impatience to thanks. I know Kari would say it's thanks, but I'm not that sure.

After Tank watered and fertilized the grass in the downpour, we returned to the private dock and stopped at *On Coastal Time*. It took Murph a few minutes to answer the door, but Tank and I were under the door alcove's cover, not that we weren't already wet. When he finally opened the door I noticed that he looked kind of funny, but it had been a stressful day.

"Hey, Murph. Kari and I are watching old movies and making cocktails, but I'm fresh out of lemons. Can I borrow one?"

"You could if I had any, but you know I'm allergic to them."

That struck me as weird, and I almost said, "Since when?" since we have had more than our share of vodkas with lemon together. But then Tank started growling, looking past Murph. I looked beyond him too, but the salon area was empty and there was no sign of Lindsay. "Oh, right, I forgot. Sorry to bug you pal."

He didn't reply, he just shut the door. Also weird. Alarms were now at full volume, ringing in my head. Tank and I returned to Tied Knot where I handed him off to Kari who followed me as I rushed past her into our stateroom, explaining on the way what had just happened. I retrieved my Glock nine-millimeter from my nightstand.

"What are you going to do?"

"I'm going to sneak aboard through the guest stateroom on the upper deck, then listen through the interior ladder hatch."

Kari asked, "Shouldn't we call the sheriff?"

"If it's Jez and he's got Lindsay and Murph, this'll turn into a hostage situation. And you know those seldom turn out well for the hostages when the cops have to follow the rule book. I'm not up for that; as far as I'm concerned, I lost the rulebook a long time ago."

"I'm coming with you."

I said, "No, I need you to call Rikki and tell her what's going on. I'm going to go see what I can find out. I'll be back."

"Marlin, be careful."

"Count on it."

I STILL HAD my key to their houseboat from back when Kari and I watched it when they were away. I snuck quietly up the outside stairs, the heavy rain helping mask any noise I was making. I unlocked the guest quarters and crept inside. The ladder hatch was closed. It led down into the galley, and this kept the cooking odors down where they ought to be. Slowly and quietly I lay down on my stomach, facing the hatch and away from the door. I cracked the hatch and could hear Jez ranting at both Murph and Lindsay. So, the good news was they are both still alive. The bad news being that he didn't plan on them staying that way for much longer, from what he was saying to them.

"You're both going to go to the same place all the others did, the bottom of the bay. Only you two cost me my Danny, my soulmate. So you're both going to go over the side for that last dip still alive and kicking. We'll see how long you two can hold your breaths.

"All you had to do was postpone the race and Danny would still be alive. But no, you two dipsticks wanted to show your friends what a pair of badass sailors you are. So you cost me Danny, my sweet Danielle. Well, now it's going to cost you, too. We've only got a few hours until dark, and then it'll be your turn to take one final cruise together."

I couldn't see beyond the galley, and his voice sounded like it was coming from the salon up forward. I'd have been even more worried if he sounded like he was talking to himself instead of an audience. I'm assuming that Murph and Linds are just gagged. Hoping that they're just gagged.

Someone put a hand over my mouth and grabbed the hatch so it didn't slam shut. My head snapped to the left and I saw Rikki kneeling next to me. She removed her hands from my mouth and the hatch then upturned both hands in a "what" gesture. I pointed up for "one" and pointed through the deck toward the salon area. She nodded, then lay on her stomach next to me. I had no idea how she had gotten here so fast, but at this point, I was glad to have someone with her experience with me.

I don't know how long we lay prone on the deck, it seemed like an eternity, but was probably only five minutes or so.

"All right now, I'm gonna go hit the head for a minute, and you two stay right there until I get back." He laughed loudly, so I was sure Murph and Lindsay were tied up. At least I hoped that's all they were.

Fortunately, Jez had left the head's door open to listen for any movement from my friends. But that also let me hear ever so slightly the sound of a urine stream start to build a pool in the bottom of the dry bowl in a marine toilet. Soundlessly I opened the hatch all the way, then Rikki and I scampered down the ladder, taking up positions in the galley. In this houseboat the head is long and narrow, occupying about a third of the width of the hull, alongside the galley. The entrance was at the end of the salon, next to the open end of the galley.

When Jez walked out and turned, I didn't give him a chance to go for his gun, which was tucked in his waistband. In fact, I don't think he even saw me before my hollow point bullet made mincemeat of the shoulder socket attached to the arm that wasn't broken. I wanted him out of commission, but not dead. He fell back against the bulkhead, screaming in pain. Apparently whatever painkillers they had given him earlier at the hospital don't work on gunshots. No doubt he'd be getting a lot of the good stuff after he got a new shoulder, but I wanted him to be in a lot of pain first so I could get some answers. Even more pain than he's in now.

Even though he wasn't going to be able to hold or aim it, I yanked his gun out of his waistband and put it in mine. It turned out to be Murph's.

"Ahm bleedin' to death!"

I stared at him, "We should be so lucky."

"Ahhhh! You gotta call me an ambo!"

"I don't have to do anything. I might just sit here and watch you bleed out." I turned and saw that Rikki had Murph and Lindsay mostly untied, or rather un *zip*-tied. With only one fully functional arm, Jez had them bind their legs with ties, then their wrists, which he tightened. They were each removing their duct tape that he had used to cover their mouths. I turned back to Jez, and what I saw on his wrist just sticking out from under the long sleeve of his shirt sickened me. I grabbed his wrist and held it up. He screamed.

"Where did you get this," I yelled, and he didn't reply. The gold watch on his wrist was unmistakable, it was Johnny's Racon Jadaux. I must've missed it when we started the race. I undid the catch and took the watch off his wrist, letting his arm fall back in his lap, eliciting another scream. "I said, where did you get this?"

Through clenched teeth, he said, "Call me an ambo, and I'll tell ya."

"Tell me, and I might call for one."

"Yeh, well, if you wanta know, I'll tell you after that ambo gets here." He glared at me, thinking he held the cards.

I turned and saw my three friends watching me, not intervening. They knew this was now about finding Johnny, and how important that is to me. I grabbed a chair and pulled it up in front of Jez. I took my time sitting down.

"Call me a bloody ambo, I'm dying!"

"Yeah, you are. Bleeding out nice and slow, too."

"If I die here, you'll never know what happened to that guy."

I smiled. "Since you had his watch, I already know he's dead, which I wasn't sure of until now. No way he'd have let this go. So, if you bleed out here, I won't know the details of what happened, so nothing will have really changed for me from this point. But you'll be dead. Yeah, I can live with that kind of tradeoff." I settled back in my chair.

"You're bloody insane! I want a doctor and a lawyer."

"You're the bloody one, and you're losing more of it by the minute. A lot of good a lawyer will do you after you're dead. But I'll have gotten justice for my friend, and you never know if that'll happen when the lawyers get involved first. This way I can guarantee it."

He looked over at my three friends, "Are you going to sit there and let him do this to me? I'm in agony!"

Murph laughed, "You should be glad we're not over there cutting pieces off of you for shark bait. He's the nicest of all of us. If it was up to me, you'd never see a doctor or set foot on land again. So, I'd advise you to tell him what he wants to know or it might end up being up to me after all."

TEN MINUTES LATER I ASKED, "Murph, you have any Quick Clot on *Irish Luck*?"

He went next door to the Merritt and returned soaked, but with two sealed pouches. I ripped open Jez's shirt then opened each pouch, removing the chemical soaked gauze pads.

I said, "This is gonna hurt, and I hope it does. A lot."

I slapped the pads on both the small entrance wound and the larger exit wound simultaneously, and he screamed. Loudly. And he didn't stop screaming for a full breath.

Plenty of sportfish boats carry decent medical kits with them for emergencies, because around here we often fish sixty and even seventy miles off the coast. That's a long way to a hospital if you get cut or hooked badly, and the number one thing to do is stop any bleeding as quickly as possible. It's why Murph keeps the Quick Clot on his boat. But folks who've had it applied to them say it feels like molten lava. Yeah, from the tears running down Jez's face right now, I'd say that's probably accurate. After what he had told me during those ten minutes, I'd be lying if I said I wasn't enjoying seeing him in pain.

25

ANSWERS

Rikki called her friend at the FBI and told him we had his prisoner as well as a ton of answers waiting for him. He showed up with two cars loaded with agents, and they walked Jez out to the parking lot. Since he was no longer bleeding and had already ducked out of the hospital once today, they were going to drive him straight to the hospital in their car instead of an ambulance. They weren't letting him out of their sight.

Murph, Lindsay, Rikki and I had moved over to *Tied Knot* to let the FBI team have room to do their investigation. Rikki had been privately assured by her FBI pal that there wouldn't be any issue over the length of time that elapsed before we called them. And since we weren't connected with any law enforcement agency, they were free to act on the information that we gathered from Jez, which I had recorded on video with my phone. I messaged a copy of the video to Kari before my phone had been taken as evidence.

Cindy was there with Kari and Tank when we walked in. She and Rikki had been about to pass by on their way back from Richmond when they got Kari's call, which is how Rikki arrived so fast. Kari stood up and hugged me fiercely. I don't know if it was just because I had come back in one piece, or because she had listened to the recording. Once Jez had started talking it was like he couldn't stop. It wasn't so much a confession as he was proud and bragging about what he and Danielle had "accomplished" together. Fourteen people murdered, and eight boats taken and shipped overseas. Not exactly an accomplishment in my book. But he told us this after giving a detailed account of what happened to Johnny.

Danielle had been lying in wait for Johnny, hooking up with him at the restaurant then talking him into taking her out for a cruise in his catamaran. She convinced him to anchor up in a cove so they could have sex. The plan had been that she would use her icepick to kill him before things went too far. Jez would pick up the outboard and ride out to meet her. They would tow the outboard back to their new boatyard with them, disposing of Johnny's body in the shipping channel. But something about Johnny had flipped all the right switches with Danielle, and Jez arrived to find the two in the middle of actually having sex. Enraged, instead of using an icepick Jez had beaten him to death, then weighted and dumped his body in the cove, wanting it off the boat immediately. He wanted to erase the memory of what he had walked in on. Corpses didn't bother him that much, but seeing someone else with his woman was his tipping point.

They brought *Wanderer* over to their boatyard that night, changing the name and the bottom color the next day. The following day they set sail for Bermuda. I remarked that they must've gotten paid quite a bit of money for the boat, and asked how they managed to get that much cash back through US Customs? He said the Broussards were major jewel fences in France, and the payment was done in stones, intentionally set in cheap settings. Customs didn't bat an eye at them, thinking they were all costume jewelry because of the settings. It was another thing he was very proud of.

I was never so happy as when the FBI took him in custody and hauled him off the houseboat. I had just looked pure evil in the eye. No remorse for having killed all those people, only grief for the loss of his woman, and concern for his wound.

OVER IN THE PARKING LOT, none of the agents even heard the shots. Jez just collapsed next to the open car door, two small holes in the side of his head. He was dead before he hit the ground, hit with two subsonic .22 caliber rounds, fired from a silenced rifle.

MARCO VAZQUEZ barely heard the click of the firing pin and the sound of the semi-automatic's slide as it chambered the next round. He was proud of his accuracy since both the wind and the rain had made both them extremely challenging shots, with these lower velocity rounds. He broke down the rifle in seconds and returned it to the flat brown waxed cardboard bait box, then walked around the far side of the bait shop and over toward his boat. Though Jez hadn't ever known that Marco Vazquez was the broker he and Danielle had been working for, Marco couldn't take any chances with him now going into FBI custody.

Marco already decided to take him out after hearing over lunch about the new boatyard setup he had been completely unaware of. He couldn't believe his luck when he saw the FBI cars tearing into the parking lot. It had to be Jez they were here for. He knew he'd have his chance when they led him to the car. By then he figured out that Jez had gone from working for him to being his secret competition. If that hadn't been bad enough, his sloppiness was what brought the feds in, making the area too hot to work from right now. But at least with Jez dead, and direct ties from him to the buyers of that last boat, they would be looking for a professional hitman, which Marco wasn't, instead of a broker. He figured they would now assume that Jez had sold all the missing catamarans directly. Since they hadn't had time to question him yet, hopefully Jez had died with his secrets intact. He was more useful now dead than he had been lately when he was alive.

~

THE AGENT BURST IN, telling us what happened and herding us away from the windows, unsure if any of us might now be targets too. While I was shocked about what had happened, I have to admit there was a little satisfaction in knowing that he had gotten what he deserved, with no delay and little cost to the taxpayers. I, along with several other people, had all gotten the news we dreaded one day might come, but we also received the closure we were scared we might never receive.

After an exhaustive search of the area in the direction they thought the shots had come from yielded nothing, the FBI let us all go on about our business. Rikki and Cindy went on up to Bayside, while Murph and Lindsay went home to start cleaning up the blood in the salon. I never did get that lemon, and I didn't see the ending to *Key Largo*, either.

THE NEXT DAY KARI, Tank, and I were having an early breakfast on the *Cove* deck. The weather had done a complete one-eighty overnight, and the day was crystal clear. We were just finishing up when Marco Vasquez stopped by our table. Tank growled quietly at him as usual.

"Es loco aroun' here lately. I think es a good time for me to get some work done on my *Zopilote*, an' let my crew have some time off. I be back inna week or two."

I said, "Thanks for your help yesterday, Marco."

He got a curious grin on his face, and I swear he was trying to suppress a giggle. "Jus' glad to help. Maybe next year jou can have a better race."

"We've got all year to plan it, so I hope so. Just a nice, boring, sailboat race," Kari said.

"Jes, I hope so, chica. Sees you two soon, an' don' rent my slip, I be back."

We watched him walk down the charter dock, and yell something at Baloney, who was in the cockpit of *My Mahi*. Bill of course returned the insult. It had gotten so they looked like they were straight out of that movie, *Grumpy Old Men*. About as comical, too.

I looked at Kari, "Maybe things will calm down now and get back to normal."

She quickly reached across and put a finger to my lips. "Haven't you learned anything about not tempting the Fates? Just let it be."

From under the table, Tank barked. We both laughed because this time it wasn't a "yip," it was a real, deep-throated bark. Our little guy was growing up. Okay, *her* little guy.

EPILOGUE

Dickie was slowly brought back out of the coma that Monday and they discovered he had suffered some slight brain damage from the attack. He's going to be walking with a cane for a few months, and having some speech therapy, but they think in a year you won't even be able to tell anything happened to him. He's also going to be a rich man, as the news of his invention has spread throughout the sailboat racing community, and he and Murph have been busy putting together licensing deals.

SPEAKING OF MURPH, he and Lindsay are getting along a lot better these days. Well kind of. He took her out for a sunset ride on *Irish Luck* the other night, dropped to one knee on the flybridge as the sun was setting and proposed. She told him she'd need a little time to think about it, that this was too close to that traumatic experience they had, and she wants to make sure this isn't just a knee-jerk reaction to that. It's driving him nuts. Now he's bound and determined to get a ring on her finger. I probably shouldn't admit it, but I'm kind of enjoying watching this.

· · ·

MARCO VAZQUEZ DID TAKE his boat in for some maintenance, but he won't be using it anymore. He took it to a small boatyard over near Norfolk that the FBI said was owned by a man he was in league with in the catamaran hijacking ring. The boats were renamed and had cosmetic changes done at the yard. The owner was also a master forger who supplied new documents for the boats which were then shipped by freighter to Europe and the Mideast for resale.

The way they know so much about it is because the owner kept a secret "insurance policy" stash of records which listed everything about the boats, from the changes, and their murdered owners to their buyers in Europe and the Mideast. They surmise that he and Marco Vasquez must've gotten in an argument over the percentage of the split and both ended up shooting each other in the office at night after hours. The yard owner died instantly after Marco returned fire. Vazquez bled out from his wound as he tried making it back to his boat. Yard workers found them both the next day.

RIKKI'S PAL at the FBI got a nice feather in his cap after they discovered the jewelry which the Broussards used to pay for Johnny's boat in a safe in the office at Aussie Cats. Interpol was able to match them to a few burglaries in a resort town in France. They then seized Johnny's boat and arrested the couple. The boat is on its way back stateside.

Funny thing about that boat. As it was on its way back across the Atlantic, I got a package from a lawyer in Richmond. In it was a letter explaining that he was the Executor of Johnny's estate. Johnny had left me *Wanderer*, along with his Racon Jadaux watch, which the FBI had released to the attorney. It was in the package as well. But the bulk of Johnny's estate was left to a trust to be used to fund grants for technology scholarships to deserving kids. The details were to be left up to the Trustee, me. The one caveat was that I had to instill in each recipient how necessary it was to not just have a goal and reach it but to have fun along the way, and I was to tell the story about how he had lost sight of that, and how it had cost him more than money.

I was honored to help do something to carry on my friend's memory, and it's a duty I look forward to carrying out. As to the boat, I've talked it over with Kari, and we haven't decided what to do with it yet, other than restore the name he gave it. On one hand, it was the place my friend lost his life. On the other, it was the one thing in his life that had brought him so much joy and reminded him of his grandfather. I think we'll wait a while before we decide if we'll keep, sell, or donate it.

The watch. As you might've guessed, it is *sooo* not me. But it meant a lot to Johnny, so I'm going to keep it in the safe on *Tied Knot* and wear it on special occasions, or when I want to be reminded of my friend.

Speaking of Johnny, a hydraulic escalator clam dredge operating near Cape Charles brought up several human bones and some shreds of fabric. Coast Guard divers recovered more bones from the site, far less than a complete skeleton, but enough to match up Johnny's DNA. The remains were cremated, and those of us that knew or had met Johnny scattered that little bit of ash just outside of Mallard Cove in the channel, about the same place where I had last seen my friend. I wanted us to think of him as we are coming and going from the marina, having the fun that he was finally starting to enjoy. Rest peacefully, my friend.

So, what's on the horizon? Well, it's not like she doesn't have enough to do, but Kari can't get that Cape Charles property out of her head. It sounds good to me, I mean, how much trouble can we get in up there, right? *Right???*

AUTHOR'S NOTES

Author's Notes

Thanks for reading **Coastal Cats**! If you read this one before reading the first four books in this series, Coastal Conspiracy, Coastal Cousins, Coastal Paybacks, and Coastal Tuna, don't worry. While it's better if they are read in sequence, each can still be read as a "stand alone" book with a minimum of "spoilers". I used the phrase *that's a story for another day* to refer to things that were covered more in depth in those other volumes.

Hey, if you liked **Coastal Cats**, I'd really appreciate it if you wouldn't mind leaving a review on Amazon or Goodreads.com. Just a line or two would be great! And I'd love to hear from you directly as well. You can reach me at contact@donrichbooks.com

I also have a newsletter where I share pictures and the stories that inspire the books. Members also get advance notice of any upcoming releases at discounted rates. You can sign up for the Reader's Group on my website, http://www.donrichbooks.com

If you're on Facebook, be sure to visit and "Like" my **Don Rich Books** page, https://www.facebook.com/DonRichBooks/
I'm also on **Goodreads:** https://www.goodreads.com/don_rich

Thanks again!
Don Rich

ABOUT THE AUTHOR

Don Rich is the author of the bestselling Coastal Adventure Series. Three of his books even simultaneously held the top three spots in Amazon's Hot New Releases in Boating.

Don's books are set mainly in the mid-Atlantic because of his love for this stretch of coastline. A fifth generation Florida native who grew up on the water, he has spent a good portion of his life on, in, under, or beside it.

He now makes his home in central Virginia. When he's not writing or watching another fantastic mid-Atlantic sunset, he can often be found on the Chesapeake or the Atlantic with a fishing rod in his hand.

Don loves to hear from readers, and you can reach him via email at contact@donrichbooks.com

ALSO BY DON RICH

(Click on titles for more information)

- COASTAL CONSPIRACY
- COASTAL COUSINS
- COASTAL PAYBACKS
- COASTAL TUNA
- COASTAL CATS
- COASTAL CAPER
- COASTAL CULPRIT
- GhostWRITER

Coming later in 2021:

- COASTAL CURSE

Click *HERE* for more information about joining my **Reader's Group**! And you can follow me on Facebook at: https://www.facebook.com/DonRichBooks

I'm also a member of TropicalAuthors.com where you can find my latest books and those of several of my coastal writer friends by clicking on the logo below:

Manufactured by Amazon.ca
Bolton, ON